PANDORA
Gets Angry

MYTHIC MISADVENTURES BY CAROLYN HENNESY

PANDORA
Gets Angry

CAROLYN HENNESY

BLOOMSBURY

NEW YORK BERLIN LONDON SYDNEY

First published in the United States of America in February 2011
by Bloomsbury Books for Young Readers
www.bloomsburykids.com

For information about permission to reproduce selections from this book, write to
Permissions, Bloomsbury BFYR, 175 Fifth Avenue, New York, New York 10010

Library of Congress Cataloging-in-Publication Data
Hennesy, Carolyn.
Pandora gets angry / Carolyn Hennesy. — 1st U.S. ed.
        p.   cm.
Summary: As Pandy, Iole, and Homer travel to Baghdad to seek another deadly
evil—rage—they face a deadly sandstorm and worse, while Alcie is aided by
Persephone, the queen of the underworld.
ISBN 978-1-59990-440-5
1. Pandora (Greek mythology)—Juvenile fiction.
[1. Pandora (Greek mythology)—Fiction. 2. Mythology, Greek—Fiction. 3. Gods,
Greek—Fiction. 4. Goddesses, Greek—Fiction. 5. Persephone (Greek deity)—Fiction.
6. Adventure and adventurers—Fiction.] I. Title.
PZ7.H3917Pac 2010   [Fic]—dc22   2010025632

Typeset by Westchester Book Composition
Printed in the U.S.A. by Quad/Graphics, Fairfield, Pennsylvania
2 4 6 8 10 9 7 5 3 1

For Donald

من شما را دوست دارم

And to the memory of Harriet Shapiro, Ph.D.,
who got my girls out of the water.
And much, much more.

PANDORA
Gets Angry

CHAPTER ONE

Out of a Clear Blue Sky

"It's gaining on us!" Pandy screamed, craning her neck to look back over her shoulder.

"Don't look at it!" Homer barked. "Pull your cloak over your head!"

"What *is* it!" Pandy screamed.

"Just keep going!" Homer yelled, his eyes frantically scanning the horizon ahead for something he knew he'd never find: someplace—any place—that he, Pandy, and Iole could hide.

Nothing.

Only sand.

Their three camels, whipped into a frenzy, were running at a speed Pandy couldn't even comprehend. Even watching wild horses race across fields back home, she'd never seen anything move as fast. With one arm wrapped tightly around Dido as he curled, shivering, in front of her, it was all she could do to stay on top of her beast as it flew across the desert, trying to outrun what was coming up behind them.

A dark mass, deep brown and thick, was now less than five kilometers away and bearing down hard and fast with a dull roar.

Two hours earlier, the midmorning sky had been a clear, pale blue—almost white; the sun beating down brutally on them as it had for the past eleven and a half uneventful days. The boredom of the Arabian desert had been broken by only two things. One was a melancholy followed by a testiness that had slowly crept into Homer's demeanor. For the first several days of their journey, Homer had been his usual quiet but courteous self as they traveled from Aphrodisias, across the lands of Galatia, Cilicia, and Syria, and finally into the endless expanse of desert toward Baghdad. Then, it seemed to Pandy, Homer had grown annoyed by the many people commenting and asking questions about their strange beasts. He had become sullen, almost rude, in answering, even when the question had not been put to him directly. Pandy thought she overheard him say something like, "We're riding these because of *her*," and flicking a hand in her direction.

The other was the fact that two days earlier, Iole had become very, very sick. Pale, sweating, and unable to keep any food in her stomach, Iole was becoming so ill that Pandy was in great fear for her friend's life. The healing powers of the enchanted Eye of Horus weren't working, and calling on the tiny bust of Athena for advice proved useless; Pandy couldn't get even a single sound out of it. There was no priestess around to intercede on Iole's behalf with Apollo, the God of Healing, and Pandy knew that her own prayers, if they were getting through, might not make much difference. Even though Apollo had been quite taken with Iole when he'd met her in Alexandria, he had saved her life once already, when she was very little, and he might feel a bit put-upon if asked to do it again.

It was only as she turned back to check on Iole for the umpteenth time that day that Pandy had seen it: the thin brown line growing steadily into a large brown mass heading straight for them.

"Homer!" she'd yelled at that moment, pointing.

With just a quick glance behind, Homer recognized what was coming.

"Get Dido up!" he cried. Pandy called to her dog, who'd been walking along beside, and at once Dido made the tremendous leap. Instantly Homer spurred his camel forward and the others had immediately followed. Now, he knew, they were in a race for their lives. And they were probably going to lose.

Suddenly, a fleck of foam hit Pandy's right cheek. As she wiped it away, another flew into her eye, and then another caught the tip of Dido's ear. She looked at her camel, its mouth covered in creamy white spittle as the creature began to tire. She looked back at Homer's camel; its eyes were rimmed with red, evidence that its heart was beating too hard. Hermes had said that a camel was the heartiest of beasts, able to go weeks without food or water in desperate conditions, but these three had been running flat out for hours and they weren't immortal: the strain was clear.

"We can't keep going!" she screamed.

"We have to!" Homer yelled back, urging his camel onward.

Pandy's mind flashed back to the deck of the ship *The Peacock* as it crossed the Ionian Sea on its way to Egypt, desperately trying to outrun a whirling black funnel that ultimately destroyed the ship and her crew. Then she thought of the great mass of the heavens forming an impenetrable wall around the Atlas Mountains, which she'd had to crawl under.

"Gods," Pandy thought angrily as another wad of spittle landed on her chin. "I am so sick of large, loud walls and masses and whatever trying to destroy us!"

Suddenly, Pandy heard a different sound: a coughing, choking gag. Glancing to her left she saw Iole, barely on her camel, her arms flopping helplessly because she was no longer strong enough to handle the reins, her head shaking violently up and down with each stride, and her tiny first meal of flatbread and dates coming up and dribbling out of her mouth. Suddenly, Iole's hands flew high in the air as she was pitched backward and hurled to the ground.

"Look *out!*" Pandy shrieked as Homer's camel narrowly missed trampling Iole's head where she lay on the sand. Immediately, both Pandy and Homer brought their camels around and were off their mounts in seconds. Without warning, Homer's camel knelt on the ground, closed its eyes, and whinnied to the other two. It was a sure sign that all three camels knew there was no outrunning the mass and would go no farther. But, as Pandy watched, the two other camels approached the first and knelt beside it, forming a small semicircle— and a barrier between her, Homer, and Iole and the storm. Pandy took this to mean that they were helping their human riders.

The brown mass was almost upon them.

"*What do we do?*" Pandy called to Homer.

"It's a sandstorm, Pan*dora*," Homer yelled over the growing din, his eyes avoiding hers. "There's *nothing* we can do."

In the middle of the desert, with a tremendous wave of sand about to hit them full force, the only thing on Pandy's mind was that Homer had used a tone with her as if she were the stupidest person in the world. As if she were someone else. For a split second, that was the entire focus of her brain.

"Get over here!" Homer yelled. Homer had carried Iole to his camel and was nestling her in a crook between its forelegs and belly, using the animal's back as a shield. "Move!"

"Dido, come!" Pandy commanded, and he was at her side in a second. Holding him close, Pandy threw herself against the camel, feeling its warmth, its chest still heaving from the hard run.

"Give me the rope!" Homer yelled, a momentary raise in the pitch and roar of the storm drowning out his words.

Pandy only saw his lips move.

"What?" Pandy cried.

Without pausing to repeat himself, Homer grabbed her leather pouch and quickly fished out the enchanted rope. He gestured wildly until Pandy understood.

"Rope," she cried, the first grains of sand crunching against her teeth as the storm bore down. "Thicker and longer!"

At once, the rope began to change in her hand. It grew thicker, but it also became much shorter. Then without warning, it turned into a tiny string. Then the rope grew longer, but it looked as if it had been burned in a fire.

"*There's something wrong with it!*" Pandy screamed.

"Give it to me!" Homer yelled, and without even looking at it, he yanked the rope from her hands. In Homer's grip, it remained long enough that he was able to frantically tie one end around his waist, then loop it in a knot around Iole, another around Dido, and finally tie the other end to Pandy.

"Hold us fast!" Pandy yelled down to the rope, hoping that whatever was wrong was just a momentary glitch.

Homer was now furiously pulling at the camel's saddle blanket, trying to wrench it free from where it was pinned underneath. With a grunt, he tore it loose and tossed it over Iole and himself.

"For Ares' sake!" Homer screamed at Pandy, his voice as full of rage and fury as the sound of the storm only seconds from impact. "Pull your cloak over your head and get under!"

Pandy wrapped her cloak tightly around herself and dove under the blanket with Dido just as the thick cloud of harsh, churning sand hit them with the force of a wall being blown apart. Pandy felt as if she were being beaten on all sides, poked with pointed sticks, and stung by millions of bees. And even though the rope was binding them all together, she could feel the unbelievable push of the wind buffeting her legs, shoulders, and head. She knew that without the rope, she could easily have been driven away from the others and out into the desert. She ran her hands along the rope's surface and found tiny metal spikes poking out. The next instant, they were gone.

And then the sand began to find its way in.

Pandy's mother's cloak, even with a thick blanket covering it, was no match for the immense volume of fine sand whirling and swirling, and soon her legs, arms, neck, face, and hair were coated in layer upon layer. She covered her face with her hands but in vain. The sand was working its way through every crevice, no matter how small—filling her ears, pushing under her eyelids and into her mouth, and, worst of all, slowly inching up her nose.

Again, an image from the past flared in her mind: falling through the desert floor in Egypt and into the Chamber of Despair and thinking she was going to drown as the sand instantly filled her mouth, nose, and ears. But that was quickly over as she crashed through the ceiling of the chamber and went plummeting through the dark, open air to the ground below.

This . . . *this* was going to be a slow, agonizing death for all of them . . . lost in a foreign land, Iole sick or possibly already dead, Homer unaccountably distant, and her quest unfinished. Miserable, she envisioned their lungs filling slowly with sand.

The only bright spot, Pandy mused, desperately trying to spit out the grit, was that Alcie wasn't here to suffer through it with them.

Alcie was already gone.

CHAPTER TWO
A New Friend

"What do you mean, you haven't *seen* her yet?" said the first shade, hurrying along the palace corridor, passing enormous dark, lavishly decorated but empty rooms, dead-end porticos, courtyards full of creeping black plants and slow-dripping fountains.

"I've been on vacation with my daughter's family in the Elysian Fields' upper campground. I arranged it with the Dark Lord weeks ago. I wouldn't have gone if I'd known there was going to be such a commotion. And who knew we'd have a guest!" said the second, keeping pace. A dim, ugly light from an unseen source barely illuminated the way for the transparent figures. "Tell me about her."

"Well, first off, she's very young. Too young to have been taken in such a horrible way."

"How?" asked the second shade.

"Snake bite."

"Ouch."

"Tragic. But she's got quite a mouth on her, especially for one so young. Swears like a warrior, but she uses fruit," the first shade continued.

"Original," said the second.

"Perhaps, though it's not going over so well with our master. But she's very pretty. Beautiful reddish hair. At least I think it's red—hard to tell in this dim light. But, oh! The best thing about her is . . ."

"Yes? Yes?" asked the second shade.

"She's got a spark! She's still got some life left in her!" said the first, pausing outside the door to a small antechamber. "I didn't realize how much I missed real 'life'—blood-pumping, heart-beating life! She's a breath of fresh air!"

"Lemon rinds! I can *hear* you, you know!" yelled a voice from inside a larger room.

The shades in the corridor quickly hushed and took up their posts, relieving two other shades that had been keeping watch over the young girl.

"And, yes, thank you, I am still pomegranate a-*live*!" they heard her cry. "At least, I think I am. Maybe. I don't know anymore. Hey! How long am I gonna have to stay here? The tapestries are cool and everything, and the lamps never seem to burn out, but can I get a window? And is there anything with color *any*where? Look, if I'm worm food already, then will somebody point me in the direction of the Elysian Fields so I can get to rompin'?"

The first shade smiled to the other.

"See what I mean?" she began whispering. "She's full of—"

But a huge figure at the entrance to the antechamber silenced her immediately.

"But if I am *not* apricot-apricoty-cot-cot-cot *dead*," the shades heard, bowing their heads as the figure passed, followed by a second, moving toward the larger room, "then somebody's gonna have some explaining to do!"

"Alcestis!" said Hades, filling the entire entryway. "You will be quiet."

Alcie, from the low couch on which she'd been lying for hours it seemed, whipped her head around to stare at the Dark Lord of the Underworld, paused a moment during which she thought better of staying down, got to her feet, then dropped to her knees.

"I know," Hades began slowly, "that this has been hard for you. It has been hard for all of us. Believe me."

"I'm sorry," Alcie said softly.

"Yes, I'm certain that you are. I also know you can't help yourself. Stand now."

As she got to her feet, Alcie suddenly felt like she was five.

"However," Hades went on, "I am working very hard

to find a solution to this whole mess. Now, while time means absolutely nothing to us here, I have just realized that you have been our . . . guest . . . for almost twelve of your days and have basically done nothing but sit."

Alcie was shocked. She *couldn't* have been sitting in this oddly beautiful but dark and dreary room for twelve days. Half a day, a day at most. She hadn't slept or eaten. Time really *didn't* mean anything.

"I do apologize," Hades was continuing, "that this is our first meeting since the day you arrived; I don't think either of us was in terribly good spirits—no pun intended—to have made a proper greeting then. You were flailing about so, you had to be enchanted into submission and I had to essentially empty my treasury to Charon so that he would ferry you across the river Styx. And I have been busy since. So . . . so I have now entreated my lovely queen to come and visit with you."

Immediately, Alcie saw the smaller figure slightly behind Hades: a young woman, sumptuously dressed and bejeweled, only a little older than Alcie, who was waving her hands up and down wildly in a very enthusiastic greeting.

Hades turned to address the woman, who instantly became still, refined, and proper, clear eyes gazing at Alcie, hands at her sides.

"Even though these are the months allotted for her

to spend with her mother on Mount Olympus, my wife, Persephone," Hades said, gesturing to the woman, "has graciously consented to return here and will be happy to engage you . . ."

Hades turned back to Alcie, and Persephone broke into a huge grin and clapped her hands silently.

Alcie's mouth started to fall open slightly as she stared at the crazy woman.

". . . in conversation. She can tell you all about her underworld kingdom. Isn't that so, my love?"

Hades turned again to Persephone and found her calm, even a little bored, nodding her head slightly in agreement.

"She will see to it . . ."

Hades continued, turning once again to Alcie as Persephone raised her hands and waggled them joyfully, mouthing the word "*Wahoo!*"

". . . that all your needs are met. Perhaps you are hungry?"

Strangely, Alcie wasn't, and she began to say so, then noticed Persephone's head bobbing furiously, directing her how to answer.

"I'm all right . . . no . . . no, I'm *not* all right. I *am* hungry," Alcie said slowly, gazing past Hades to Persephone, who gave her a thumbs-up and grinned madly. "I am very . . . very? . . . *very hungry*!"

"Right, then," said Hades. "We shall see that food is

prepared. And now if you will excuse me, I think I know how all of this may be concluded to everyone's satisfaction. Wife," he said, turning around as Persephone solemnly bowed her head, "I leave her in your care."

With that, Hades strode from the room, dismissed the shade guards, and passed through the antechamber and into the corridor. Persephone crooked her neck to watch him as long as she could, then put her finger to her lips as a sign for Alcie to be quiet, waited several seconds more, and then finally whirled around.

"Hi!" she exclaimed, throwing her arms about Alcie in a tremendous hug that nearly knocked the wind out of her. Alcie caught a faint scent of roses and lavender, and saw flickers of fuchsia and light pink in the threads of her gown.

"Oh my gods, oh my gods, oh my gods! I am so happy to see you! He says I consented to come back down here . . . *phah*! I begged, do you hear me, I *begged*! You know my story, right?"

"Uh," Alcie began.

"Oh, of *course* you do! Here sit, sit!"

Persephone playfully pushed Alcie back down on the couch and plopped beside her.

"Maiden, meaning me, strolling in the fields. Big, dark, scary but handsome-in-a-pale-kinda-way god, Buster—oops, that's his nickname—I mean Hades, sees me, falls in love, and drives his chariot up through the earth from the underworld and kidnaps me, yeah, yeah. Brings me back down here, marries me—I *know,* like I had a choice—and then my mom, Demeter, Glorious Earth Mother, starts looking for me, can't find me, blights the earth with winter all year long. Bad news for mankind. Then there's this whole pomegranate-seed incident, and finally Zeus decrees that I spend six months up there, which makes Mom happy, and that's why you mortals have . . . c'mon, say it . . ."

"Uh, spring and summer?" Alcie said.

"Right! And six months down here, Mom gets weepy, and you guys get . . . ?"

"Fall and winter."

"Right! Okay, what*ever,* right? My mother and my husband are fighting over me . . . weird, huh? I *know*! Talk about issues, I *got 'em*! So it's boring enough down here, but then I have to go back home and Mom won't let me out of her sight, even for one tick on a sundial. I can't even go to the baths alone. Mothers! I *know*! Absolute torture! So can I tell you—can I just *tell* you—how thrilled I was to find out that you were down here? Someone new and *interesting* to talk to! A mortal maiden who's had a *life*! I just went right up and begged my mom to let me come back down for a little bit. Told her it would be to help you adjust until Hades gets you out of here, but really, it's for me . . . to keep me from going stark raving mad! I *know*, call me selfish."

Alcie, in spite of the fact that this woman was obviously bonkers, started to smile.

"Well," she said to Persephone, "I'm really glad you did. Thanks."

"Are you kidding? Thank *you*! I mean, considering your whole death, or whatever this limbo state is that you're in right now, was for nothing, I figured you'd need a friend, right? A good ear to talk to about what a hateful she-dog Hera is."

Alcie had no idea what she was hearing, exactly, but knew enough from what Persephone was saying to be shocked.

"What?"

"What do you mean 'what'? You died, or whatever, for nothing."

"Uh, excuse me, but I *died* because Aphrodite demanded a life in order to give up the golden apple with Lust hiding inside. What do you moldy olive, pardon me, mean it was for *nothing*? She gave the apple to Pandy, right? Pandy put Lust in the box?"

"Well, yes, ultimately she did, but the Aphrodite you saw in the temple in Aphrodisias was really Hera in disguise, and after you were dead, or whatever, she gave Pandora a clay apple."

Alcie's jaw dropped. What did this mean? Was Pandy's quest to recapture all of the evils in the world now ruined?

"But wait! Wait!" Persephone went on. "Then the real Aphrodite appeared with the real apple, and after Pandora set Hera on fire—"

"HUH?"

"I *know*! Yep, on fire. Mom says she's still bald as an eagle egg. Anyway, after Zeus appeared and took Hera away, Aphrodite gave Pandora the real apple, so everything's fine!"

Alcie just gaped at Persephone for a long time. Then her eyes began to wander all over the room. Her thoughts were a complete jumble.

"I'm guessing you didn't know."

"How would I? No," Alcie said softly. "No."

"Pandora has her dog back, so that's good, right?"

"She's got Dido?" Alcie said, tears filling her eyes with no warning at all.

"Yep! Apparently Zeus brought the dog down from Olympus himself. Mom said that Zeus told Pandora something like: if she had to lose one friend, she might as well get another back. Hera was ticked."

"How does your mom, I mean Demeter—"

"Glorious Earth Mother."

"Huh?"

"You have to say that after her name," Persephone said. "Hey, I'm not making this stuff up. It's protocol. Even I have to say it . . . even when it's just her and me— and I'm her daughter! Okay, you don't have to say it all the time, but just say it now, in case anyone is listening. Make me feel better."

Alcie looked at Persephone, her mouth open to say something, but she paused.

"Okaaay," Alcie said at last. "How does Demeter, Glorious Earth Mother, know so much about it? I mean with Hera and all?"

"Because, they're best friends. They do everything together. Mom and Hera are inseparable."

"Really?" Alcie said, a suspicion growing in her mind.

"Really! I *know*!"

Alcie was silent for a while. Then she sighed.

"You know, I think I am hungry."

"Want a pomegranate?" Persephone said with a laugh. "Oh, *stop me*, I'm just kidding. Actually, they're not big on vegetables and fruit down here, but if we want something dead, no problem. I don't know what Buster has them preparing, but it'll be something yummy. And don't worry about the color. Everything is gray, but it's good."

"Great. Can't wait," Alcie said. "So, you think I'm getting out of here, right?"

"Buster says he'll do it, so he'll do it," Persephone said, leading the way into the anteroom. "Look, if you're not supposed to be here, then it will throw everything off if you stay. Stars will collide, fire will rain down, animals will start talking, and the dead will walk the earth . . . your earth."

"Really?" Alcie said, feeling bizarrely proud that she could be the cause of all of that. "Gods!"

"I *know*!"

Persephone was silent for a second, then burst out laughing.

"I'm kidding! Please! I have no idea what will happen." Persephone giggled, moving into the corridor. "But trust me, if you're supposed to be topside, you will be."

"Pears." Alcie sighed. "I wish I could get word to Pandy. Just to let her know I'm coming back."

"Oh," Persephone said. "I can help you with that."

"You're joking."

"Nope. We'll just make sure the coast is clear, and then we'll go talk to Buster's Big Bowl of Borrower's Bile!"

CHAPTER THREE

Waiting

"Next."

The first few figures all began to move forward one space, but the large, blue-robed woman standing at the very head of the line didn't budge, causing instant confusion.

"Next."

Three wizened men, all wearing official red robes and caps, stood at posts behind a counter at the far end of the room: log books, maps, sightseeing brochures, visas, and date stamps at the ready. Two were still in conversation, going over policies and procedures with individuals on the other side of the counter, but one space was now open.

"Next."

The vast but stuffy room was packed with immortals of every shape and size, all waiting patiently (or not) in a line that wound around itself, then stretched back out of the room and down a spiral staircase, past four floors of offices, and down into a crowded lobby. The interior of the room, which occupied the entire fifth floor of its building, was dominated by twenty-one open windows, seven each on three sides. Twenty windows were bordered by row upon row of inlaid diamonds, rubies, emeralds, topazes, amethysts, and sapphires following the curvature of the window arch. Each large gem was flawless and brilliant; the stones would catch the rays of the sun and reflect rainbows of light. But the twenty-first window was left unfinished and undecorated. When an immortal chanced to ask about the ugly window, bereft of any beauty, and why it was allowed to mar the grandeur of the room, the officials would reply that "nothing in the world should ever be perfect; it would be too much for even the immortal mind to comprehend. And, since the works of art and architecture that come closest to perfection are, of course, to be found in Baghdad, an imperfection must be built in, so that none would be driven to madness."

The floor was an immense mosaic: tiny squares of colored stone and glass that were set in such a way as to depict the moment when Haroun al Rashid (the first of many), then Prince of Baghdad, received his crown.

But many immortals didn't bother appreciating the windows or the floor, choosing instead to spend their time in line looking up. The ceiling was a massive map, which stretched from wall to wall and laid out the entire region of Persia, including deserts, oases, cities, and seaports. The map was dotted with dozens of white, blinking lights, each one representing an immortal conducting any business in the land. Frequently, the lights would flash green and a name would appear close by, a signal that some deity had used a power, curse, or enchantment legally. Rarely, the light would flash red, indicating an illegal use of power. At that moment, the sound of much commotion and alarm bells could be heard ringing in the unseen rooms behind the great counter.

Outside the carved white marble and bloodred porphyry doors was a unique view of the rooftops, spires, and turrets of Baghdad that no human ever saw, because the huge, ornate building housing the Bureau of Visiting Deities–Department of Permits and Visas was, in fact, floating over the city, invisible to the mortal eye (although the architects had taken care to make it perceptible to flying birds, for safety reasons).

"*Next.*"

"Hey, lady, you're next!" came a call from Forseti, a mid-level Norse deity, two back from the front of the line. "Lady, he's open!"

"*Next!*"

"*Is* it a lady?" asked a Celtic tree nymph. "Because if not, I say kick him."

"I believe it is," said a small Chinese spirit, standing

directly behind the sleeping figure. "Although I think she, or he, is bald, so it is difficult to tell."

"Shove her out of the way," called a minor Indian god.

From under the hooded blue cloak came a delicate snore.

"That's it!" said Forseti.

"I'm gonna start screaming!" screamed Cloacina, the Roman Goddess of the Sewers.

"Start?" sniffed Aji-Suki-Taka-Hi-Kone, covering his nose against her stench. The Japanese God of Thunder was baffled that someone or something could actually be louder than he was.

"Oh, that's great—just what I need—more noise," said Alu. Even though the Mesopotamian demon had no legs, ears, or mouth, somehow everyone heard him.

The official who had been calling out was so shriveled in size he could barely see over the flat marble countertop; he clambered on top and surveyed the crowd.

"What's going on?" he shouted. "No one wants a permit?"

"This one won't move," called Forseti, indicating the sleeping figure in blue, then he looked at the Chinese spirit in front of him. "Give her backside a slap, why don't you?"

"Aren't you Forseti?" asked the spirit. "Aren't you the Norse God of Justice?"

"With places to go and people to see," he replied. "Now give her a good whack!"

"That would be impolite," said the spirit.

"Poke her with a stick!" screamed Cloacina.

"Why don't *you* go stand close to her," boomed the Japanese thunder god. "That would wake anyone."

"Go around her," purred Ailuros, an Egyptian cat deity, in line off to the side.

"The yellow line on the floor says, 'Please do not cross until it is your turn,'" said the spirit.

The snoring from under the blue cloak was now punctuated with grunts and snorts.

"It just became your turn!" said Forseti as he picked up the Chinese spirit and threw her over the yellow line.

Rising up off the floor, the Chinese spirit turned, her eyes narrowing into slits, her long black hair now standing on end, brushing against the high ceiling, as she summoned a magic spell to punish the one who had manhandled her. Flinging out her hands with a loud cry, the spirit produced tiny sparks at the ends of her fingers and then . ... nothing.

"Fool!" laughed Cloacina.

"You won't get anywhere with that nonsense," said Forseti. "You can't. You're forgetting, that's why we're all here."

"Oh," said the spirit. "Of course you are correct. But you may expect to see me outside."

"Right. I'm frightened," laughed the god as the spirit turned to the counter.

A second space at the counter opened up and Forseti stepped easily around the sleeping, blue-robed woman. And then another bypassed her, then another. For the rest of the day, as other foreign immortals circumvented her without reservation, all wanting permission to practice their powers in Persia, Hera stood at the front of the line, deep in slumber.

CHAPTER FOUR

A Full and Frank Exchange of Views

Pandy's lower body was completely encased in sand; she could still wiggle her toes, but moving her legs in the dense grit was difficult. Now, as it began to pile up and around her back and arms, she started to panic: they were all going to be buried alive. Suddenly she realized that Iole wasn't even sitting up, the way she and Homer were; Homer had laid Iole down against the camel . . . on her side! Pandy began flailing her arms, trying to brush away some sand in order to free herself. She had to get to Iole, if she wasn't already buried.

As she freed one arm, the wind caught hold of the fabric of her cloak and nearly ripped Pandy's arm out of its socket. Pandy was dragged almost wholly out of her sand casing and flung on her stomach, her legs pinned awkwardly and painfully underneath her. Almost immediately, the sand began covering her again. She felt Dido struggling away from her and then she felt a strong tug on the enchanted rope tied around her waist. Completely blind, her eyes shut tight, her hands now exposed as the wind tore the cloak away, she groped the air in front of her, grabbing nothing but sand and air. She didn't even know which direction she was facing. Suddenly, the rope snapped in two and Pandy felt herself flung backward and her hand hit something hard but pliant. She felt a huge pair of hands grab for her arm and pull her slowly across the sand. Feeling her way along as Homer dragged her up and over the sand covering his own legs, Pandy's finger touched Iole's shoulder, and then her head, which was lolling to one side. Homer had righted her, Pandy thought, thanking the gods.

Pandy's clothing was now twisted against her body. As she crouched down beside Iole, the edge of the camel blanket Homer had used as a covering flew up and slapped Pandy on the side of her head, dazing her for a second. She thought she felt Dido climbing over her at one point. Then, the fraying ends of her cloak (a prize possession of her mother's that her father had given to her the night before she began her quest) got caught up in another particularly violent gust and nearly strangled Pandy as it was blown backward before it was thrown over her head and pinned against her face, suffocating her.

Then . . .

. . . it all just stopped.

The wind and the sand died out and the thunderous roar dimmed to just an obnoxious noise.

Pandy didn't know what was happening exactly and brought her hands up inside the cloak, trying to make a little breathing room. Suddenly, she realized that she could move her arms and her shoulders freely. She heard Dido yelp once, then Homer's voice calling to her. Slowly she pulled her cloak off of her head.

There were still a few grains of fine sand spiraling through the air, so she shielded her eyes as she opened them, staring down at first.

Looking up, she saw the enormous brown mass of whirling, choking sand now about five meters away and slowly moving off to the east. With only a glance at Homer, who was extracting his legs from their sand tomb, Pandy looked toward Iole . . .

. . . or where Iole should have been.

She was almost completely covered. The only thing Pandy could recognize was the shape of Iole's head and a few hanks of black hair poking out from the sand hill stacked against the camel.

"Iole!" Pandy screamed as she began flinging sand away from Iole by the handful, just as Dido, somehow freed from the rope, rushed over and began shaking himself furiously.

"Homer! Help me!"

Homer was at her side in an instant, but instead of scooping away the sand, he rammed both arms, elbow-deep, into the sand hill on either side of Iole and slowly lifted her out. Part of the camel blanket was caught in Iole's hair clip, and Iole's neck was stretched at an awkward angle. Pandy quickly freed the clip. Homer laid Iole on her back, and Pandy searched her face for any signs of life, but Iole was ashen.

"She's warm," Pandy said, putting her hand to Iole's forehead while she pushed away Dido's nose. "Stay back, boy!"

"She's breathing," Homer said, pointing to the very slight rise and fall of Iole's chest.

The next moment, Iole coughed and opened her eyes. Then she closed them again.

"Iole?" Pandy asked gently.

"I'm here," Iole answered, almost inaudibly, her eyes still closed.

Pandy sighed and turned to Homer.

"Thank you," she said, mindful that he was deliberately not looking at her. "Gods, that was fast thinking!"

"Oh," he said, then paused as if weighing his next words very carefully, "I'm sure you could think that fast. I've seen you do a lot of things fast."

He moved to stand, untying his end of the magic rope and dropping it on the ground.

"When you want to."

Pandy jerked her head to stare up at him, seeing only his back as he walked away, shaking the sand from his cloak.

"What?" she called after him.

He didn't reply.

Pandy felt confused, as if he'd physically hit her for no reason, or no reason she knew of. But beyond that, she was just plain curious. Homer was behaving as if he were a totally different person.

"What did you *say,* Homer?" she yelled, her growing confusion and frustration causing her voice to rise unevenly.

Homer was shaking out his toga as if he hadn't heard her at all.

"We'd better get moving," he said calmly. "The storm shifted all the dunes and—"

"Stop it!" Pandy cried. She fumbled at the rope knot around her waist, then realized the rope had snapped and she was no longer tied to Iole.

Pandy stomped toward Homer. She stepped in front of him and spun to face him.

"What is going *on*?" she yelled. "What did you say about me being fast or quick or whatever? What's with you?"

Sensing Pandy's anger, Dido rushed in and was about to leap on Homer.

"Dido! Go! Go stay with Iole!"

Dido growled but trotted away.

"So?" Pandy hissed.

"I just meant," he said, gritting his teeth, and Pandy saw that he was not calm at all; his whole body was shaking slightly, "that you can be fast when you want to be. You can move fast and think fast . . . and *answer* fast. When you want to."

"What are you *talking* about?" Pandy cried.

"And hey," he yelled back at her, "we didn't, like, lose Iole, so I guess it doesn't really matter which of us was fastest this time, right?"

Pandy felt like she was being slapped. But why? This was code. Homer was talking in some sort of code that she couldn't decipher. She vaguely heard Dido bark in the background. Who cared who was fastest? He'd made a point of hammering the word "answer" as if it meant . . .

And suddenly the realization hit her so hard that she staggered backward and fell to the ground.

He blamed her for Alcie's death.

Pandy just stared at Homer, tears filling her eyes, her lower lip beginning to quiver without her knowing.

In Aphrodite's temple in the city of Aphrodisias, when Hera, disguised as Aphrodite, had demanded a life in return for the golden apple, Pandy, Alcie, Iole, and Homer had huddled together to try to think of a way out. There was nothing to be done, however, and Pandy, of course, had spoken first: she had to be the one to die; after all, this whole thing was her fault. Homer had spoken, and Iole—Pandy let them all have their say—but she knew that, in the end, as the leader, she would be the one to make the sacrifice. Then Alcie had demanded her turn to speak, and Pandy was fully prepared to hear her out, then gently tell Alcie there was no way and raise her own voice to volunteer. What she had not prepared for was Alcie suddenly calling loudly that she would give *her* life and Hera seizing the moment. Pandy tried to override Alcie, but Alcie was instantly transported to the steps where Hera stood and bitten by a huge snake, before Pandy could do anything of consequence. Worse still, the other three had been forced to watch, immobilized, as Alcie writhed in agony.

And now Homer was putting Alcie's murder squarely on Pandy's shoulders, insinuating that Pandy had deliberately been slow to call out her own name and had willingly let Alcie die. No, more terrible, that Pandy had, essentially, killed Alcie.

Pandy sat in the sand and sobbed. She covered her eyes with her hands, getting more tiny grains stuck underneath her lids. In the next few moments, she realized that she, herself, had never really grieved, never really come to terms with the loss of a best friend.

And then, in the blink of an eye, she became angry. Not quite as angry as she'd been with Hera, but very close.

"How dare you!" she screamed at Homer, startling him.

Dido was on the move.

"Stay back, boy!"

Dido backtracked and sat, tensed, over Iole. Pandy glared at Homer.

"You blame *me*? You think I *let* her do that? You think I wanted my best friend to die? It was always going to be *me*, Homer. Always! I was the one! I let the rest of you speak because that's . . . that's what a good leader does. And I was . . . I am trying to be a good—"

"Oh, yeah, you're good, all right," he started.

Pandy took a swing and landed a blow on his arm, which caused her hand a great deal of pain.

"SHUT UP!"

Homer did.

"You think you're the *only* one who loved her? Huh? We—Iole and me—we loved her a long time before you even knew she was a living, breathing person. We had her first! And we had her best . . ."

She was breathing so hard that she was beginning to lose her air, and her head was getting light.

"Well, you didn't have a whole future with her ahead of you!" Homer screamed back at her.

"Like Hades we didn't!" she panted. "You think she was gonna give us up and run away with you when she got older? FAT LEMONS!"

"Stop it," came Iole's voice across the sand, too weak to even be acknowledged.

"As a matter of fact, I do!" Homer cried. "You think she wasn't gonna grow up?"

"Of course she was gonna grow up, you clod! We all are, but just because you love somebody else doesn't mean you give up your friends!" Pandy spat back.

"Why don't you just do the only thing you do really well and set me on fire! Then I can join her!" Homer yelled.

"Stop it!" Iole shrieked.

"Maybe I will!" Pandy said, the energy leaving her voice. Then her lightheadedness turned into dizziness, and she pitched forward as Homer caught her.

Then Iole mustered every ounce of strength she still had and let out a long, pitiful scream as Dido, panicked, spun in a circle.

"Oh Gods," Pandy mumbled as Homer carried her quickly to Iole.

Iole lay with a line of sweat beaded across her forehead, her hands absently clawing at the sand.

"I'm okay. Put me down. Put me down," Pandy said, her head clearing a bit as Homer stood her upright.

"For Hermes' sake," Iole whispered, her eyes still closed. "For anyone's sake. For Alcie's sake. Both of you, *stop*."

"Iole, don't try to—," Homer began.

"Be silent, Homer," she said. Each word was a struggle, and only every third or fourth was audible. "You too, Pandy. Gods, Alcie . . . spitting at the two of . . . she were here now. . . . loved her and we all . . . miss her. No one . . . monopoly. Homer . . . not Pandy's fault. You know . . . because . . . knew Alcie. . . . enough to know . . . was a perfect Alcie thing . . . she did. Desist . . ."

She fell into a cough that lasted several seconds.

"Can't you appreciate? . . . comprehend? If . . . at each other like this . . . no point in going on. And we promised Alcie . . . Don't . . . both understand? We're all we've got!"

Homer and Pandy were silent. Then Homer turned away, pounding one fist into the other hand, again and again. Pandy saw his shoulders heave and when he began to turn around, she was certain that it would be to blast her again with another reproach. But his big, beautiful face was scrunched tight and overrun with tears. His mouth was open and slack.

"I'm . . . I'm sorry," he said, staring at the sand, shaking his head back and forth.

"It's okay, Homer," Pandy said. "I get it. I do."

"I'm sorry," he repeated.

Then he reached down and grabbed Pandy into a hug that brought the dizziness back with a rush. Dido jumped up and put his forepaws on Homer's hips.

"Homer. Homer," she wheezed, patting Dido's head and Homer's back. "We're good. We're good."

He set her down.

"We're a team, remember? And everything we do now, we do in part for Alcie, okay?"

"Okay," he agreed.

"Right, Iole?" Pandy asked.

But Iole had passed out.

"Gods," Pandy said. "We have to get her to a physician."

"We have another problem," Homer said.

"What?" Pandy asked.

"Look," he said, pointing.

Two camels, already on their feet, were pawing at the sand over and around the third; Homer's camel lay on the ground, a mountain of sand piled high against her back, quite dead.

"Oh, no," Pandy said, following Homer as he went to make certain.

"Hermes said the camel was known as 'The Ship of the Desert,'" he said softly. He patted the camel's neck, feeling her body growing cold.

"They're supposed to be able to withstand anything," Pandy said.

"Maybe," Homer said, "it was just her time."

Pandy was silent for moment.

"Like Alcie," she said, putting her hand on Homer's.

"Like Alcie," said Homer, rising and glancing down at the animal, her fur moving faintly in the lessening breeze.

"She was a good ship."

He wasn't aware that Pandy was staring at the crest of a newly created sand dune.

"We need another camel," he said.

Then he followed Pandy's arm as she raised it to point off into the distance.

"Maybe we could use one of theirs."

CHAPTER FIVE
Unwanted Epithet

It had been amusing for a while, watching the other deities laugh, poke, pinch, and prod Hera as they stepped around the sleeping goddess, still slumped at the front of the line, her hip thrust sideways at an awkward angle. Each immortal chided her after their own fashion, spitting unintelligible curses or whispering snide remarks.

But now it had become tiresome to everyone. Finally, one official whose place at the counter had just opened up, held his hand high and halted Cloacina, the Roman Goddess of the Sewers, just as she was crossing the yellow line. With a glare at the official, she stepped back but not before waving the sleeves of her stinking cloak underneath Hera's nose, which caused the goddess to cough in her sleep.

"This has gone on long enough," the official said for the benefit of everyone in the large room.

Slowly, he began to make small circles in the air with his right forefinger. Out on the floor, Hera lifted a few centimeters off the ground and began to spin lazily. Faster and faster the official twirled and faster Hera spun; just as she was becoming a blue blur, the official clenched his hand and Hera dropped to the floor, the energy of her spinning sending her sprawling across the tiny, intricate mosaic tiles.

"*Ohp!*" she cried as her eyes flew open. She lay motionless for a second, not realizing where she was.

"Next!" called the official.

All eyes went to the large mass of blue robes on the floor. Hera lifted her head, still partially covered by the hood of her cloak, and stared back, dazed.

"Is that me?"

"Yes!"

"It's you, lady."

"Has been for a while now."

Hera tried to pick herself up off the floor gracefully but instead stepped on a corner of her robe and everyone within earshot heard a soft *riiiiiip.*

"All right, then," Hera said nonchalantly, lifting her robe and walking, as stately as she could, up to the counter.

The official didn't even glance up.

"I would like to—," Hera began.

"Name?" the official cut in.

"Oh, yes, of course. Hera. Wife of—"

"Excuse me?" the official said, now gazing up at her. "What was that?"

Hera was caught off guard and did what she normally did when caught off guard: she became impatient and even more imperious.

"I *said*, 'Hera, wife of—'"

"Zeus?" asked the official. "King of the Gods of Greece?"

"Naturally you heard of him—and me."

The official began to chuckle softly.

"Oh, we've heard of you," the official said, then he called off to his left. "Haven't we, Saad?"

"Haven't we what?" Saad called back.

"Haven't we heard of Hera, wife of Zeus?"

"You're kidding?" Saad said, ignoring his own visa petitioner for a moment. "Don't tell me she's . . ."

"Standing right in front of me, big as life. Bigger!" said the official.

"I find it impolite to talk about—," Hera said.

"First of all, you're gonna lose the *attitude*. Let's not forget why you're here, *Hera*. Do we know you? I should say we do, wife of Zeus. Queen of Heaven."

The official left his stool and walked back a few paces to a wall with several portraits drawn on papyrus sheets hanging on it. Never taking his eyes off of her, he tapped at a decidedly unflattering charcoal sketch of Hera hanging in between a sketch of Loki, the Norse trickster, and the Hindu goddess Kali, the murderous destroyer.

"Chosen One," he continued as he moved back to the counter, rattling off Hera's other nicknames in a voice that sounded as if he had crushed, dried leaves in the back of his throat. "Cow-eyed, Big-eyed, Peacock Lady, Pea-brain, *Bird-brain*."

"No one would venture to call me that! How do you dare . . . ," Hera cried.

"No attitude! Now, around here, we have another name for you. Can you read what it says underneath your picture? No? I'll tell you. It says: 'WARNING! Hera aka Queen of the Gods, wanted in Egypt for questioning in connection with misuse of immortal powers regarding the setting of traps, deadfalls, pits, and other assorted schemes without permission from the local deistic authorities.' "

"What?" asked Hera, trying her best to act innocent.

"Oh, you're fun, you are, Sandtrap. That's what we call you around here. And now you're actually applying for a permit? Well, this is gonna take some time. Lots of paperwork. We have a special room for difficult customers. Follow me."

CHAPTER SIX
The Caravan

"What are they doing?" Pandy asked softly, staring at the crest of the large dune as she untied the length of rope from her waist and slipped it into her pouch.

"They're studying us," Homer said. "Seeing if we're dangerous."

"As if," Pandy said, echoing one of Alcie's favorite phrases.

The five men, three on camels, two on horseback, had not moved for a long time. Snippets of conversation had been carried on a light wind down the dune, but neither Pandy nor Homer could understand what was being said. Suddenly, the three men on camelback and one on a horse broke away and began galloping toward them down the dune.

"Homer?" Pandy's whispered voice shot up in pitch. "*Homer?*"

"Don't move," Homer said firmly. "Stand still."

Dido barked ferociously.

"Dido! Sit!" Pandy ordered. "Not another sound!"

He looked at her, panting, but remained silent.

"Why aren't they all coming?" Pandy asked.

"They're leaving one as a marker," Homer said. "So they'll know where they came from."

There was absolute silence from the men, all dressed alike, with neatly trimmed black beards, each one alert and scowling. The only sound was the heavy breathing of the animals.

"Their weapons are drawn, but not raised," Homer said, his voice still even.

Pandy noticed the scimitars flashing in the sunlight, almost as bright as the single giant rubies studding each man's turban.

Two men stopped their mounts only a meter away from Homer and Pandy, the other two circled behind.

"Yeah, right," thought Pandy, "as if we could escape."

"Your names?" said the man on horseback to Homer.

"I am Homer of Crisa. This is Pandora of Athens. We have a friend with us who is very sick."

"They are but children," said another man to the horse rider. "They are harmless, certainly."

"They are old enough to cause trouble," replied the man on the horse, clearly the one in charge. "They might be spies. They might be a decoy. Who knows what tricks the Physician might use?"

"But," said one of the men behind Pandy, "we would never have found them if not for losing our way in the storm. As guards, we would not have been sent to scout. We should not have seen them."

"They might have been on their way *to* us. To free the Physician," said the man in charge. "You say someone is sick?"

"Very sick," answered Homer, pointing to Iole. "She's there."

"She might be dying!" Pandy cried.

One of the men on camels dismounted and knelt over Iole.

"They do not lie," he said, looking up.

"How convenient," said the horse rider. "When we have the Physician with us."

"This child's illness is not a ruse," said the man, feeling Iole's forehead. "Her fever is great. She does not have much longer."

"How would you want your child treated in a foreign land?" another man asked quietly of the one in charge.

"Is not the generosity and hospitality of Persia known everywhere, even if we are, at present, stuck in this terrible Arabian desert?" questioned a third. "As representatives of that gracious country, are we to let these children die in such a place?"

The man spun his horse around in a circle, thinking a long moment.

"Please!" Pandy cried out at last, not caring what would happen to her, as long as they could help Iole.

The man in charge, looking from Iole's prone form to Homer, then to Pandy, finally sheathed his scimitar.

"Bring them," he said, turning his horse.

The man standing over Iole quickly remounted, then called to Homer.

"Hand her to me."

Homer gently lifted Iole into the man's arms, and he cradled her, unconscious, in front of himself. Pandy saw the magic rope, still around Iole's waist, now dragging in the sand.

"Rope," she mouthed, hoping the severed section was still enchanted, and more importantly, that it would do as she asked. "Circle Iole's waist only."

In less than the blink of an eye, the rope shrunk itself to the point where Pandy thought it was going to slice Iole in two. Pandy nearly shrieked as Iole moaned. Then the rope expanded to just the right size and actually took on a decorative sheen, as if it were part of Iole's clothing.

"Please, I don't know what's going on," Pandy thought to the rope. "But please don't kill Iole."

Pandy and Homer, quickly checking their belongings, mounted the two remaining camels and, surrounded by the rest of the guards, galloped up the dune as Dido ran easily alongside. Reaching the crest, Pandy peered down into a deep valley that she would have sworn had not been there before the storm. Now, instead of a view of the endless desert, she saw a camp of many differently sized tents in various stages of assembly, some undergoing repair from the effects of the storm. Each was constructed of multicolored stripes of brightly dyed canvas. She could also see a long line of camels tethered together, and columns of smoke from several fires as people scurried about, shaking sand from carpets, cooking pots, and clothing.

As he raced his horse toward the caravan, a shout went up from the man in charge, now in the lead and heading toward a half-erected gold and white tent. The other guards took it up and the air was filled with short, high, loud cries, as if they were laughing deliberately. At once, other guards came to the perimeter of the camp, scimitars drawn, and answered back. Pandy could see a few women join the crowd, staring at the approaching strangers over thin veils covering their noses and mouths. As the group reached the tent and began to dismount, a large man approached the horse rider. He was wearing the same garments as the other guards but more richly embellished. There was gold trim on his sleeves and gold fabric woven through his turban, and instead of a ruby, it was held together with a giant emerald. Pandy watched all five guards give a formal salute and greeting to this man as he began to question them about the new arrivals.

Suddenly, a shout went up from somewhere in the growing crowd.

"Pandora!"

Pandy was so startled that she didn't know where to look. Two guards instinctively drew their blades.

"Let me through. Pandora! I know her! I know them!"

Pandy finally spotted a head of black hair close to the edge of the crowd and moving fast, but she couldn't see the face. The woman was waving her arms and would have fallen upon Pandy's feet, since Pandy was still on her camel, if several guards had not stopped her and were about to roughly throw her back.

"Pandora, it is Mahfouza!"

Pandy's mind went blank. Did she know this woman? How?

"Wang Chun Lo! I taught you to dance!"

Instantly, Pandy remembered everything: Wang Chun Lo's Caravan of Wonders, a gathering of strange and wonderful living oddities that had stopped for the evening just outside of the abandoned temple in Egypt when Pandy was hunting for Vanity. All members of the troupe had put on their show especially for Pandy and her friends, and that performance had included one of the most stunning things Pandy had ever seen: Mahfouza and three other Arabian girls, all of incomparable beauty, dancing as if each one had her own personal muse on her shoulder. Their movements, the music they made with tinkly bells on the ends of their fingers had overwhelmed Pandy. But then, at the very end of the performance, they had invited (dragged, in Alcie's case) Pandy and the others onto the floor and had taught them each to "belly" dance—or had tried to at least. Pandy did remember spinning and falling down a lot.

"Mahfouza?"

"Yes! Yes!" the girl cried, then she pushed her way past the guards. "She knows me! Let me through, you donkeys!"

Pandy was off her camel in a heartbeat, and she flew into Mahfouza's arms. Although she really didn't know this girl at all, to Pandy she was a touchstone, something even slightly familiar in an unknown world.

"Why are you here? Where are the other dancers? Is Wang Chun . . . ?" Pandy asked when they finally let each other go.

"No, no. We will talk of me later," Mahfouza answered quickly. "The guards have told their captain that one of you is sick?"

"Iole," Pandy said.

"And only three of you came off the desert, but I see the youth. Where is . . . oh, her name? I have forgotten her name!"

"Alcie."

"Alcie! Of course. Where is Alcie?" Mahfouza asked.

Pandy took a deep breath and felt the tears well up.

"Alcie is dead," Pandy choked out.

Mahfouza's shoulders dropped and her face went slack as she stared at Pandy.

"Stay here a moment," she said, then she marched toward the captain of the guard. Pandy saw Mahfouza gesturing toward her and Homer, then back into the caravan. At last she saw the captain nod and wave her off as if Mahfouza's words were insignificant and a bother.

"Come," Mahfouza said, racing back to Pandy. "You will all stay in my tent. Tell the youth. I will have them bring Iole."

As Pandy and Homer collected their things off the camels, she told him of their coincidental, unimagined link to the caravan in the form of the beautiful dancing girl.

"Pandora, this way!"

They saw a guard carrying Iole in his arms, following Mahfouza.

"This way!" Mahfouza called back to Pandy and Homer as they hurried to keep up. Dido wove his way after them, his pure whiteness causing whispers and stares.

Passing many tents, Pandy could not help but notice the wild color combinations: black and olive and cloud gray, lemon and blue and silver, bloodred and lime and brown. They came to a large tent, striped in colors of plum and cherry, and found Mahfouza inside, commanding the guard to be careful as he placed Iole on a pile of floor cushions. Pandy motioned Dido to a spot on the floor out of the way, indicating he should lie down and stay.

"I know a little medicine," Mahfouza said, bending over Iole as the guard left. "We shall see."

Several minutes later, after much gazing and gentle poking, Mahfouza looked up, stricken.

"It is beyond me. Any potions or elixirs I know would be useless. I am sorry."

"Do you know what she has?" Homer asked. "Why she's so—"

"Wait just one tick on the sundial!" Pandy interrupted. "There's someone here called 'the Physician,' right? Some big shot, ooby-dooby guy, right?"

Mahfouza gasped slightly.

"Right?" Pandy went on insistently. "Well, let's go get him, for Apollo's sake!"

"The captain would never allow it," Mahfouza whispered.

"We don't know that until we ask!" Pandy said.

"The Physician is under constant guard."

"I don't care!" Pandy said through gritted teeth. She stormed out of the tent with Mahfouza on her heels.

"Dido, *stay*! Homer, please look after Iole," Pandy said over her shoulder. "Which way?"

"Come," said Mahfouza, heading toward the front of the caravan. When they reached the two guards at the entrance to the gold and white tent, Mahfouza began to speak, but Pandy put a hand on her arm, silencing her.

"Let me," she said. "It might mean more if everyone thinks that a stranger, even a maiden, has respect enough to learn their language."

"Save that for the captain," Mahfouza said. "I will get us past the guards."

Mahfouza expertly negotiated their entrance into the captain's tent by explaining that Pandora, as leader of her group (an extremely rare position for a woman in Arabia), wished to pay her respects and express her gratitude to the captain for allowing them into the caravan. Once inside, she did this with several other groups of guards until at last she and Pandy stood in front of the captain, who remained silent and motionless.

"Exalted is He," Mahfouza said, making a gesture of greeting and respect.

"Exalted is He," Pandora quickly echoed, attempting the same movements.

The captain of the guard looked surprised at hearing a young girl, dressed in strange garments, obviously from far away, speaking his language.

"Your Persian is flawless," he said. "How is this so?"

Pandy began to lie on the spot. She didn't consider it a large lie, but rather a necessary bit of cunning: part of that set of powers that included a growing intellect fueled by a bad situation, which her father alluded to the night before she left her home.

"The power to think things through, to see the big picture, not just the small scene. To use your wonderful mind to its absolute fullest. And don't forget, sweetheart, you're semi-immortal . . . so the power of your mind might manifest itself in interesting ways . . . You'll ask, you'll ponder, you'll learn."

Pandy heard her father's words clearly in her head.

So instead of telling the captain that she'd drunk the ashes of the evil magician Calchas in an abandoned temple in Egypt, she said respectfully, "I attended an excellent school in . . . in my native homeland, of Greece. I am Pandora Atheneus Andromaeche Helena of the House of Prometheus. It is, um, well known in Greece, as it is everywhere, that Persian is a beautiful language, but not easily mastered. Therefore, I made it my personal goal to speak it as well as possible. I am honored that you find me . . ."

What *was* the word? She'd heard Iole use it a hundred times!

". . . *adept*, sir."

"I do," he replied. "Now what is it you wish? Although, I think I already know."

"One of my companions is very ill and there is in this camp a physician."

"No," said the captain flatly.

Pandy took a deep breath and pleaded her case again and again, using various stratagems, fabricating a rich tale of Iole being of great importance, the daughter of a statesman and very wealthy. The captain remained resolute. Finally Pandy, seeing Iole's life slip from her grasp, stopped the lie. She looked at the captain, a small sag in her shoulders.

"She is one of only two friends I ever had," Pandy began. "The other is dead. Please, please don't let me lose this one, too."

The captain, moved by the single tear coursing down her cheek, relented.

"He will be brought to you in chains and they are not to be removed," he said. "The dancer's tent will be surrounded with a man every five paces and two at the entrance. Two will be inside the tent with their backs to the proceedings, as I am aware there may be some examination. If any of you attempts to help the Physician escape, you will regret it. Is all of this understood?"

"Yes, yes!" Pandy cried. "Thank you!"

She and Mahfouza bowed low and ran out of the tent.

"Well done, Pandora!" Mahfouza said.

"It was the truth that worked. Who knew?" Pandy replied. "And, please, call me Pandy."

They burst into Mahfouza's tent to find Homer, sitting over Iole, fanning her with a small cushion.

"She's burning up," he said.

"Douban is on his way," said Mahfouza.

"Who's that?" asked Pandy.

"Douban," Mahfouza replied, then she looked incredulously at Homer and Pandy. "Douban the Physician? Surely you have heard of him?"

Pandy and Homer shook their heads.

"He is the greatest physician in the known world. I cannot believe his fame has not traveled to Greece."

"Well, we have Apollo," Pandy replied.

"At any rate, he will be here soon," Mahfouza said. "So now we will wait."

Settling themselves close to Iole, the group was silent for a long time. Then Pandy looked at the lovely dancer, whose concern for Iole seemed to match her own.

"Mahfouza, why are you here? Now? Why aren't you with Wang Chun Lo? Did something happen? Where are you going?"

"Pandy, please," Mahfouza said, smiling. "Let me answer these questions before you ask any more."

"Oh, sorry," Pandy said. "I'm just curious."

"Wang Chun Lo's Caravan of Wonders is doing well, I must assume. Instead of four dancers, they now have only three. I received word of trouble at home, so I have left to be with my family."

"I'm sorry," Pandy said. "How far are you traveling?"

"To Baghdad."

"That's where we are going," Homer cut in.

"I thought you were Arabian," Pandy said.

"That's only for advertising." Mahfouza smiled. "Wang Chun Lo thought it would be simpler to bill us as four exotic Arabs, but in truth, we were from all over. Pandy, you are still on your quest to find the remaining evils, yes?"

Pandy nodded.

"Baghdad is such a small, backwater town on the Tigris. I cannot imagine a great evil taking up residence there. It was only my father's business, providing goods to ships in port, which forced my mother to make a home there. The house still stands, I believe, but I fear my parents are dead."

"What?" Pandy cried. "How do you know? What was the message? Who told you?"

"No one told me. It was not that kind of message."

Mahfouza rose off of her floor cushion and went to a wooden trunk from which she pulled a carved box, not unlike the box that Pandy carried in her leather pouch.

"The day I left to join Wang Chun Lo, my father gave me a dagger. He told me that no matter where I was, if the blade was clean when I pulled it from its sheath, all was well with him. But if the blade was bloody, he had been terribly injured or worse. On that same day, my mother gave me a string of pearls, saying that if the string remained loose and I was able to slide the pearls back and forth, she was fine, but if the string was fixed and unmovable, she too was either injured beyond hope or already dead. For several years I kept both items in this box. I had pulled the dagger from its sheath many times and found it clean, and I had draped the pearls around my neck. Then, for several months I actually forgot to do these things, thinking that all was and always would be well. Shortly after you came to us in Egypt and we all learned what had happened and why you were on your quest, I became frightened."

Sitting again, she placed the box on the ground in front of her and lifted the lid.

"As it turns out, I had good reason to be."

Mahfouza held up the dagger and slowly drew the blade from the sheath. Blood began dripping everywhere, staining the carpets and cushions. She sheathed the dagger again and put it in the box. Then she took out a strand of large pearls, frozen in a straight line, not one pearl loose.

"I don't even know the exact day these items became like this," she murmured.

Replacing the pearls and closing the lid, Mahfouza looked at Pandy.

"Do you know what 'Baghdad' means?" she asked.

"No," Pandy said softly.

"*Bagh* means 'God' and *dad* means 'gift,'" she said. "It is a gift from God. That is how I always saw it. The city is a trash heap, really, but I loved it. It is my home. And now I fear it is my parents' grave."

Once again, Pandy felt the tremendous weight of the responsibility of her actions. If Rage was in Baghdad and Mahfouza's parents had suffered because of it . . . it was all her fault.

"I'm sorry," she began. "I'm so very sorry."

But she was interrupted by the sound of heavy foot-steps approaching and encircling the tent. Seconds later, two guards entered and took up their posts. Shortly after that, four guards shoved their way through the entrance. They surrounded a small, frail man and a youth appearing to be only slightly older than Homer; both were clothed in simple white robes. Shoving them into the center of the room, the four guards departed.

"Don't try anything funny," one guard said as the tent flap closed behind him.

The older man turned and looked from Mahfouza to Pandy to Homer, then his eyes came to rest on Iole.

"Did someone call for a physician?"

CHAPTER SEVEN

The Tale of Douban the Physician

With his eyes trained on Iole, the man glided across the floor of the tent. Pandy noticed that neither he nor the boy were in chains, as promised. Perhaps even the captain realized there was nowhere to escape to. Mahfouza rushed across her tent.

"Thank you, Douban," she began.

"Not now, my dear," he said quietly, patting her arm as he passed her. "Come, my son."

The youth, with only a glance at Pandy, followed his father. They knelt over Iole and studied her face, flushed and beaded with sweat.

"What do you see?" Douban asked the youth.

"There is no visible trauma," the youth replied. "Her

fever is high. Her lips are cracked, so she has lost much fluid. It is either an infection or digestive."

"Good . . . for a start. And I concur," said the elder man, and then he looked up. "Who can tell me of this girl?"

"I can," Pandy spoke up. Then she looked at Homer. "We can."

"Do so," said Douban.

"We've been, uh, days in the desert," Pandy started.

"Eleven," said Homer.

"Eleven. And she was fine up until two days ago. Then she couldn't keep her food down, she can't drink. . . ."

"From where have you traveled?" asked Douban.

"From Greece," said Pandy. "I mean, originally. But we were most recently in Aphrodisias."

Douban looked up at Pandy.

"How are you called?"

"Huh?" asked Pandy. "Oh, you mean my name. I am Pandora of Athens."

The youth's eyes widened and, suddenly, Douban's entire face became a mixture of pure astonishment, disbelief, concern, and joy; yet only the corner of his mouth moved, rising upward slightly.

"Can you believe it?" Mahfouza said suddenly. "And I was speaking of her only the other night!"

"Yes, my dear," said Douban, speaking to Mahfouza but staring intently at Pandy. "But her fame preceded her long before you recounted the dancing lesson. This may explain much."

He turned his attention back to Iole.

"What has been your diet?"

"Huh?" Pandy replied.

"Food."

"Oh! Well, we started out with fresh supplies, but we ran out of those about a week ago. So we've been eating flatbread and dried fruit."

"Show me your stores," said the Physician.

"Well, we don't really have stores," Pandy said, reaching for her leather pouch. "It's all in here."

"You cannot possibly keep enough food in that small space."

Inadvertently, Pandy looked to Homer.

"He's gotta know," Homer said.

"Right," Pandy said, turning back. "Athena, the goddess . . . she's Greek."

"I'm acquainted with your pantheon," Douban said.

"Oh, yeah, well, when we first started out, she enchanted my carrying pouch so that it would always give us dried fruit and flatbread. So that we wouldn't starve if we ever got into trouble."

"Let me see what it can produce."

Pandy reached in her pouch and brought out a handful of dried dates, apricots, and figs and several small pieces of flatbread, then handed everything to Douban.

Carefully, the Physician turned the bits over in his hands, sniffing them in short bursts that wrinkled his nose like a squirrel's, examining each and every morsel in the filtered purple and crimson light of the tent. Then he handed them to his son, whose reaction, while slower, was the same.

"These are tainted," Douban said at length. "In fact, they are spoiled to the point of being poisonous. I have no doubt that your friend succumbed before you because she is relatively small and seems rather frail, but the two of you would soon follow had you continued to consume this."

"What? But Athena . . . ," exclaimed Pandy.

"All will be explained," Douban said. "Now, I require hot water, a small dish, and a little space. And quiet."

Quickly, Mahfouza poured a cup of hot water from an urn nestled in a glowing pile of coals. Pandy watched as Douban pulled a few dark glass bottles from hidden pouches in the sleeves of his robes. He emptied tiny measured amounts of the oddly colored, foul-smelling contents of the jars into the dish: powders; blue, milky white, and amber liquids; seeds; crushed dried leaves. Occasionally, he would murmur an instruction to his son, or ask what the youth thought would be the next step. At last, he added some hot water and quickly mixed together a greenish-white paste. Then, opening Iole's mouth, he coated the inside of her cheeks and her tongue with the concoction.

"Do you see what I am doing?" Douban asked his son. "Mixing this with this. Do you understand why?"

"Yes, Father," said the youth.

Then Douban brought out a small role of white gauze.

"Knife," he asked of Mahfouza.

"Here," she said, fetching a petite blade.

Douban cut several strips of the gauze and dipped them into the rest of the hot water, then laid them carefully across Iole's mouth and nose. As his son found a place to sit behind his father, Douban settled back onto a large black cushion and closed his eyes.

"So . . . ," Pandy began after many moments had passed.

Douban opened his eyes.

"Is she going to be all right?" Pandy asked.

"Of course," Douban said. Then he shook his head. "I humbly ask your forgiveness. I did not mean to keep you in suspense regarding your friend. I was simply giving in to a momentary love of the art of healing . . . and thinking how much I shall regret having to give it up. But of course, your friend will be perfect come sunrise. The poultice is being absorbed through the wet membranes of her cheeks and into her blood, where it will have a restorative effect, I promise you."

"But the food?" Homer said.

"Yes," Douban said. "Let me explain. You have left your native homeland of Greece, ruled by your own gods. You are now crossing the Arabian desert on your way to . . . ?"

"Baghdad," answered Pandy.

"Ah. As are we," he said, his face falling slightly. "Oh! Be merciful! Again, forgive my rudeness: allow me to introduce my son Douban."

The youth nodded toward Homer, who greeted him back. Then he looked at Pandy and smiled . . . and didn't look away.

"Are you called Douban the Younger?" she asked. "I mean . . . doesn't it get confusing?"

"At home we call him Dou-dou," said the elder man.

At this, the youth pursed his lips and looked at the ground.

"Do not fret, my son," said Douban. "Shortly, you shall have my name all to yourself. And my work shall become yours as the art of healing is handed to you as my father handed it to me, and his before that. It is only a little sooner than I expected."

"I am sorry, Father," said his son.

"I can't bear this," said Mahfouza, causing Pandy to look at her with curiosity.

"At any rate, Pandora," said Douban, with a wave to calm Mahfouza. "You need to know that the rules, the gifts, the enchantments of your lands and your gods have no sway here, and what was once beneficial can often become deadly. There is still an enchantment on your pouch and should you ever return to Greece, or someplace where your gods hold power, your pouch will start producing nutritious food once again. Until that time, well, we have our own higher powers here, and they must be respected."

"But it gave me a lot of food just a few weeks ago when I was in the Atlas Mountains," Pandy said. "That's not Greece!"

"Indeed," Douban answered. "And those of us who have been hearing of your exploits were most impressed by the way you handled your uncle and captured Laziness."

Pandy was suddenly aware that the younger Douban was again gazing at her.

"But you see," his father continued, "Zeus banished your uncle to that high peak, forcing him to hold the heavens for eternity. Therefore, your Sky-Lord must have some sort of power trade with the other gods or spirits of that land, and the enchantments of other Greek gods would still be in effect. We have also heard of your adventures in Egypt. I am certain there must be an arrangement with those gods as well."

Pandy thought of the enchanted rope and understood the reason it was behaving so strangely.

"But wait! Dido ate this food," Pandy said with a sudden realization. "He's smaller than Iole. Kinda."

"The unclean can eat anything," Douban said.

Dido raised his head.

"Ex-*cuse* me?" Pandy said, dropping her voice.

"I am sorry," Douban said. "I did not mean to offend. It is simply custom to call a dog—"

"Father," interrupted his son, "if I may. In this part of the world, there are those who still cling to backward thinking. Dogs are considered unclean and some of the lowest of the low."

Dido cocked his head to one side.

"However," the young man continued, "there are others, such as myself, who understand that dogs are wonderful and loving companions. I know my father agrees; it was simply a slip of the tongue. And your dog, if I may say so, not only looks remarkable but seems to be a wonderful animal."

The younger Douban looked at Pandy and smiled. Pandy felt her stomach drop toward the floor.

"He is," she answered, quickly shifting her gaze back to Iole.

"How were you able to tell this food was bad just by sniffing it?" asked Homer.

"That is a gift I have been given," Douban said, smiling wistfully.

"He is the greatest physician in the known world!" Mahfouza exclaimed, startling everyone.

"For the moment," Douban said sadly.

"Then why did you say you have to give it up?" Pandy asked. Then she became bolder. "And why are you, um, a prisoner?"

Again, Douban stared at her for a long time. So long that she became uncomfortable and was about to speak, when he suddenly shifted against the cushion.

"I shall tell you my story," he said. "I think there will be much benefit for you in it. But first let me tell you, Pandora, that you are to be greatly admired. Word of your quest has reached scholarly ears far and wide; you and your friends are much discussed in the libraries, senate halls, throne rooms, and, yes, even the gambling dens. Wagers on your success or failure are placed almost every moment."

"For or against?" asked Homer.

"The majority against, I'm afraid."

Pandy was silent. It was so much better when she thought that her quest was a big secret almost no one knew about. Now, to find out that most of the whole world already believed she was going to fail . . . Suddenly she felt very, very small. Smaller than she'd ever felt in her entire, miserable life.

"I don't seem to be saying the right things to you, do I, my dear?" Douban asked, reading Pandy's face. "Very well, then let me tell you a tale that might be of great interest."

"I'm sorry," Mahfouza said, pulling a small pillow to her side. "But this story makes me so mad that if I have to hear it again, I need to hit something."

Pandy could not imagine what it was that Douban had to say.

"The current ruler of Baghdad," Douban began, "Prince Camaralzaman, contracted leprosy several months ago. He tried every remedy at his disposal: baths, salves, burning the affected areas, freezing, but no cure could he find. The case was so severe that at last, having heard of my skill, he sent for me. When I arrived, the prince was close to death, but by means of various potions and herbs, cloth bandages soaked in special oils and the like, I was able to cure him completely. He was initially so grateful that he gave me wealth such as I had never known—jewels, land, fine garments, and a host of slaves to do my bidding. I told him that I was thankful for his kindness, but that I really wanted nothing more than to return home to my family. Yet the prince demanded that I remain as his personal physician; he built me a palace next to his and elevated me to a position at his court equal to that of his grand vizier."

"What's that?" asked Pandy.

"The vizier is the most important, most trusted, and usually the wisest of the prince's advisers. Except in this case. The grand vizier, seeing me ensconced in my new palace and in such favor with the prince became extremely jealous and, I am convinced, began to whisper into the prince's ear that I was secretly plotting against him. The prince held a good opinion of me for many days but finally surrendered to the slander. One day, only a few weeks ago, the prince summoned me into his presence, but he did it with none of his usual graciousness: there were no roses strewn on the path before me; no lovely women leading me on, scenting the air with perfume; no musicians playing me along. This time, I was grabbed by my arms by two huge guards and dragged from my palace and thrown at the feet of the prince. The prince then said that he was aware that I was plotting to assassinate him and that he was going have me executed the next instant. I begged for only one thing."

"What? What!" cried Pandy, horrified and completely rapt.

"That I be allowed to return home to my family for a stay of one week and set my affairs in order, arrange my funeral, bestow some charity, and acquaint my eldest son with the books and papers that he will need in his new position. I promised that I would return by the next caravan and he could carry out his sentence."

"No *way*!" shouted Homer.

"You gotta be kidding!" cried Pandy.

"He's not," said Mahfouza, punching the pillow.

"But you were, like, in the *clear*," Homer said in disbelief. "You could have taken your family and run!"

"Your name is Homer, yes?" Douban asked.

"Yes," said Homer.

"Well, Homer," Douban said. "Yes, you're right, even though the prince sent a guard into my home, I could have easily made my escape anytime I wanted to. But I gave my word. In the end, it is the only thing that is ever wholly ours, and when we speak it must be only the truth. I said I would go back and back I am going. I am bringing my son so that he may return my remains to our home."

"Not cool," Homer said quietly.

"Do not despair," Douban said, smiling. "Now that you all are here, I know I have made the right decision. You see, Pandora, I believe that my death will help you."

"Okaaay. Kind of a big leap. Not really seeing it," Pandy said.

"While I am going back to fulfill a promise, have no fear, the prince will also be punished. I know that you are not only searching for the great Evils, but for lesser ones as well. I believe that the prince is consumed with several, four to be exact: weakness of character, gullibility, deep ingratitude, and a lack of mercy. If you will join me at the palace at the moment of my execution, you may be able to capture a few of these. Now, you must pay attention to my head when it—"

"Uh, y-y-your head?" Pandy stuttered.

"Yes, my dear. That is how it will be done. The prince is demanding my head."

CHAPTER EIGHT
Paperwork

The old official led Hera through a series of back rooms and corridors, each sumptuously designed and detailed, and each staffed with workers who whispered and gawked as the Queen of Heaven walked by. There were, Hera noticed, a curiously large number of small monkeys clothed in colorful, bejeweled vests and caps, racing to and fro—carrying papers, fetching cups of hot liquids to the workers, pushing large carts full of papers or small, white rounded stones. And, she observed, each monkey had a collar around his neck with the same fat, milky white stone at the center.

From under her hood, Hera nodded graciously to everyone as if she were bestowing a great gift simply by being in the room. Then she caught two women giggling by an urn of cooled water as she strode by. Glaring at them, she heard another man snicker as he sat hunched over sheets of papyrus, copying information from one page to another.

"Guess I'll be checking over a lot of forms with this one," he called out to the official who was now leading Hera down a darkened hallway.

"Sorry about it," the official yelled over his shoulder. "Hope you didn't have any wine-and-hummus plans after work."

He led Hera into what was, comparatively, a plain room, large and windowless except for a row of tiny, ruby-bordered windows along the very top of one wall, letting in only a small amount of light. In the center of the room was a long table on which were placed several stacks of paper, each a few centimeters high.

"And here we are," said the official.

Hera looked down at the piles with disdain.

"Declaration of All Powers Outside Persian Borders," she read aloud from the heading on one page. "Purpose of Visit to Persia, Agreement of Non-Malicious Intent."

She picked up a pile, thumbed through it, and roughly tossed it down again.

"I have to sign all of these?" she asked.

"There's that attitude again," said the official. "And no, of course you don't have to sign all of these."

"I should hope not."

"You have to sign all of these *and* all of these," said

the official, pointing across the room to two monkeys moving toward them, pushing a cart twice their size, full to the brim with piles and piles of papyrus sheets, most in small bundles.

Hera opened her mouth, but the official cut her off.

"It's so simple. You either sign all of these forms, in triplicate, which means three—count 'em, three—times, or you will be denied access into the country and all rights and privileges granted therein. You won't get an egg, and for you there's no way out of this building without one except a one-way express back to your country of origin. Where, I can only imagine, they miss you terribly. Moudi and Houdi . . ."

He pointed at the monkeys, who jumped up and down and clapped their hands.

". . . will be watching just to make certain you don't miss anything. And if you leave, that's it. At a later time, if you decide you do want to behave, you'd have to go back and wait in that long line again. No cuts."

The man's tone was almost more than Hera could bear. She desperately wanted to be furious, and for a moment she was until she was distracted by something the man had only glossed over.

"Egg?" Hera said, glancing at the collar around one monkey's neck.

The official looked at her as if she were crazy.

"Of course," he said, then he paused. "Didn't you see

all of the others walking away with shiny white objects when they left? Didn't you pay any attention when you were standing in line? Oh, that's right. You were so excited to be here that you fell *asleep*."

"Yes," Hera said slowly, her teeth clenched. If only she had this man in her clutches back in Greece. "Yes, I am sorry about that, I feel as if I have been waiting in line such a very long time."

"Time is irrelevant here," the official cut in. "Very much, I believe, like your underworld. You may have been here only several ticks of a sundial. Or you might have been here for weeks. You were sleeping, you know."

"Yes, and again, I do so apologize, but what does an egg have to do with—?"

"*An* egg?" he said loudly. "Not just *an* egg. My word, you really didn't do your homework, did you? Every immortal visitor must, at all times, be in possession of a roc's egg."

"What's a roc?"

"What . . . whaaaa . . . *what's a roc?* Do you know *anything*?"

"How to turn you into an oil lamp," Hera thought.

"A roc is the most sacred of all our birds, and an unborn roc, still in its egg, is the most powerful creature in Persia, able to bestow abilities great and small on whoever possesses one. The unborn roc has two functions. One, it is the source of a visiting immortal's powers while in Persia; or, in other words, it will allow you to use your powers while you are here. And two, it is the master of all genies. You have heard of genies, yes? Well, I can't imagine *you* actually have, since you seem to know so little about Persia, but our main group of immortal beings is made up of genies and peris, or female genies. An unborn roc has one or several of these in his service. Yes, a genie or peri may be enslaved to a human, if a human is lucky enough to capture one that is being punished and is condemned to a ring or a lamp or a slipper or a chair or some such. But the unborn roc is the ultimate source of their powers, it is their 'god' if you will, and the death of a roc means disaster. This is why the egg must be guarded so closely by visiting immortals, and why it must be surrendered upon leaving."

Hera noticed the monkeys, now sitting on top of the table, picking things off each other.

"You give an egg to a monkey?"

"You mind dropping the snide tone?" said the official. "You know I have half a mind to kick you out right now. We're a tolerant and hospitable land, but you're just a pill."

"I am . . . sorry," Hera squeezed out. "I was only wondering."

"The monkeys you see all around are disobedient genies or peris. They either defied their human masters or, worse, defied their roc. One of the alternative punishments to being pent up in a lamp or a ring is that the roc sends them here to the Bureau, changed into animal form, very mortal I might add, which is rather debasing for them, and they are forced to do odd jobs and busy work until they finish off their punishment. The eggs around their necks are a constant reminder. And the unborn roc can communicate without words, so they are continually providing guidance. When the genies or peris have been properly rehabilitated, we take the collar off, they are restored to immortal form, and everything is back to normal."

"So that's what I would—will—get if—when—I fill out all this paperwork? A roc egg?" Hera asked sweetly, her mind racing. "That's what's going to help me truly experience the wonders of your beautiful country?"

"I see you're a quick study," the official said with a smirk. "Fortunately, we are blessed with a surplus of roc eggs, and those with no genies to command elect to come to the Bureau and help with Persia's immortal visitors. You can't get around without one and with it, you have the potential to do almost anything. That's why you have to put your big 'H' on all of these. And now I'll leave you to your signing. I'll see you in about a week—mortal time."

"And I'm going to be monitored by monkeys?"

"I'll bet you were the sharpest one in your class," the

official snapped, his back now turned on Hera. "I'll have a snack brought to you in a few days. Don't eat the monkey food."

Hera watched the man go until one of the monkeys threw a quill pen at her with such force that it stuck in her forearm. She looked down at the feather, its point stuck in her immortal flesh. She looked at her robes, still singed from Pandora setting her ablaze. Pulling the quill out, she reached up and felt her skull; red hairs were beginning to grow back, but it was still short enough so that, without her hood, she looked like a man. She had no idea when her glorious locks would once again cascade down her back. At that moment, her hatred of Pandora swelled to such a point that Hera instantly brought her hands up to her mouth to stifle a scream.

She paused for only a second, her hands clenched until her nails dug into her palms, then she composed herself and turned toward the table and the growing piles of papers. She spread her arms wide, surprising the monkeys, one of which was unloading the cart.

"Are you going to help me? Is that what you're going to do? Come here, my little friends," she cooed in a soothing voice. Houdi and Moudi were instantly enchanted and came forward to the back edge of the table.

"What should I start with, huh? What do you think?" she said, as if coddling an infant. "Should I start with

'Emergency Contacts in Case of Detention or Dismemberment'? Or 'References'? How about 'How Did You First Hear About Persia?' Yes?"

The monkeys shook their heads in disagreement and Houdi grabbed a handful of papers from one stack.

"Those?" she cooed, not seeing what was written on top.

The monkeys nodded with delight.

"That's what we'll do then, all right," she purred. "Will you bring them to me? That's right, that's right."

Houdi raced across the table to her and Hera only glanced at the bottom line. Signing three times, she looked at the other monkey from under lowered eyelids.

"Why don't you both come here and make certain I'm doing it correctly."

As Moudi approached gleefully, in one swift motion Hera grabbed Houdi, snapped his neck, and tossed him on the table. Moudi instantly leapt to the black marble floor, racing toward a door in a far corner of the room. Hera shoved the table out of her way, scattering papers everywhere. Large and bulky as she was, she tore after him and soon had his tail in her hands. Even though her powers were severely diminished, he was no match for her strength.

She carried his body back to the table and placed it by the other one, ripping the collars off each monkey's neck. She thought for a moment how she could carry two eggs; she had no pouch, no headdress, and putting them in the folds of her robe might cause them to smash together and crack. She tried wrapping one collar around her wrist but it was too small. And then an idea struck her.

She removed her ornate gold and emerald earrings, the ones that set off her red hair brilliantly—when she had hair. She carefully detached the bodies of the earrings from their hangers. Then, slowly and meticulously, she took one of her intricate hairpins, now adorning her cloak, and began to pry away the tiny gold egg cage from the first collar.

CHAPTER NINE

You Mean, You Eat That?

Alcie couldn't tell exactly how long she'd been following Persephone through the darkened hallways of Hades' palace. It could have been only five ticks on a sundial, or five hundred, or five thousand. And "following" wasn't really the right term anymore; it was more like racing to keep up, slowing down when something caught Alcie's eye, then speeding up again in the direction Persephone *might* have gone and occasionally, luckily, catching a glimpse of Persephone's robes as she rounded a curve or a corner, or hearing Persephone's voice as she kept up an almost ceaseless running monologue.

Three things were against her, Alcie knew: Persephone was much larger than she was, than any mortal girl really, and her strides were mammoth. Second, Alcie was now definitely feeling both hungry and tired and had to stop often to rest. But third and most interesting, the rooms of Hades' palace were—there was no other word for it—bizarre. There was no color anywhere and yet Alcie was certain that if she were to take the tapestries, floor cushions, or frescoes into the upper world, they would be alive with wild tints. It seemed that everything in every room was perfectly physically whole, but quite, quite dead, and Alcie simply had to stop and stare. Or, in the case of the several arboretums, reach out and touch. These were enormous rooms, glassed in on three sides, filled with blooming black flowers and black vines that were, quite literally, crawling all over the floors and walls. Yet, when Alcie stepped in and gently reached up her fingers to a gorgeous, enormous black rose, the petals crumbled into dust at the slightest touch.

There were many fantastically decorated rooms with one or two sleeping cots. One room held an array of various bottles, jars, and devices used in the healing arts. Another room was filled with scrolls. Still another seemed dedicated to music and musical instruments. Every so often, Alcie thought she'd seen a human form sitting or standing or walking in one of the rooms, and then, as soon as she blinked, the apparition was gone.

But the most astonishing thing about all of these rooms was that out of every window, sealed with glass, Alcie would catch flashes of the most radiant, breathtaking green she'd ever seen. Three times she raced to a window to get a better look, only to have the blackened trees and bushes outside close up and block her view.

It was while standing at one of these windows that Persephone, having backtracked a good distance, found her.

"Okay," she chirped, feigning impatience, "someone said they were hungry and that same someone is daw-dling!"

Alcie turned from the window with a feeling like she'd been caught with her hand in the oatie-cake jar.

"This place is . . . is . . . ," she began. With so many adjectives she could use, she couldn't pick just one.

"I *know*! And we haven't even covered half of it yet! Come on."

Alcie rejoined Persephone in the hallway, but she hadn't gotten two steps before Persephone whirled on her.

"Mother's little toe! Did you see out the window?" she cried with alarm.

"Well, I looked out the window," Alcie began.

"No, but did you *see* out the window?"

There was a new urgency in Persephone's voice.

"Not really," Alcie answered, now a little scared. "I mean, I saw something green."

"What was it?"

"Figs! I mean, golly, uh, I couldn't tell," Alcie replied. "Just a flash and then the bushes got in the way."

"Okay," Persephone sighed. "Okay! Good. See, I knew you weren't really dead! And now it's time for fooooooood!"

As she strode away, Alcie stood stock-still for a moment in utter bewilderment.

"All right," Alcie called out, forgetting entirely that she was, after all, yelling at an immortal. "Just hold up there a tangerine moment!"

She tore after Persephone.

"What is *that* supposed to mean?"

But she'd only run several meters when a glint of gold, silver, and bronze caught her eye and she turned her head. Three shadowy figures in full battle dress sat at a small table in a room chock-full of weapons of every size and shape. Without knowing exactly how she recognized them, she knew instantly who these men were.

"Whoa," she whispered.

"Are they still there?" Persephone asked as she walked back toward Alcie. "Are they letting you see them?"

Alcie just nodded her head, staring at the three rugged faces that now stared back.

"Well, they're warriors, after all," Persephone said. "What do they have to fear from you, right?"

"Achilles?" Alcie whispered.

"And Ajax and Hector. Hi, boys!" Persephone assented, now standing next to Alcie and waving. Achilles and Ajax just ignored her, but Hector gave her a sly little nod of his head.

"Three of the greatest heroes of the Trojan War," Persephone said, slightly fawning. "And cutest. They've been here for centuries, yapping about how it *should* have gone, how it *could* have gone if only someone had drawn their sword earlier or fired their bow later. Blah, blah. Boring, I *know*!"

"Okay," Alcie said firmly, out of patience and very confused. "Time for a chat."

"That's cool," Persephone said. "Fire away."

"Why are they here?"

"They're dead."

"I know they're *dead*, but why aren't they in the Elysian Fields?" Alcie asked. "Isn't that where the heroic and . . . and . . . ?"

"Glorious dead."

"Yeah, thank you," Alcie said, feeling like she was talking to Iole. "Isn't that where they go?"

"Well, not *all* the time."

"What?"

"Alce, sweetie, think about it," Persephone said, startling Alcie by using the nickname only her still-living friends knew. "It's a field. They go out, they run around and scamper like bunnies; they toss a discus or a javelin. That's fine for a bit, but then they need someplace to lie down and recover from all the eternal fun.

Buster . . . Hades . . . has rooms in the palace for all the really heroic and glorious dead. Warriors, physicians, poets, scholars."

"Politicians," Alcie added.

"Oh, gimme a break!" Persephone laughed. "Well, all right, a few, but not many. The really good get to stay here. And the really bad, but they don't take up much space."

"The really bad?" Alcie asked. "They're *here*? Not Tartarus?"

"Hah! Are you kidding? Tartarus is for rookies!" Persephone snickered. "Tartarus is for amateurs! This place makes Tartarus look like a three-day 'Hey, It's Spring!' festival. C'mere, I'll show you."

Persephone walked a few paces, then abruptly turned a corner Alcie knew was not part of the original route.

"By the by," Persephone said, "the EF is the green you're seeing outside the windows."

"EF? The Elysian Fields?"

"I *know*! Cool, huh? But only the heroic and glorious *dead* get to actually view the splendor. Now, you and your friends might be heading toward heroic and glorious, but you're not there yet, and if you can't see the fields, you're definitely not really dead! It's all good."

A hundred meters farther, Alcie could hear men's voices shouting, moaning, and wailing. And, more softly, underneath, she heard women's voices; some sharp, some monotone, but while the men's cries rose and fell, the women's voices were a constant drone.

"We're walking, we're walking, we're walking," Persephone said, mock-officiously leading the way down a corridor of, Alcie guessed by the short spaces between each barred door, very small rooms. "And we're stopping. Here we have not necessarily the most brutal of criminals, but the most despicable. Not your average murderers or fiends, but the truly wicked. Those who went against their conscience. Those who betrayed family or country, especially those who did it for money. We have a couple of kings who wiped out entire civilizations, either theirs or someone else's, because they were power-hungry. And we have a man who sold his wife and daughters into slavery."

"Orange rinds," Alcie said softly.

"I know."

"But it just sounds like they're having a fight with someone," Alcie said.

"Yeah, isn't it grand?" Persephone smiled. "Who do you think is also in each of these rooms with each of these monsters?"

Alcie was baffled.

"I give," she said.

Persephone grinned.

"Their mothers."

"No!"

"I *know*!"

"For eternity?" Alcie whispered.

"Sometimes Buster gets impish and sticks their mother-in-law in there as well. *And,* they're not allowed to sleep."

"Get out!" Alcie cried.

"I *know*! Let's eat," Persephone sang out, striding back the way they came.

🍇

"Cym? Cyn? Com? It's a 'C,' I know *that*. What *is* it?"

"Are you talking to me?" Alcie asked as they approached a wide set of open double doors. Delicious scents floating on puffs of smoke were emanating into the corridor.

"Huh?" Persephone responded, startled. "Oh, no, I'm just trying to remember something."

Through the open doors ahead, Alcie could see figures rushing back and forth, carrying urns, platters, and bowls. Someone saw Persephone coming and sent out a great shout.

"Cookie! What've you got?" Persephone called cheerily as she entered the vast food preparation rooms. Shades, wearing splatter-smocks, were frantically forming a reception line.

A heavy, wrinkled, gray-haired shade turned quickly

from a hot oven, a tray of freshly roasted black things in her hand. With a kind smile, she set the tray on a long table and bowed deeply, as did the entire line.

"My queen."

"Cookie?" Alcie asked quietly.

"She's the chief cook. She cooks. She's a cookie," Persephone answered. "She doesn't mind, right . . . Cookie?"

Before the woman could open her mouth, Persephone had turned slightly to Alcie.

"*I've forgotten her name,*" she mouthed.

Alcie caught a slight movement in the polished silver of a large serving bowl and saw the cook's reflection. She had seen exactly what Persephone had whispered and was now smiling softly.

"My mistress may call me whatever she desires," she said.

"There, you see?" Persephone said. Then she gestured grandly toward Alcie.

"We have a guest!"

"So I have been told," said the cook.

"This is Alcie!" said Persephone. "She's mortal and not really dead. She's not going to be here long, and I'm showing off the place."

Alcie suddenly felt as if she were on display, as if she were a piece of fruit or a bolt of silk in a marketplace.

"Hello," Alcie said.

"Welcome," said the cook. "I am Cyrene."

"I *knew* it started with 'C,'" Persephone muttered softly.

"But you may call me 'Cookie.'"

"Cookie, what's good today?" asked Persephone.

Cyrene gestured to the long tables in the center of the room.

"In honor of your off-season visit and in honor of our very unique guest, I have prepared some of your favorites!"

"Oh, goody!" Persephone squealed.

"Wilted field greens with oil and vinegar."

"Plucked right out of the Elysian Fields!" Persephone crowed to Alcie.

"Roasted garlic and snail custard in phyllo dough. Liver pudding on day-old flatbread rounds."

"Yum! Which liver?"

"I forget whose."

"Whaaa?" Alcie gagged.

"She means *which* animal," Persephone said.

"Cream of tripe soup," said Cyrene.

"Can't wait!"

"Lamb's entrails stuffed with minced kidney and sweetbreads."

"Have mercy!" Persephone moaned with delight.

"And your favorite . . ."

"Here it comes!" cried Persephone.

"Blackened dove hearts with walnuts," said Cyrene, pointing to the tray of tiny dark nuggets she had just removed from the oven.

"Now it's a festivaaaaal!" yelled Persephone, clapping her hands and turning to Alcie. "What shall we start with?"

"Oh, wow," Alcie said, having no idea what to say. She followed Persephone to a small table set for two off to the side of the room. "Um, oh, grapes."

"Dried or pickled?" asked Cyrene.

"Oh, no, I meant . . ." Alcie looked over the platters of food heaped on the table. She *was* famished and she felt, somehow, that Persephone's mood would alter toward her a bit if she turned up her nose at all of it. The least disgusting item on the menu was the pile of soggy green leaves.

"I'd love to try those," she said brightly, sitting down.

"Good choice," said Cyrene, heaping a plate high and setting it before her.

Alcie poked at her wilted greens as she watched Persephone devour enormous quantities of everything. Then, and only because Persephone was looking directly at her as she spoke, she actually put a bite in her mouth.

The sour, oily limp leaves . . . were the best things she had ever tasted in her life.

"Gotcha!" Persephone smiled. "Didn't think you'd like it, right?"

"Oh Gods," sighed Alcie.

"I *know*! It sounds disgusting! I mean, really, why do you think I basically starved myself the first time I was down here. I only ate six pomegranate seeds when I could have been stuffing myself. Here, try the dove. Don't think about it . . . just taste."

Alcie hesitated, then popped a tiny black morsel into her mouth. In that instant she made a silent vow to be as noticeably heroic as possible for the rest of her natural life, just so she could spend eternity in Hades' palace eating delicious food.

When her very mortal stomach was distended over and under her girdle, Alcie pushed back from the table. Then she gave a thunderous belch.

"Oh, lemons, I'm sorry."

"That's the best compliment you could give them!" Persephone said.

The shades, having hovered in the corners of the great room, all nodded appreciatively.

"Right-o! And off we go," Persephone said, rising. "Now, let's see if we can talk to your friends."

CHAPTER TEN

Out and About

Fastening the hooks through her ears, Hera shook her head gently.

"And now for a little test," she said, satisfied the earrings were secure

She willed the thousands of unsigned papers to rise out of the cart and hover in the air while the bodies of the two monkeys floated off the table and dropped into the bottom of the cart. Then she let the papers fall on top with a sickening thud.

"It's good to be alive!"

She strode back through the offices of the Bureau, catching from the corners of her eyes the smiling faces and nodding heads; after all, if she was wearing an egg, she must have been approved. She ignored everyone. Confidently, she walked out into the main room, cut directly through the long line of deities waiting to apply, and descended the staircase.

But when she stepped out of the building, there was nothing below except the rooftops of Baghdad.

She would have, at that moment, simply used her restored powers and dematerialized, but in the next instant, a new stairway appeared before her; step by step, Hera moved downward, negotiating twists and curves as the building overhead, now invisible, moved over the city.

Finally, with her feet firmly on the ground, Hera decided to test the full effect of the eggs.

"I wonder, where *is* my dear girl?"

CHAPTER ELEVEN
On the Dunes

It had been eight days since Douban the Physician had placed the strange poultice in Iole's mouth and, true to his word, she had been completely healed the following morning. Since then, the caravan had moved slowly across the Arabian desert and now, finally, it was within sight of the small town of Baghdad, situated on a bend in the Tigris River.

Pandy and Iole sat atop a large sand dune as the last thin crescent of the sun sank below the horizon. Overhead, the stars began to twinkle in the twilight sky and lamps were flickering throughout the city, only several kilometers away.

They were watching Homer toss a large bone to Dido far below in a trough of the desert dunes. After one particular toss, Dido raced back to Homer, the bone in his mouth, and, instead of dropping the bone at Homer's feet as usual, Dido sped past him, nearly knocking

Homer to the ground. Iole giggled, but when Pandy didn't, Iole turned to her. Pandy's face was serene, her gaze far away to the west.

"And you are cogitating?"

Pandy turned a puzzled expression to her friend.

"What are you thinking?"

"Oh," Pandy said, gazing again at the intense red glow where sun had been only an instant before. "I am wondering, since nothing else from our homeland seems to work or make sense in this country, who or what is pulling the sun across the sky? Is it still Apollo? Or, when the sun gets to Persia, does he have to hand it over to another god or . . . or someone . . . or something . . . until the sun crosses back into Greece and then he gets to pull it again. What does he do with his chariot while the sun is somewhere else? Does he just fly around for a bit? Is it like that in every different country in the known world? Do the gods of different countries have to share the major responsibilities?"

She turned to look at Iole.

"I have no idea," Iole replied, smiling. "But your mind is working wonderfully. Do you realize that, months ago, you would never have even considered these possibilities?"

"But I don't have an answer," Pandy said.

"Not the point. Your mind is expanding. That's big news."

"I guess," Pandy sighed, grabbing a handful of desert sand and letting it trickle through her fingers. "I'm just homesick. I want this over, no matter how it turns out."

"Don't say that," Iole cautioned.

"It's true, Iole. Alcie's gone. We almost lost you. Tomorrow I have to watch a man get his head lopped off just because he thinks there might be some lesser evils lurking somewhere."

"We've been through it, I concur. But you have four big evils in the box. You are over the hump, as it were. You didn't lose me; I feel better than ever. You have Dido back, and Homer and me. I have no words about Alcie. There are no words . . ."

Iole's voice trailed off for a moment.

"And as for tomorrow, we've seen horrible things. I cannot imagine that this will be any worse."

"But his execution makes no sense!" Pandy cried. "And he could have escaped! That's the most horrible thing!"

"May I join you?"

A soft voice from behind them had floated on the light breeze.

"Oh," Pandy said, jumping slightly. "Oh, yes, of course. Please."

Douban's son made his way across the top of the dune and sat down close, but not *too* close, to Pandy.

"Hey, Little D," she greeted him.

"Good evening, Pandy. Iole," he said.

"And a good evening to you," Iole answered.

There was silence for several minutes. When it finally became uncomfortable, Iole got to her feet.

"Well," she said, "I'm going to go see what Mahfouza's concocting for evening meal."

"We already had evening meal," Pandy said.

"I'm talking about the *second* evening meal," Iole said, walking down the dune. "The one we have after the first evening meal. Like we do all the time . . . back home. All right then, see you later . . . you . . . two."

Pandy looked at Douban's son and smiled. For some reason, she felt at once nervous yet comfortable around this handsome youth who was watching her, as he'd done for days, so intently.

"I'm sorry to have interrupted," he began.

"You didn't," Pandy laughed. "She's just being a goof. Hey, you don't mind me calling you Little D, right? I can't say Dou-dou."

Without thinking, she playfully swatted at his arm with the back of her hand. Her hand dropped to the sand and he covered her little finger with his, and didn't move it.

"It's fine. It will all change tomorrow anyway."

Pandy was silent, staring at their fingers touching. She'd had a few crushes on youths back in Greece but had never known what it was like to have that feeling reciprocated. For the first time in her life, she felt . . . "crushed." And it was wonderful. There was nothing in the world except this handsome young man and his little finger touching hers. In the next instant, the full weight of their situation came rushing back in and Pandy was a little ashamed at having let herself go, having forgotten why she was where she was, even for a moment.

"You know, we've been camped here a full day and a half," Pandy said, slowly putting her hand back in her lap. "The caravan could have gone into the city already."

"I know," said Douban's son. "For all of his bluster, the Captain of the Guard deeply respects my father and is taking more time than necessary. He knows that what is going to happen is a corruption of justice. I think he himself is trying to think of a way out of this. But it is all useless, I'm afraid. The lookouts in the highest city towers have seen us here, and the Prince of Baghdad has sent more guards to discover the delay. There is to be no more stalling. It is to be tomorrow."

"This is the stupidest thing I have ever heard of, and if you knew what some of our gods have done back home, that's saying something."

"Pandy," Douban's son said, "do not think for a moment that the prince will get away with this."

Pandy looked at the youth, surprised.

"My father is a man of honor," he went on. "But he is

not without the desire for vengeance. My father is not the only one who will die tomorrow. Pay close attention to the instructions my father has for the prince. And be ready to seize the prince's blood . . . and there will be blood."

"I'm so sorry," Pandy said softly. "This is my fault."

Douban's son waited a bit.

"Nothing happens without a reason. My father believes, and so do I, that every choice we make is the right one, even though we might not know it at the time."

"Where I come from, everything is set from the moment you're born," Pandy countered. "It's all predetermined and we don't have choices. Although I can't imagine you or your father being subject to our rules."

"Then our two different views have conspired to allow you and me to meet. And for you to be able to recapture some of those lesser evils."

He paused again.

"It will all be rather hectic tomorrow and I just wanted to say that I have enjoyed knowing you. I have enjoyed listening to the stories of your adventures. You are very . . . impressive."

"Thank you, Douban. So are you."

After another long silence, the youth spoke. There was a tremor in his voice.

"That is the first time I have heard my new name on another's lips. It is . . . bittersweet."

CHAPTER TWELVE

Buster's Bowl of Borrower's Bile

Looking backward, Alcie knew that without Persephone, she would be lost in the maze of the palace forever. But as they had been walking together through yet another long, complicated labyrinth of palace corridors, Alcie had been marveling not at the endless gray sumptuousness, but at how much Persephone could eat.

She had cleared every one of the platters and bowls that had been set out (for which Alcie was actually grateful. She'd loved everything she'd tasted, but could not bring herself to try the entrails or the tripe soup), and still Persephone was now traipsing along with a large silver goblet of dove hearts ("Just a little something to go," she'd said as Cyrene had heaped the cup full only minutes ago. "In case we get peckish.")

"So I am guessing that you don't get food like this on Olympus?" Alcie asked, a flash of green outside a window turning her head for a moment.

"Have you ever had ambrosia?" Persephone asked by way of a reply.

"Uh, no."

"Can I even begin to describe how disgusting it is? And it's the only thing up there! If I never see a piece of it again, it will be too soon. All right, now slow down a little."

Alcie dropped back as Persephone cautiously approached a small doorway with a plain white privacy curtain at the end of a corridor.

"You just never know when Buster might be using it," Persephone whispered, poking her head into the room. "Of course, I can use it anytime, but he might not be so keen on letting someone else, if you get me. Okay, all clear."

They entered a windowless room illuminated only by soft torchlight. It was completely empty except for a large, shallow basin on a stand in the very center. Standing across from Persephone, Alcie stared down into the bowl brimming with a hot, milky, yellowish (she thought) liquid. The aroma of the steam rising off it made Alcie gag almost instantly.

"I know, I know," Persephone said. "But don't bring up the dove. Just back off a little; you'll get used to it."

"Bile?" Alcie asked.

"Borrower's bile. Powerful stuff. I don't even want to think how Buster harvests it. But, mind you, it's only from those who don't pay their debts. Of course, you mortals get to lean on each other every once in a while . . . normal stuff. 'Hey, lend me a drachma for an apple' or whatever. This bile is from those who take and take and don't give back."

"I can talk to Pandy through this?" asked Alcie.

"Wait till I tell you . . . it's brilliant," Persephone said. "Buster doesn't like to leave the underworld, right? Right. But he also likes to talk to Zeus and Poseidon. The Big Three have to keep in contact, blah bitty blah, and Buster can be very chatty. So he devised this, and all he does is call out the name of whomever he wants to contact, and blammo! There they are."

"Well, that doesn't seem so magical. I mean Pandy has shells that do the same thing—"

"Not done."

"Sorry."

"Because no one else has a bile bowl and Buster never knows where anyone is at any given time, it's only Buster's voice that they hear when he makes contact. His voice is channeled through the closest living mortal thing. So if Zeus is standing next to a horse, or Hermes is sitting next to a cat or Artemis is relaxing underneath an olive tree, the horse or the cat or a tiny green olive will start speaking for Buster."

"That must be weird," Alcie replied.

"I know! It's too weird, and it's too much for them, or anyone. After the conversation is done, the experience of channeling Hades, the Dark Lord of the Underworld, causes complete and fatal physical collapse."

"You mean . . . ?"

"Yep. Instant death. That's why Buster really works hard to channel through vegetation, but sometimes we lose a mouse or a frog or worse."

"People?"

"Sometimes. Hey, we're gods, nobody said we were perfect," Persephone said. "So? You wanna give it a try?"

The thought of being able to contact Pandy was exhilarating, but what if the closest thing to Pandy at that moment was Iole . . . or Homer? The idea that Iole or her dear Homie or even Dido might be the channel and lose their life was too much to bear.

"I can't risk it," she said.

"Oh, come on! You mean to tell me we came all this way, spent all this time, and now you don't want to do it? *I did this for you!*"

"Interesting," came a low voice from the doorway.

Persephone didn't take her eyes off of Alcie's face.

"*You made me do this!*" Persephone cried after a second.

Alcie's jaw dropped.

"Persephone," said Hades, now blocking any light from the corridor.

There was a pause, and then Persephone burst out laughing.

"Kidding!" she said, then she turned to her husband. "Kid-*ding*. Oh, of course it was all my idea. Don't be angry with Alcie. Punish me all you want! I deserve it."

She flounced her way toward Hades and flung her arms about him. He was solid and unmoving for a moment, then relented at her touch and held her face to his.

"I simply asked you to entertain her," he said. "To engage her in conversation, I believe, was my exact phrase. Yet you brought her here . . . one of my private chambers to see one of my most treasured devices . . . on a whim. And still I forgive you. I always forgive you, my wife. Why can't I ever be angry with you?"

"I don't know, but I love it! I'll use it and abuse it!" Persephone giggled, kissing him lightly.

Suddenly, Alcie noticed that Hades was not alone. He moved farther into the room and was followed by a tiny, white-haired, wrinkled creature. Had to be a woman, Alcie thought, but she couldn't be sure; the figure was bent with age at a severe angle. Suddenly Alcie thought she knew who this was. But why was *she* here?

Gods, Alcie thought with a start, had *she* died while they'd been gone?

"Sabina?" Alcie said, certain that this was Pandy's house-slave.

At once, the old woman raised her head and stared Alcie down with her pus-colored eyes. Then she smiled wide.

"You know my sister, do you?"

Alcie was stunned; the resemblance to Sabina, whom Alcie had known ever since she'd known Pandy, was astonishing. Of course, Pandy had told Alcie that Sabina was, in reality, one of the Fates (albeit the Hapless Fate. The Fate nobody talked about because she was the only one who couldn't really *do* anything); Alcie had known this for years. Then the hard fact hit Alcie and nearly knocked the wind out of her: if this wasn't Sabina, it was one of her sisters, which meant that Alcie was now in the presence of one of the three true, terrible Fates.

The woman began to laugh softly.

"Alcestis," Hades said, "this is Lachesis, the Disposer of Lots."

Alcie was frozen. Each of the Fates was supremely powerful in her own way. Clotho, the Spinner, spun a thread from a great wheel when someone was born. Atropos with her enormous shears would cut the thread at the end of someone's life. But it was Lachesis who decided what went on in between: king or slave, warrior or potter or scholar or thief; it was she who decided their destiny.

"I told you, Alcestis," Hades said, "that I would find a solution to your problem. And I believe," he said, turning to Lachesis, "that we have."

He gazed down at the wizened woman with a conspiratorial smile.

"Eh," said the old woman with a shrug.

Alcie remained silent, her eyes moving from Hades to Lachesis. Her mind went back to her first day at her preschool, Medea's Mini Muse and Happy Hero Day Care. There had been a big sign over the teacher's head and the teacher had pointed to it, shouting to make certain everyone understood. Growing up, the message was everywhere. It was embroidered on floor cushions, painted on the back walls of market stalls, and verbally woven into greetings and farewells. It was the one thing that was seared into everyone's brain from the time they could comprehend the meaning of words, because it was the coldest, hardest, most cruel fact in the whole known world.

There was no bargaining with the Fates.

They decided and that was it. Period. They paid attention to the wishes and desires of no one. Not even Zeus could sway them if a destiny or death had been set.

And yet, here stood Lachesis, smiling and giving a little shrug of her shoulders as if to say "whatever."

Lachesis hobbled toward Alcie, one hand stretched out and the other balled into a tight fist. For a second, Alcie thought she might need a lavatorium. Lachesis stopped only centimeters from Alcie's face; her breath wheezed out in a mist, rank, fetid, and the same yellowish color as her eyes.

"We aren't often surprised," she said, her voice sounding like sap-filled wood burning with pops and little explosions. "In fact, my sisters and I have never been surprised. And then, there's *you*. *You* we were not prepared for. *You* are a mystery. But, thanks to Hera, you happened. I might have been able to redesign a different destiny, but Clotho had already cut your thread."

Alcie gasped. That was it . . . there was no escaping. A cut thread meant only one thing.

"Fortunately," Lachesis continued, "when our dear Hades arrived and told us of your situation, we had not yet tossed your thread into our fire. Had we done that, we would not be standing here discussing it. After much debate—you must realize that this is new territory for us as well as you—and after a generous bargain made by the Dark Lord, we have come to a conclusion."

Lachesis opened her tiny fist, revealing a long white thread. For a moment, Alcie thought Lachesis had pulled a hair out of her head. Then she realized it was much thicker.

"This, maiden, is your life."

Alcie's stomach flipped over hard.

"A mortal only gets one. Since yours was cut short before its time, the pathway I set for you is gone and you cannot return to it. However, since this was a mistake, even Atropos agrees with that, we have spun a clean thread and woven it onto the end of the original. This section is blank. It is wholly and only yours. You may do with it what you will. I cannot believe I am saying this, but you are in charge of your own life."

She held the thread out to Alcie. Alcie didn't move. There were so many questions filling her mind that they all blended into bright whiteness.

"Is she rather dense?" Alcie heard Lachesis ask out of the side of her mouth.

Alcie reached forward and, as if she were holding a butterfly by its wings, gently took the thread between her forefinger and thumb.

"Here!" Persephone said, rushing up. "Here, put it in this."

Out of thin air, she plucked a small cobalt blue enamel and gold box and handed it to Alcie. The words "Alcie's Life!" were engraved across the top, with the word "Wahoo!" in smaller script underneath.

Alcie opened her mouth to speak. How much time did she have left? What *would she have been* if not for Hera's attempted murder? Was Pandy going to succeed in the quest? Was there any special care of the thread?

"My dear," Lachesis said, reading Alcie's thoughts as she turned away to leave, "if I won't answer any of those kinds of questions for anyone else, why would I answer them for you?"

She stopped and turned back.

"Besides, and this I can safely say where you're concerned, I really don't know. It's all up to you. Just live!"

And she was gone.

"Buster!" Persephone squealed. "A Fate . . . *here*! And me looking like five kilometers of chariot road! You might have at least warned me so that I could put a little berry juice on my lips!"

"You're gorgeous, my wife."

"Oh, stop. Don't stop!" she cried, and kissed him again.

Slightly uncomfortable, Alcie started looking off into the corners of the room.

"Alcie!" Persephone turned to her. "You have to put that box someplace safe."

"All I have is my pouch," Alcie replied, thrusting the box deep inside.

"Well, guard it with your life!"

Suddenly Persephone started laughing so hard at her ridiculous joke, Alcie thought the goddess might throw up. Then Alcie started laughing, but stopped when she saw Hades just staring at her.

"Ahhh, I amuse, I amuse. So, what bargain did you

make with the Fates?" Persephone asked when she had calmed down a bit.

"They never get to have any fun, so I invited them all down for a picnic, and they asked if, perhaps, we might do it on a regular basis. We decided the day after every third full moon, they're showing up for a little sunbathing without the sun, and some lamb. Clotho wants to throw rocks at Tantalus in his pool. Lachesis wants to watch Achilles toss a javelin. Things like that."

"You're so good!" Persephone said.

"No, wife," Hades said, attempting to loosen up and be casual. "*You're* good!"

"I *know*! Oh, but Buster . . . we have another problem. Alcie's going back now and she wants to let her friends know that she's coming. Otherwise they may fall down dead at the sight of her and then we'd have to do this all over again. Do you think that she could use the Borrower's Bile?"

"I think that might be arranged. Although your friends, Alcie, are in Persia. It will be quite a reach. I cannot vouch for the clarity."

"S'okay," Alcie replied.

"But she's worried," Persephone continued, "about the whole channeling thing and one of her friends losing their life."

"Wife, do you not think that I take that into account every time I communicate with another immortal?"

Hades looked at Alcie.

"While I, perhaps more than any other immortal, understand that all life is precious, there is a hierarchy of living things. This device singles out that which is the closest but lowest form to the recipient. I'm always hoping for a fly or a snail or a slug."

"Hera," Alcie blurted out before she realized what she'd said.

She looked quickly at Hades, who was now staring hard at her. Persephone's head was whipping back and forth as she looked between the two. Alcie was certain insulting the Queen of Heaven in front of another Olympian was, perhaps, the worst thing she could have done. She was about to ask Hades if he wanted her life-thread back when he started laughing.

Hard.

He threw his head back, his black hair falling out of his eyes, and opened his mouth wide, revealing perfect white teeth. He bellowed so loudly that Persephone was stunned into silence. He laughed so long that he doubled over, and Persephone finally had to pat him on the back several times.

"Oh, Alcestis," he said at last, when he had caught his breath. "If only there was a way."

He shook his head as he focused on the floor.

"If only."

Then his face became even more somber than normal.

"Now," he said approaching her, "you have a choice to make. If I send you back to the world of the living—your world—*our* world, then I can control exactly where I deliver you. Your own home perhaps? I can set you down right in front of your mother and father. You may contact Pandora now and tell her that you will be safe and sound in Athens and that you will be waiting for her when, or if, she ever comes home. Or, you may join her where she is, a place called Baghdad somewhere in the Persian Empire. If this is your decision, however, I cannot vouch for what will happen. My powers are limited as to what I may do, and while I believe I can get you there, you may materialize in a wall, or in the bed of a deep river, or you may be altered in some way, the specifics of which I have no way of knowing. The choice is yours."

Alcie was dumbstruck. She had just been given something no other mortal had: her own life to do with as she pleased. Yet, within the next few moments, she might end up at the bottom of a river. *Soo* . . . why shouldn't she play it safe and wait for Pandy back home; after all, Pandy was certain to get them all into more life-threatening situations, and she, herself, had just been so close, *too* close, to death. Pandy would be able to recapture the evils without her. Pandy was doing just fine. No one would ever blame her if she chose the easy way, and the hills above Athens were so pretty this time of year.

"I'll go to Persia."

"Yesssss!" said Persephone.

"Wait!" Alcie said, a thought popping into her head. "Apples! If I'm in a wall, how will Pandy know? How can I get to her or contact her once I'm in Baghdad? I mean, you know, if I'm 'altered'? Or even if I'm not?"

"Alcestis," Hades said, a scowl deepening his brow. "Much has been done for you! The Fates have been swayed for you! Must we continue to solve all of your dilemmas? Can you not figure this out on your own?"

"I'm sorry," Alcie said. "I'll find a way."

Persephone, however, had recognized a tone in her husband's voice. It was one of pure defeat and it was very rare that she or anyone heard it at all. She knew that her husband had absolutely no idea how Alcie could contact Pandora. He was a giant of a god, strong, powerful, and robust, but he was unused to commotion in the underworld; it exhausted him and he just didn't have any answer for Alcie. But Persephone did.

"Are you ready?" Hades asked Alcie.

She nodded, then Hades motioned her to the center of the room.

"Now, step up to the bowl and call to your friend."

CHAPTER THIRTEEN

Prince Camaralzaman

"Aside from everything else," Iole said, looking at Pandy, "why are you frowning especially deeply this morning?"

"I'm a little worried about Dido," she answered.

"But Mahfouza paid the guards very well to take him directly to her home. You know he could never have come with us," Iole replied. "Not considering the prevailing populace perspective on canines."

"That's my point. I think," Pandy said. "I just hope the guards take care of him and that Mahfouza's family treats him well. Did you know she has, like, eight brothers and sisters?"

Then she jerked her head back on her neck as if surprised by a thought.

"Mahfouza!" Pandy said suddenly, whipping around quickly and walking backward to be able to talk softly to the dancer. "Why are *you* still here? Why haven't you gone to your family? I got the little map to your parents' house that you left on top of my pouch. Why aren't you there?"

The walk from the caravan encampment, across the river and into the city of Baghdad, had been more of a march than anything else. Douban, his son, Pandy, and the rest, including Mahfouza, had been forced into a single-file line and "escorted" by many guards. Now the gates of royal palace were in sight.

Mahfouza stopped glaring at the guards to either side and stared at Pandy, her eyes hard and cold.

"The guards have heard me speaking out for days against this travesty—this injustice—that is about to take place. So, when I tried to leave early this morning, because I am desperate to know what is happening in my home, I was informed not-so-politely that I am now considered a threat. That I might actually rally common citizens to come to the aid of the Physician. I am not to be at liberty until he is dead."

Mahfouza spit, hard, at one of the guards walking alongside. He deftly dodged the white wad and kept walking.

"I'm sorry," Pandy replied, her fault weighing heavily upon her again. "We'll get to your home as soon as we can. I'm sorry."

For an instant, Pandy thought she saw a flicker of resentment in the older girl's eyes. Then Mahfouza closed her lids for a moment, a tear rolling down her cheek and a sad little smile playing upon her lips. Without a word, she reached out and took Pandy's hand, giving it a squeeze. Pandy turned and walked forward again but let her arm stretch out behind her, holding on to Mahfouza's hand for a long time.

🍇

The main reception room in the palace of Prince Camaralzaman of Baghdad was not the largest room that Pandy had ever seen. That honor, she firmly believed, would always belong to the great hall in Zeus's palace on Olympus, and not far behind was the hall of the palace of King Peleus on Mount Pelion where his very dramatic wedding was celebrated.

Although immense to be sure, the feature that set this room apart from any other Pandy had experienced was . . .

. . . the jewels.

There was not one square centimeter that was not covered with or carved out of jewels, including, Pandy realized with awe, the windows, which were huge, flat, finely faceted diamonds. Emeralds, amethysts, and pearls were opulent ornamentation around the windows and doorways. Floor rugs and wall murals were mosaics constructed of the teensiest semiprecious stones, and the "plaster" on other walls was a thin sheet of deep amber. The mortar holding together the sapphire bricks at the edges of the room and in between the "rugs" was crushed topaz. The curtains were of jade, sculpted to actually appear as if they were rippling in a breeze. The only decorative piece of fabric in the entire room was the brilliant red cushion atop the prince's large throne, which was cut from a single mammoth ruby.

When Pandy, Iole, Homer, and Mahfouza entered, following closely on the heels of Douban and his son, it seemed that every citizen of Baghdad must have been present. The perimeter of the room was teeming with people, peering to get a good view of the execution. Even the center of the hall was crowded, but the Captain of the Guard brusquely shoved onlookers out of his way as he cleared a space for Douban the Physician.

Pandy couldn't get a decent view of the prince and his attendants, in their official places at the far end of the room, until the captain and the rest of his guards fell to one knee. Douban did the same and then his son and Mahfouza, and suddenly Pandy found herself staring across a vast space into the dark eyes of Camaralzaman . . . who was staring back at her.

Slowly she, Homer, and Iole got onto one knee and bowed their heads.

Silence filled the chamber.

Long moments passed.

Someone, somewhere, coughed.

And still there was silence.

Just as Pandy's curiosity was beginning to boil, Camaralzaman's voice carried across the room. And Pandy, without thinking, grabbed Iole's hand to keep from laughing.

While the prince was clothed in dark, elegant robes with a white and gold turban on his head, the very picture of masculine authority, the voice of the Prince of Baghdad, absolute ruler and arbiter of life and death, was high and squeaky. It sounded to Pandy as if he had a terrible cold and his nose was stuffed up. He also sounded as if he were about five years old.

"You brought . . . guests, Physician?"

"Prince," replied Douban, "my son attends me as I said he would. When I realized that, after my death, my son would be alone and friendless in your city, I decided to bring a few . . . cousins to help him in his grief."

A large man, dressed almost as royally as Camaralzaman, leaned forward and whispered something into the prince's ear.

"You do not fool me," said Camaralzaman, when the man finished. "You have brought a host of friends to speak in your favor, hoping that their voices combined will sway me. You are mistaken. You introduced yourself into this court on the pretense of curing me of leprosy and yet I know now it was merely a veiled attempt to assassinate me. You will die."

"I ask you again for proof of my treason, Prince," said Douban.

"Silence!" Camaralzaman whined. "Codadad, my grand vizier, has told me enough. You cured me, yes, but I now fear your cures will produce the most pernicious effects in the end. The drugs you gave me may be eating away at my entrails this very moment! Therefore, prepare yourself."

Douban and the rest glanced at the man who had leaned forward. Codadad gave only the faintest hint of a smirk.

"Prince," said Douban, "one moment more."

From the folds of his robe, Douban produced a small book.

"In going through my books, I found one that is extremely rare and precious. Though I am to be punished for saving your life, I wish you to have it as a remembrance of me and of my gratitude at the kindness you did show me once."

"What sort of book is it," replied the prince, "that is so valuable as that?"

"It contains the answers to some of mankind's most eternal, troubling, and profound questions. It is for you, Prince."

"Don't think that by giving me this I will grant you any mercy," the prince said, rising to receive the book.

"I would not dream of it," said Douban, handing the slim volume to a waiting guard, who in turn bowed and handed it to the prince.

But the book would not open. Try as hard as he might, Camaralzaman couldn't pry apart the cover.

"What trickery is this?" he cried.

"If you will be patient," answered Douban. "When my head is severed, my son will place it on a small rug."

Douban's son rose and placed a small rug on top of a large jeweled area "rug" that was a few steps back from the prince's throne.

"The blood will cease to flow, my eyes will open, and I will instruct you on the wonderful mysteries of the treasure you now hold."

There was a single gasp from all those assembled and people actually began stepping on each other to get a glimpse of the event. At a wave of the prince's hand, Douban was forced to his knees as a ferocious-looking man with a huge scimitar stepped into place. Douban's son slowly reached down and took Pandy's hand. She squeezed back tightly.

The Physician's head was severed in one stroke. There was no blood. Douban's son paused only for a second before rushing forward, taking up his father's head, and placing it gently on the small rug. Almost instantly, the eyelids fluttered open and the mouth began to move. Pandy flashed on her bust of Athena, with its green eyes and tiny tongue that got stuck every once in a while.

"Prince . . . ," the head began.

In one corner of the room, a man fainted.

". . . you will now be able to open the book."

Camaralzaman did so easily.

"Please turn to the sixth page," said the head.

As the prince began to turn the pages, he found that the first page was stuck to the second. He brought his finger to his mouth and wetted it in order to be able to turn it over. The second page was stuck to the third and so on, so the prince continued to wet his forefinger to loosen the pages. When he came to the sixth page, it was blank.

"There is nothing here," said Camaralzaman.

"My apologies, Prince," said the head. "It must be only a few pages further. Please continue."

The prince turned page after page, always putting his finger to his mouth. Suddenly, Camaralzaman felt as if his body were on fire; the sight went from his eyes and he fell back against his ruby throne with a hard smack.

"Ahhh!" he cried, putting his hands out before him.

The head of Douban the Physician began to laugh.

"Tyrant! Now who is the fool?" it cried. "The pages of that book are coated with a deadly poison that you have ingested with every turn. And now you see what becomes of those who abuse their authority and murder the innocent. Brutality and injustice are always punished. And in case any of you are thinking of retribution against my son or my family, let me warn you that I will have power beyond my grave and I will be watching this court from now on!"

No one stepped forward to help Camaralzaman as he lay writhing in agony. Pandy was noting that the grand vizier was not only *not* aiding his prince, but was actually smiling, as if someone had just done him a great favor. After several seconds, the prince gave a tremendous heave, sat straight up, then fell back onto the floor at the foot of his throne, dead.

Slowly but steadily, blood began seeping from the ears, nose, eyes, and mouth of the dead ruler.

Now people began to rush frantically toward the door of the hall, taking care to stay as far away from the head of the Physician as possible. Codadad was yelling at the guards to stay away from the prince's body and physically blocking anyone who tried to get close. Yet, over the great noise of the crowd, Pandy heard the Physician's voice.

"Pandora! NOW!"

❦

"Just focus on the person you wish to speak to," Hades was saying as Alcie stared into the milky bile. Alcie concentrated on Pandy's face, with her golden teardrop just under one eye, her long brown hair, and her smile with the overbite that wasn't so prominent anymore. Suddenly, two clear pools in the shape of eyes appeared in the yellowish liquid. Then the pools became confused with color and motion and Alcie realized she was looking into a room or a space where there was much commotion; people were racing past in the background, but in the foreground, there was the unmistakable figure of a man lying on the ground, motionless but bleeding profusely. Alcie realized with a start that she was looking through someone else's eyes.

🍇

"Let's go," Pandy whispered to Iole.

Making their way against the throng, she and Iole were pushed and pulled as they inched past Douban's son, talking in low tones to his father's head, on their path to the lifeless prince. Seeing his body only a meter away, Pandy pulled the box out of her carrying pouch. Then she and Iole stopped short.

The blood oozing from every opening on Camaralzaman's face was coagulating in puddles and those puddles were slowly but surely taking the form of shiny red scorpions.

Instinctively, Pandy reached into her pouch and

grabbed the adamant net. Watching the scorpions, she flashed back to Jealousy, in the form of a black goop that then formed itself into a spider.

"This is like the first time, with Jealousy," she said to Iole, raising her voice to be heard over the din.

"That was just one Evil," Iole answered. "There are three of these that I can see!"

"Thank Zeus that we've gotten good at this," Pandy said, handing the box to Iole. "On a count of three. Ready?"

One by one, Pandy threw the net over the scorpions and, as Iole lifted the lid of the box with perfect timing, threw them inside without so much as a wisp of smoke from any other captured Evil ever curling out.

"That was easy," Iole said, but she wasn't smiling.

"Too easy for my drachmas," agreed Pandy. "Wait! Douban said he'd counted or he'd guessed that there were four lesser evils in the Prince. We only got three!"

At that moment, Homer let out a bloodcurdling scream.

Iole took off, still clutching the box, but as Pandy rose to her feet and turned to run, a giant weight fell on her left shoulder. Turning back, she saw the grand vizier, Codadad, towering over her, his right arm flopping against her neck, his eyes a yellowish white and his mouth beginning to move.

"Hey!" the vizier said.

But it wasn't his voice, Pandy thought; that *couldn't* be his voice.

"Hey, figs, how do I know if I'm getting through? Pandy! Where are you?"

The vizier's head jerked around until he was almost face-to-face with Pandy.

"There you are!" came the strange voice out of his mouth. "Pandy, it's me! It's Alcie!"

Pandy dropped the net.

"Look, it's crazy, I know, but I'm okay! I'm alive and I'm coming to join you."

"Whaaaa?" Pandy gaped.

"Don't go all wonky on me. I'll explain everything when I see you. I may be sticking out of a wall, but I'm gonna get there! I'll be in Baghdad, oranges, when?"

Although it was taking all of Pandy's concentration just to stay standing, she thought she heard a deep voice behind Alcie saying "soon."

"Soon," said Alcie through Codadad's mouth. "I'll figure out a way to let you know where as soon as I get there. Hades says—"

Pandy, quite involuntarily, did a double take.

"—that right now my voice will be coming out of the lowest form of life close to you, so, pomegranates, I just hope it's no one we know."

"Let Pandora talk, Alcestis," came the deep voice again, from somewhere behind Alcie.

"Okay, you talk now!"

Pandy stood stock-still in front of the vizier, his body rigid, as if it had been stuffed.

"Alcie?"

"Right here!"

"Is it really you?" Pandy whispered.

"Yep, and right now I think there's *more* of me," Alcie replied. "I've been eating really well.

"And Hades is there?"

"Well, he, like, lives here. And Persephone is here too!"

"Hi, Pandy!" came a distant female voice out of Codadad's mouth.

"This is a trick," Pandy said, shaking her head, not knowing whether to cry or to be incredibly angry. "It's one of Hera's tricks!"

"So not so, my friend," came Alcie's voice.

Pandy thought fast.

"Tell me something that only Alcie would know!"

The figure of Codadad was silent, then suddenly the mouth broke into a wide grin.

"Okay," said Alcie. "About a year ago, we found out that some of the youths from the Apollo Academy were gonna go swimming after wrestling practice and we stole all their clothes just so we could see . . ."

"Oh Gods!" said Pandy, feeling the tears welling up in her eyes. *"Alcie!"*

"Hey, no cryin'. This is all great stuff. And I have so much to tell you about the underworld! I'll start with the food. Okay, apples, I don't know where you are or what you're doing, but you look like you're busy, so I'm gonna go. I'll see you and Iole soon. Tell Homie I miss him. Love you!"

The vizier's eyes cleared as a huge tremor shook his body. Pandy staggered back as the man gagged once, then pitched forward to lie stone dead next to the hardening, bloodless body of Prince Camaralzaman.

CHAPTER FOURTEEN
A Lesser Evil

"Pandy!" Iole was yelling. "Pandy, bring the net!"

Pandy looked at the body of Codadad until Iole's voice penetrated. She jerked her head up and caught glimpses, through the crowd, of Douban's son carefully placing his father's head in a silk sack, Homer sitting on the floor clutching his ankle, and Mahfouza and Iole standing over him screaming for her attention. Pandy quickly picked up the net and fought her way through dozens of people still frantic at witnessing a talking head and the painful death of Camaralzaman.

"What's up?" Pandy said, reaching them.

"Look!" said Iole, pointing to Homer's lower leg.

Homer was squeezing his calf muscle as hard as he could, trying to form a barrier. Below his hands, at his ankle, Pandy saw a bloody gash, as if something had jaggedly sliced his flesh. Then she saw something lumpy moving under his skin.

"The fourth scorpion?" Pandy said.

Iole nodded.

"It didn't just sting him, it punched a hole large enough to crawl inside. Pandy, what were you doing over there?"

"Talking to Alcie," she said thoughtfully, staring at the hidden scorpion scrambling over Homer's ankle-bone, not noticing Iole's mouth fall open.

"I *beg* your par—"

"We have to get it out of him," Pandy interrupted. "But we can't do it now. We've got to get out of here before the guards start taking over."

"Don't let it reach his heart!" came the Physician's voice from inside the bag. "The effects will be permanent, I'm certain. As they were with the prince."

"If he takes his hands away, it will crawl up his body," said Mahfouza.

Pandy hastily scanned the room, then, seeing the perfect solution, raced over to the body of Codadad and hurriedly removed one of his many ceremonial sashes. She brought it to Homer and began tying it around his upper calf.

"Iole, Mahfouza," she called. "Help me pull it tight!"

The crowd in the room was beginning to thin and the guards, with fewer people to guide safely from the hall, began to take notice of the scene in the middle of the floor.

"This should keep it from moving, Homer," said Pandy, actually having no idea if the sash would work.

"Oh, I believe you. I believe you," Homer said softly, taking his hands away from his leg.

"Nice job," said Douban's son, looking at the neatly tied sash and the scorpion, unable to get under it. "It's perfect. Let's get him to his feet."

Slowly, the group ambled toward the entryway of the hall. When any guard looked at them oddly or tried to approach, Douban's son would hold up the silk sack and the voice of the Physician would bellow forth, scaring the wits out of anyone close by.

"Where are we going?" asked Iole.

Pandy looked at Mahfouza.

"Suggestions?"

"My house is on the other side of the city. It is too far," Mahfouza said, shaking her head. Then she brightened with an idea. "Come. Come! I know a silver merchant with a shop close by. He has dealt with my family for many years. He is an old friend and I am certain he will help us."

Mahfouza guided them through the streets of Baghdad and into the bazaar. Pandy and Iole gawked at the wonders of the marketplace as they tried to keep Homer from falling over in pain. Bolts of silks in colors and patterns she'd never seen in the Athens agora, bowls of spices so bright they made the colors of the silks look dull by comparison, and so many gold and silver merchants with their wares glimmering in the sunlight, she thought she would be blinded. As Mahfouza led them into one particular shop, Pandy glanced into the stall of a rug merchant and could have sworn she saw a man standing on a rug that was floating half a meter off the ground, yelling, "I'll take it! I'll take it!"

They found the silver merchant standing on a tall ladder against one wall of his shop hurriedly displaying, on a high shelf, silver bowls and platters with Prince Camaralzaman's face etched deep into their bottoms. Word of the prince's death had traveled fast and the merchant knew that these pieces had now become expensive collector's items and tempting for thieves. After Mahfouza greeted him and hastily exchanged introductions and a few pleasantries, she asked for his permission to take Homer into a back room. The merchant agreed without question but was then somewhat shocked when he got a good look at the two maidens supporting a big blond youth with something squiggling under the skin around his ankle, followed by another youth talking to a large, heavy sack.

On their way into the small room, Pandy noticed a thin, mottled, tired-looking cat snoozing on top of a short stack of silver platters. The cat barely opened its eyes as the group passed, calling out with a faint whimper at being disturbed.

The merchant led them to several couches, then politely excused himself, telling Mahfouza that he would be at the front of the shop if she needed anything.

"If the authorities pass by, it will look strange if he is not visible," she said to Pandy. "Then they will search the entire shop. He is doing us a favor."

"It's a favor," said Homer, nodding his head as he sprawled on a low couch. "I agree."

Pandy and Iole looked at him.

"My son, remove me," came the Physician's voice from within the sack.

Douban's son removed his father's head and gently placed it beside Homer. The eyes were bright as the Physician looked down at Homer's ankle. Then he gazed up at his son.

"Your first patient, Douban," said the head.

"*You* are the great Douban, Father," said the dark-haired youth.

"Enough! We both know I do not have much time. Do you have your bag?"

"Always; as you taught me."

"Then let us see how you will treat this case."

For the next half hour, young Douban, the new Physician, mixed herbs and blended them with strange liquids, uttered odd words, made clean incisions, and burned foul-smelling sticks of wood. It was only every so often that his father's head would chime in with a word or two. "Remember to . . . ah, good . . . that's it!" or "You are dealing with a lesser evil, this is not an average pox; you can't simply . . . yes, yes, there you go!"

Finally, Douban looked at Pandy.

"Ready your net, if you please."

"Oh, right! Right," she said, jolted out of her fascination with his treatments; then she realized she'd been holding the net tightly in her hand ever since she'd left the bodies of the prince and his grand vizier lying at the foot of the ruby throne.

"Iole, where's the box?" she asked.

"Here," Iole answered, drawing it out of her own pouch.

Gingerly, using the tips of his fingers, the young Physician began to force the blood scorpion down Homer's calf, where it had been crawling around desperately trying to get under the sash. Slowly and delicately, he inched it toward a large, clean incision he'd made just above the jagged wound torn by the scorpion. When Pandy saw it was about to appear, she threw the net over Homer's ankle and grabbed the first tiny, bloodred claw as it poked into sight, drawing the animal slowly out of his body.

"Now," she said.

Iole flipped the clasp and opened the lid. Pandy tossed the scorpion inside and Iole snapped the lid shut as everyone listened to the faint fizzling sound as the evil dissipated. Pandy quickly put the net and the box into her carrying pouch as Douban smeared Homer's wounds with an orange paste and began wrapping his leg with clean linen. At last Pandy looked at Iole.

"Which one do you think it was?" Iole asked.

"Could have been any one of them," Pandy replied. "Could have been 'deep ingratitude.'"

"That's it," said Homer softly.

"Or it could have been the lesser evil of a 'lack of mercy,'" Pandy continued.

"That's it," Homer said. "That's what it was."

"How do you know?" asked Pandy, now looking at Homer, curiosity all over her face.

"Because . . . because," Homer fumphered. "Because, like, you *said* that's what it was."

Pandy stared at the floor for a moment.

"No," she said flatly, testing a theory. "No, it was 'deep ingratitude.'"

"Right!" Homer agreed, nodding furiously. "You're right."

Pandy looked at Iole, then at Mahfouza and the young Douban.

"My hair is the color of straw," said Mahfouza, picking up on Pandy's intent and twirling her pitch-black curls.

Homer stared at her, his eyebrows furrowing and unfurrowing.

"Okay," he said at last. "I probably would have said black, but if you say straw, then I believe you."

"Your name is not Homer," said Pandy.

"Yes it is," he replied.

"*No,* it's *not.*"

Homer paused.

"Okay."

Everyone else began to smile.

"Gullibility," they all said at once.

"Right!" said Homer.

"If it had to be one of them," Mahfouza said, "I am glad it was that one."

"How long do you think its effects will last?" Pandy asked Douban.

Douban turned to his father's head, but the eyes and mouth were closed.

"Not long," said the youth, turning back, a delicate authority creeping into his voice. "Prince Camaralzaman had these embedded in his heart for months. Homer only had it in a lower extremity for a much shorter period of time. I would say the effects will wear off sometime before sunrise tomorrow."

He was even beginning to sound like his father, Pandy thought.

"Very good, my son," mumbled the head, but the eyes remained shut.

"Pandora," Iole said, standing up. "I must speak with you privately. Will you all excuse us briefly?"

Mahfouza nodded as Douban checked his dressing of Homer's ankle.

"'*Pandora*'?" Pandy asked as she and Iole stepped into the shop and stopped by the old cat. "What's with the proper name?"

Iole whirled on her, her face was so intense and there were so many emotions flashing on it that Pandy didn't know if she was mad or frightened or bewildered.

"What do you mean you were talking with *Alcie?*"

CHAPTER FIFTEEN

Good-bye

Alcie stared at Persephone and Hades.

"So . . . ," she began, and then stopped.

"So . . . ," answered Persephone. "Okay! Time to say bye-bye. But, oh, wow . . . I wish you didn't have to go."

"Yeah. I mean, this place is fantastic and I've had a great time . . . I guess. I mean . . . I don't know what I mean."

"I know. I *know*!" Persephone turned to her husband. "Buster, would you be a hero and get Alcie some dove hearts to go. Just have Cookie—no, wait . . ."

Persephone tossed a look to Alcie.

"Cyrene," said Alcie.

"Right! Cyrene! Sirens, will I ever remember? Just have Cyrene wrap a few in a cloth, so she can share them with her friends."

Then she turned to Alcie.

"If those tasty morsels actually make it that far, am I right?" She giggled.

"You are asking me," Hades said, gaping at Persephone, "the Lord of the Underworld, in the presence of a mortal, no less, to play delivery boy and—"

"Honey, she has only a few moments left here, and we want some girl time. Even if I tried to explain it to you, you wouldn't understand 'cause you're all burly and rough and tough and strong and—"

"I get it," said Hades. "I'll go."

"Thanks, love-bucket! I'll make it up to you, I promise."

Persephone stood absolutely still for the few moments it took the sound of Hades' footsteps to recede, then she hurried to the entryway and stuck her head into the corridor to be certain. She whirled on Alcie.

"Not much time!" she whispered as she raced to the bowl of Borrower's Bile.

Out of thin air, she created a small, blue glass vial and lowered it slowly into the ugly liquid. Once the vial was full, the yellow liquid turning the blue glass green, Persephone manufactured a glass stopper and corked the vial. Then she blew on it softly.

"Sealed tight until you need it," she said, handing it to Alcie. "Now, here are the rules. One use only; Buster won't know this tiny amount is missing, but I don't want to take any chances. Don't blame him for being a little snappish before; you wouldn't believe the pressure he's under. He probably would have thought of this himself if he hadn't been on the spot. I'm just glad I did. All right, one use. Pour it into your drinking cup, but then make sure you wash it clean. Contact Pandora when you get to Baghdad; afterward, toss this vial into the air and clap three times and it will simply disintegrate. I'd tell you to heave it into the nearest river, but Zeus only knows what might happen if this stuff ever got into a water supply. Okay?"

"Got it," Alcie said, then she inadvertently sucked her lips into her face.

"What?"

"Sorry. Nothing. I—I'm just worried about ending up in a wall or a lake or something."

"Oh don't!" Persephone cried. "Buster just said that to cover his own butt, on the off chance that something will go wrong and you'll come back down here and be all grumpy because your forehead is stuck to a turtle or your foot is in a temple column or whatever they have in Persia. He's never missed when it comes to sending someone back—no matter where it is. You'll be fine!"

Persephone gave a big sigh and put on a frowny-face.

"I miss you already," she said. "This has been the highlight of, maybe, the last three centuries for me."

"Well," Alcie began, "I'd like to say I'll be back, but I don't know."

"Yeah, but now *you* get to decide." Persephone smiled, patting Alcie's pouch containing the box with her life-thread.

"Thank you," Alcie said as Persephone gave her a tremendous hug. "Thank you for everything."

"I'll be watching you and Pandora and everyone," Persephone said, her eyes moist. "Or at least I'll try to— if my mother ever lets me out of her sight again."

"You would really like Pandy," Alcie said.

"I know!"

"Very well, Alcestis," said Hades, entering the room. "Two dozen dove hearts packed to travel."

"Oh, Buster, you're a champ."

"Thank you," said Alcie, placing the cloth bundle in her carrying pouch.

"Are you ready?" asked Hades.

"Lemons," Alcie said to herself, then she straightened. "I am."

"Good luck to you, niece of Medusa. I hope"—and here, Hades lowered his head to stare hard, but kindly, at Alcie—"that someday you will walk in the Elysian Fields."

Persephone began clapping in agreement behind her husband. As Alcie was forming the words "thank you" for the umpteenth time, Hades, Persephone, the bile bowl, and the walls began to fade into blackness. In the dimming scene, Alcie saw Hades turning his head to say something to his wife. Then the room was gone and Alcie was losing consciousness. But not before she heard a clear and distinct . . .

"I know!"

CHAPTER SIXTEEN
Another Chat

"Helloooo? Known world to Pandy. Come in, Pandy."

Pandy stared at the striped silk siding of the market stall. Then she stared at the rugs covering the dirt floor. She had no idea how she was going to explain her conversation with Alcie to Iole. Finally she looked up.

"Uh . . ."

"Let me repeat the question," Iole said, a look of genuine concern on her face. "What did you mean when you said you were talking with Alcie?"

"Alcie's voice was coming through the mouth of the—the—the grand . . ."

She trailed off.

"Very well," Iole said, crossing her arms. "Commence at the beginning."

Somehow, that shook Pandy out of her confusion.

"What beginning? You were *there* at the beginning," she said, her voice raised. "You saw everything. The prince was poisoned and we got three blood scorpions in the box before Homer started yelling and you ran over to him. I was about to follow you when Alcie— Alcie's voice—it was Alcie's voice, Iole, by Athena it *was*! And it started coming out of the grand vizier's mouth. She's alive, Iole! She was telling me things that only she could know. She's in the underworld."

Pandy's voice had become so loud and passionate that Mahfouza crept from the back room to see what was the matter.

"But she's coming to join us. She said she was going to contact us again as soon as she got here. She said it over and over. It was *her*, Iole. And she said she'll explain everything."

Iole paused, her brow knitted into a black line.

"You're fabricating this."

"I am *not* fabricating this," Pandy yelled. "Whatever that means, and I know it's not good."

Homer and Douban, carrying the sack, hurried in from the back as the shopkeeper quickly left his post at the front to see what the commotion was.

"I'm not saying you're doing it deliberately," said Iole. "I think the stress of this whole quest has finally gotten to you and—"

"And *what*? I've snapped? You think my lamp's outta oil? Fire's out in the oven? Chariot's lost a wheel? I know what I saw!" Pandy cried.

"I think you're tired," Iole said.

"Girls," said Mahfouza, reaching for both Pandy and Iole at once. "Girls, what is—?"

"*Hey!*"

The call came from somewhere nearby in the shop. Mahfouza gave a tiny shriek and dropped her arms.

"*I leave you guys alone for a few weeks and already you're fighting?*"

Iole froze, Homer gasped, and everyone looked around the market stall, hunting for the source of Alcie's unmistakable voice.

"Alcie?" said Pandy.

"Here."

The old, mottled cat was rigid as stone, sitting stiff on her hind legs, her eyes now colored the same yellowish white as the eyes of the grand vizier.

"The cat?" Pandy asked.

"Is that what I'm comin' through this time?" Alcie asked in return.

"She wouldn't believe me, Alce," Pandy said, pointing at Iole as she looked at the animal. Then she turned to Iole. "Alcie said her voice would come through the lowest form of life close by. Before it was the grand vizier, and now it's a cat, so there."

"And *that's* why I am your *real* best friend," said Alcie. "I would have believed you."

Iole's mouth hung open as she watched the cat's

mouth move in time with Alcie's voice. The cat roughly jerked her head around the room.

"Hi, Homie!" said Alcie.

"Khaaaa," choked Homer as he stumbled backward, practically falling on top of Douban.

"Inconceivable," said Iole softly.

"Tangerines, I don't have much time," said Alcie. "Okay, I'm here, I think, but I don't know where that is exactly, so you have to come and find me."

"Why don't I tell you where we are and you can come to us?" Pandy asked.

"I'm kinda stuck. Persephone said that Hades never misses when he sends someone back . . . but he . . . uh . . . missed. So you have to come get me down."

"Down?" asked Pandy.

"I'm in a tree. I *knew* I was gonna end up somewhere funky. But it's dark—like, black—so I think I'm in a room or a cave or something. There's one tiny light at the far end of this big space, but I can barely see around me."

Mahfouza and the silver merchant both inched toward the cat.

"A dark room with a tree in it?" asked Mahfouza.

"Hey, I remember you! From that crazy circus, right?" said Alcie as the cat swiveled her head.

"Yes, you are right, Alcie," Mahfouza replied. "But tell me more about the room now. Is there one tree or are there many?"

"Many," said Alcie. "Lots. And there's weird fruit on the trees. Shiny stuff. And it makes noise."

Mahfouza turned to the silver merchant, who was staring incredulously at his cat.

"Are you thinking what I am thinking?" she asked him.

He turned uncomprehending eyes on her.

"The Garden of the Jinn?" Mahfouza said. "Could that be it? She has described it perfectly according to the legends. But no one knows where it is!"

The merchant shook his head, trying to clear his mind of the fact that a strange girl was talking through his cat and focus on the new information regarding trees in a dark room.

"Yes," he said at last. "She has described it well."

"Pears," said Alcie. "Wherever I am, Pandy, you have to get me outta this tree!"

"Don't worry, Alcie," Pandy said. "We'll find you and we'll get you down!"

Suddenly, there was a soft noise behind Alcie, a sound like wind chimes clinking together.

"Hear that?" said Alcie. "A wind just blew through here from nowhere and the branches around me are hitting each other and making that noise."

"Young girl," the merchant said, "please describe the fruit on your tree."

"Oh, that's easy 'cause I have some sticking out of my shoulder, which, by the way, is why I can't get down.

It's . . . uh . . . well, I think they're red and smallish and sparkly. They look like cherries."

"Yes," he said. "She is in the garden."

"Okay," Pandy cried. "We know where you are and we're on our way! Sit tight!"

"I got no choice," Alcie said. "All right then, I'm signing off. And this is the one and only time I can talk to you, so hurry! Bye, Iole! Bye, circus lady . . . bye, two men I don't know. Bye, Homie!"

The cat jerked up on her hind legs as her eyes cleared. She gave one loud sigh as she shuddered, then fell back onto the pile of rugs on which she'd been lying—dead.

"Safie?" cried the merchant, dashing to his cat. "Safie!"

"I'm sorry, sir," said Pandy. "That is exactly what happened to the grand vizier."

The merchant cradled his lifeless pet in his arms.

"I want to be angry," he said at last. "But I cannot. She was old and in pain and this was to be desired. I have witnessed a great deal here that I cannot explain, but I think Safie's life was given in the cause of something much greater."

"Much," said Mahfouza, gently placing her hand on his arm. "But I fear that Alcie said farewell too quickly. We have no way to find her! All my life, I thought that the Garden of the Jinn was merely a legend."

"What is this garden?" asked Pandy.

"The Garden of the Jinn, if you believe the legend, is the most enchanting place on earth," Mahfouza answered. "It was created by the jinns, or genies, solely for their own recreation. It is said the fountains run with diamonds. And even though it is forever in darkness, the plants are eternally in bloom. But it is the trees that are truly incredible. It is also the place where the genies keep their vast treasure. No mortal man has seen it or knows where it is."

"You have been away from Baghdad for many years, dear Mahfouza," said the silver merchant. "The location has been known for some time. Only now fewer and fewer seek it out."

"What?" Mahfouza said. "How did this happen?"

"As with each ruler before him, the genies told Prince Camaralzaman the location of the garden, as a gesture of goodwill and respect for his position. The genies simply assumed that, like his ancestors, he would never divulge its whereabouts. But the foolish dolt told the guests at a banquet one evening several years ago, after he had drunk too much sweet wine. The very next day, the garden was looted and gold was taken from the genies' treasury. It didn't make even the tiniest dent in the huge amount, but it is said that the thief was able to build several palaces before the jinns destroyed him as punishment. The genies knew instantly what had happened. They were angered at Camaralzaman's stupidity, but instead of moving the garden, they protected it with deadly spells. At least that is what everyone believes. No one who has attempted to enter has ever returned."

"I know every inch of this city," Mahfouza said. "There is no room in any building I have ever seen that could hold such a place."

"That is because the garden lies underground," said the head of Douban from inside the cloth sack.

At the sound of this new voice, the silver merchant turned around just in time to see young Douban withdrawing his father's head before he keeled over facefirst into a neatly stacked pile of silver-polishing rags.

"Yes, it is enchanted and dangerous," said the head. "Prince Camaralzaman, being ultimately a coward, never dared to enter, but he allowed me free use of the garden because he knew I would never offend the jinns and take advantage of its treasures. It is beautiful, but now it has been almost completely abandoned by the genies, who cannot bear the thought of humans in their sacred place. There is only one genie left, by the name of Giondar. His crime was so terrible in the eyes of his master that he was condemned as punishment to live in a small lamp at the far end of the garden. But it is also said that he learned how to escape."

Although Pandy was curious as to what the terrible

crime was, it was clear to everyone that the head of the Physician was now truly dying. His eyes were open only slightly and a brownish crust was starting to form on the lids. His lips were blue and his tongue sounded thick in his mouth. Pandy's heart went out to his son. "The entrance lies but a short distance on the outskirts of town, very close to my old palace and gardens. I don't think I have strength enough to show you, but I can tell you the way. However, there are precautions you must take before you enter."

The silver merchant opened his eyes and sat up slowly. Peering over the pile of polishing rags he stared at the talking head, forcing himself not to faint again.

"Walk away from the river until you come to the edge of town," said Douban's head. "Then walk another one hundred meters until you come to the ruins of an old palace. You shall know it by the crumbling fountain in the center of a dilapidated courtyard flanked by two tall palms."

"I know this place," Mahfouza said quietly. "I used to play there as a child with my family. But mother always warned us to leave before dark."

"Each evening," the head continued, "as twilight rests on the desert, spirits will emerge from the unseen palace and soon the courtyard will be in full celebration. You will see musicians playing and servants rushing to and fro. There will be eating, drinking, and dancing.

You will be asked to join in but you must refuse, for if you give in to temptation, you will join the spirits forever and there will be no saving you. When the sun is almost set, the final rays will illuminate a bronze ring set into a slab midway between the two palms. This is the location the genies chose for the entrance to their realm. Lift the slab away and you will see stairs descending downward. Follow them. You must pass the gatekeeper and then the dreadful corridor; however, only one of you may enter at a time. The rest must remain behind. You will come to three rooms: the first will contain jars full of copper coins and several black stones lying about. The second will contain jars full of silver and many more black stones. The third room will have hundreds of jars overflowing with gold, rivaled in number only by the black stones. Touch none of the treasure. Not one coin. Keep your mind focused only on getting through the rooms. You will then come to the garden itself and you will be able to find your friend—but only if you do exactly as I say."

"Got it," Pandy said. "Let's go!"

Douban placed his father's head gently back in the sack as Mahfouza walked to the silver merchant and bowed low. Then, with a promise to return and give him a full explanation of all the events he'd just witnessed and perhaps a new cat (if he wished), she raced to catch up with Pandy and the others as they headed toward the entrance of the shop.

Realizing they didn't know exactly which way to turn, Pandy, Iole, Homer, and Douban turned back and waited until Mahfouza came rushing out of the shop.

"You must follow this street," she said. "I can take you only part of the way but then I must leave you. I must get to my home and my family."

"Of course," Pandy agreed. "We'll get Alcie and be there as fast as we can."

Then they turned in the direction Mahfouza had pointed and, with only the slightest gasp from Iole, they all froze. Douban and Mahfouza had no idea who the enormous blue-robed woman blocking their way actually was, but they could tell from the look on Pandy's face that she was no friend.

CHAPTER SEVENTEEN
We Meet Again

"Well, well," Hera said, her eyes narrow but bright, her mouth set in a fierce fake grin. "You know I was just thinking, being so far from familiar faces and places, how much fun it would be to run into someone I know—and here you are! How thrilling to see you, Pandora. Quite a way from home but looking well. And I see you've made some new friends."

Hera leaned in as if sharing a sacred truth.

"But they can't ever replace the ones we lose, am I correct?"

Mahfouza shrieked, then quickly covered her mouth.

"Oh," said Hera, turning and reading her thoughts. "Do you like my earrings? They slosh a little, but they're a tremendous help. As if I need to tell you—you live in these parts, right? So you know all about the *power* I now have!"

Then she turned back to Pandora, glaring.

"How shall I do it? How *shall* I do it? Now that I have you, what's the best way to *kill* you?"

"You have no power here, Hera," Pandy piped up, surprised at her own audacity, although there was panic in her voice. How did Hera know where she would be? How did she get out of Zeus's sight long enough to get to Baghdad? What did she think she could do with her powers limited or gone?

Hera could barely contain her laughter. She shook her head from side to side, earrings bouncing off her puffy cheeks.

"Oh, don't I? I have no power? What do you think these are, sweeting? Candy?"

"What are they?" Pandy asked out of the side of her mouth.

"She's wearing the egg of an unborn roc," Mahfouza said.

"Two," said young Douban.

"That's right, my little oatie cakes. Not one but *two*!"

Pandy had no idea what the significance of the eggs was, but their tone was enough to make Pandy's stomach drop. This was a moment like several others on her quest, where Hera was literally threatening to kill her. In the past, like the most recent time in the temple of Aphrodite in Aphrodisias, Aphrodite herself had intervened, and then Zeus. This time, however, Pandy was certain that Aphrodite or Hermes or Athena or anyone else who might help her was far, far away. This time, Hera was actually going to do it.

"Put my head on the ground," Douban the Physician said softly to his son. Slowly, young Douban removed his father's head from the sack and set it down.

"Step away," said the head.

"Father?" his son whispered.

"My studies and powers were not limited to the physical. I advise you to be learned in all things. Distract the goddess Hera for but a moment. This is goodbye, my son. Tell your mother I love her and always do right by the world."

The younger Douban slowly walked around the back of the group now under attack by Hera. He grabbed Pandy's cloak, forcing her to sidestep a little, which in turn forced Hera to turn her back on the head sitting on the ground only a meter from her right foot. For the moment Hera was looking at Iole, trying to read her thoughts about Alcie, who naturally had sprung into Iole's mind at the mention of lost friends.

"My father says to distract her," Douban whispered to Pandy. "Keep her talking."

"Why?" Pandy asked, but there was no time for an answer. Hera whirled on them.

"Private conversations? Those don't please me. Not so much. Back to business; yes, I have two, count 'em, two eggs. I thought just having one would be fine, but I can do anything with these. Eyes here, please."

Suddenly, no one could look away from Hera. Their bodies from the neck down could move freely, but their heads were immobilized in space and all eyes were forcibly trained on her malevolent face.

"So, she has eggs on her ears. What does that *mean*?" Pandy asked aloud, brazenly stalling and honestly curious at the same time.

"Roc eggs give visiting immortals their powers to use while in Persia," said Douban.

"Smart lad," said Hera. "Don't believe me?"

Without a moment's hesitation, Hera sent a ball of fire directly into the shop of the silver merchant behind them. The merchant barely had time to escape with his life. Although they couldn't actually see the destruction, within seconds, all the silver was liquified into one large pool and the precious metal was flowing in a shiny river into the street.

Boom!

She set a milk stand ablaze over her left shoulder, which everyone saw.

Crash!

She leveled a tavern, a jeweler's, and a spice shop, all crowded close together nearby.

BANG!

Over her right shoulder, she destroyed a lamp shop and all the lamp oil stored in the back.

"Oooops." Hera giggled like a fat baby. "Sometimes I get carried away."

"All right! All right," Pandy said, putting her hands up, still unable to look away. "I believe you! We all do. You can do anything here, Mighty Hera, just like you could do anything back home. But—but you don't want anyone else but me, so please, let them all—"

"Wrong!" Hera shouted, loudly enough that the desperate, terrified customers and merchants trying to flee the devastation stopped for a moment at the sound of her terrible voice.

"Wrong I say!" Hera screamed even louder at Pandy, who realized that this was the final moment. This was where it was all going to end, in a dirty street of a marketplace far from home.

"Now everyone dies!" Hera spat. "You, of course. But now the two miserable friends who still remain will get to accompany you on that long walk to the underworld, where you can be reunited with the other brat—the gimpy, blind one. Won't that be fun? The question is, how to do it? Boiling, roasting, wild dogs tearing you apart. All boring. And who gets to go first? Who gets to watch?"

At that moment, a giant shadow fell across a portion of the marketplace and Hera, surprised, lost focus on her enchantment. Everyone's head and eyes could move freely, and they saw that, where once Hera had been silhouetted in the afternoon sunlight, now a mammoth figure rose up behind her and blocked the sun.

At first Pandy thought it was some type of creature, a beast of some sort. Or a series of animal skins sewed together and inflated. Then she saw the enormous eyes ringed in a brown crust, and the lips, huge but still tinted blue. The turban itself was also oversized, along with the severed stump of the neck.

The head of Douban the Physician was now the size of a small temple. Everything was in proportion but the skin was stretched tight and shafts of sunlight penetrated inside, indicating that the skull was gone. For an instant, Pandy thought of the large, translucent slug tent that circled the perimeter of Wang Chun Lo's caravan, and the sentries that could be seen moving about inside.

The huge mouth now in front of her opened wide, showing teeth the size of writing tablets.

"What I have always enjoyed most about wrong-doers," bellowed Douban the Physician in a voice that caught Hera so off guard that she nearly stumbled forward, "is that before they act, they *talk* about what they are going to do! And talk and talk and talk."

Hera spun to face the head as the mouth opened wider and wider. The head tilted forward on the cleanly sliced neck and Hera could only stand, stupefied, as the mouth surrounded her, sucked her in, and swallowed her whole.

Pandy and the others watched as Hera slipped over the tongue and down the throat, but instead of passing out through the severed neck, she took a strange turn and ended up, head over heels, where the Physician's mighty brain would have been. Suddenly realizing what had happened, Hera could be seen getting to her feet and pounding relentlessly on the inside of the Physician's head.

"Which gives plenty of time for the heroes to act," said the head with a huge smile. Douban the Physician forced a violent gulp, which threw Hera completely off balance and sent her robes flying over her head, threatening to reveal more of the goddess than anyone wanted to see. At that moment, the head began to lift into the air. "Although I have learned to communicate with unborn rocs—a skill you should cultivate, my son—and the ones she possesses are currently cooperating, I don't know how long I can hold her. And I don't know how long I shall want to because, if I may add, she tastes foul."

Pandy and Iole smiled in spite of themselves.

"Hurry, my children. The sun is sinking fast," said the head as it floated over the rooftops. "Good thoughts to you in all that you do."

After only a few steps Mahfouza, with a squeeze

of Pandy's arm, ducked down a side street as Pandy, Iole, Homer, and Douban—now, truly, Douban the Physician—rushed headlong toward the edge of Baghdad, each of them looking back every so often to see the giant head, with the Queen of Heaven furiously stomping about inside, gently gliding on a southbound breeze.

CHAPTER EIGHTEEN
Three Rooms

In almost no time, Pandy spotted the two palms and even though her breath was catching hot in her throat, she ran across the cracked tiles of the courtyard toward the dry fountain. The sun had just begun to dip below the horizon. Douban was the first to reach her as she paced back and forth by the fountain, trying to find the ring in the slab. Homer helped Iole to sit on a large stone, patting her back as she struggled for breath.

"With all the running we do," Iole panted, "you would think I'd have just a little more stamina."

"It was only a few days ago," Pandy said, still searching the ground and heaving a little herself, "that you were so sick you couldn't move. I think you're doing great."

She kicked at a spot and sent up a cloud of dust. All of a sudden, the faint jingle of a tambourine caught her ear. She looked up quickly.

"I heard it too," said Douban.

Almost imperceptible shimmers of heat and color were starting to flicker off in the desert. Pandy would focus on one color or a movement, and the next instant it would disappear. Then the flickers would hold steady for just a little longer and everyone knew, as Douban's father had foretold, the spirits of the palace were moving in for the evening.

"Here they come," said Iole, watching several young boys, nearly transparent, dash onto the courtyard, tossing about a small black ball.

"Don't pay any attention," cautioned Pandy. "Don't even look at them."

But the sounds and color of the musicians, the filmy beauty of the women and young girls dancing passionately, the troop of horses and the flash of scimitars clanking about in mock duels was so enticing. The courtyard even smelled wonderful as some cooking stoves appeared with spits of meat and pots of many different kinds of food bubbled away.

"Mmmm," Homer said, inhaling the spicy scents. "I'm hungry."

"No, you're not," Pandy said.

"Right, I'm not," he agreed completely.

Within moments, however, as the sun dipped lower, the spirits of the ruined palace were approaching the four friends, encircling them, and beckoning them to join in the dancing and fun. There was no language, exactly, only laughter and strange sounds that emanated from open mouths. As if the spirit's speech had been reduced to rounded, lopped-off words. Douban forced himself to turn away from the marvelous spectacle. He closed his eyes and sat on the ground next to Iole. Iole followed his lead and closed her eyes as well. Pandy was still busy glancing between the setting sun and the ground between the palms, hunting for the ring and waving away the outstretched arms of the tittering girls who tried to get her attention.

Without warning, Iole thought of Homer. Her eyelids flew open just in time to see Homer only one tick away from taking the hand of a lovely dancer whose black hair was so long that the very tips trailed on the ground.

"Homer!" she screamed, startling him, his hand dropping to his side. "Don't look at her. You don't like her and you don't like dancing!"

"I don't?" Homer asked. Then he nodded his head. "That's right. I don't."

"Come sit by me," Iole commanded. "That's what you want to do."

Without another word, Homer plopped down on the other side of Iole. She draped her arm around one broad shoulder and let her fingers loosely enclose the back of his neck. If he moved again, she'd know it.

The pitch of the celebration had nearly reached its peak and Pandy, who knew she couldn't close her eyes for fear of missing the one flash of light that would reveal the ring, was having difficulty avoiding the myriad hands and arms that wanted to pull her into the crowd. She found a path in the throng of spirits and darted to one of the palms, throwing her arms around the trunk and holding tight. Then she realized that the spirits weren't actually making contact with her, merely tempting her to join in. They had plenty of opportunity to try to pry her from the palm; yet all they were doing was beckoning. She walked away from the tree, directly into the crowd—and it parted in front of her.

"Hey," she called to the others. "If you don't touch them, they can't—or won't—touch you. It's okay to move around."

Iole opened her eyes and turned to look at Pandy. The sun was forming a soft red crescent as it started to slide from view and a shaft of light flew across the desert, piercing through any spirits in its path.

"Guys! Hey, guys!" Pandy called. "It's time!"

Iole, Homer, and Douban leapt to their feet, making their way around the ruined fountain. The sunbeam marked a spot on the ground and there suddenly appeared a large bronze ring.

"Everybody!" Pandy cried, and the four friends fell upon the ring. Homer and Douban each got a firm grasp and shooed Pandy and Iole back. They tugged hard and the slab lifted easily out of the ground, as if it were made of feathers, revealing a dark hole and the top-most steps of a narrow staircase leading into the earth. The spirits now lost all interest and wandered away to other activities.

Pandy led the way but paused only a few meters down.

"We need light," she said, looking backward, up past the others to the darkening sky.

"Can you set something on fire?" asked Iole.

"I don't have anything."

"It cannot be too much farther," Douban said. "If it were so far underground, my father would have told us."

In almost pitch-black, Pandy made her way down the stairs, her hands feeling the narrow walls on either side. Soon, she saw a dim light ahead and a glint of light on metal. She headed straight for it, but cautiously.

The dark pathway leveled out, and within moments, Pandy and the others found themselves in a little alcove lit by a tiny lamp in a niche above a golden door with no handle or knob. She stared at it intently. Then she pushed on the door with all her might.

"Homer," Pandy said with a bit of authority.

Homer threw all of his considerable weight against the gleaming metal, using every ounce of his strength. When he couldn't budge the door even a millimeter, Douban joined him and together they strained for several minutes before they fell forward, spent.

"I don't see any way of getting in," Pandy said, now slightly frantic, acutely aware that Alcie was on the other side.

"Nor would you," came a thin, raspy voice from her left. Everyone turned to see a small, old, impossibly thin man clad only in a tattered undergarment. He was sitting cross-legged on a large stone.

"I am the only one who knows the secret of the door," he said. "I am the only one who may open it, besides the jinn to whom the garden belongs. Who are you and why should I let you enter?"

Pandy began to approach him but faltered after her first step as she saw something slither out of a hole in the wall just above the man's head. She stared as a thin black snake disappeared behind the man's shoulder, then reappeared as it wrapped around the man's neck and climbed over his head. Then another snake, white this time, caught her eye as it popped its head out of another hole. Pandy looked around, her legs frozen, as she realized that most of the room—the uneven walls, part of the ceiling, and much of the floor—was crawling with hundreds of snakes.

"Guys, stay very still," Pandy said.

"Oh Gods," Iole whispered in a tiny voice, seeing the snakes covering the walls. "Homer, will you— would you?"

Without finishing her question, Iole grabbed the shoulder of Homer's cloak and hoisted herself up his body, until he helped her to sit on his shoulders.

"They're just snakes," Homer said.

"Yes, they are," Iole answered.

"I will ask again," said the old man as a red and brown snake slithered under one arm and across his sunken chest. "Who are you and why do you wish to enter?"

"I am Pandora Atheneus Andromaeche Helena of Athens, and this is Iole—"

"You," said the man, cutting Pandy off and pointing to Douban. "Who are you?"

"I am Douban," said the youth. Then as if the meaning of the words was only just hitting him, he said very slowly, "The Physician."

"You lie!" said the man sharply. "I know the Physician. He visits frequently. You are not he. You lie."

In unison, all the snakes that Pandy could see turned their heads toward Douban and bared their fangs.

"No," said Douban, far more calmly than Pandy would have expected. "I do not lie. The great Physician, the man you knew, is—was—my father. He is now dead. And I have taken his place."

The snakes closed their mouths and went back to slithering as the man stared at Douban for a long time.

"That saddens me," said the man. "He was the best of men."

Then he looked again at Pandy.

"Why do you wish to enter, Pandora of Greece?"

"My friend is stuck in a tree on the other side. In the garden," she answered.

"She's in a cherry tree," Iole said.

"We only wish to get her down and be on our way," Pandy said.

"My father has instructed us on the enchanted garden and the three rooms of coins," said Douban.

"Then you know you may not touch a single piece," said the man.

Everyone nodded their heads.

"You may enter to find your friend," the man said, turning his filmy eyes back to Pandy. "But only you. And beware, the danger to which you will expose yourself is greater than you imagine. Attacks may come from any side. Many have tried to walk through the rooms of copper, silver, and gold, and they have all met a terrible end, I can assure you, for not one of them has ever come back. Except, of course, for your father, young Physician. You would all be better to turn back and let your friend stay in the cherry tree."

Pandy huffed at the suggestion. Remembering her power over fire, Pandy squared her shoulders. "I can defend myself if someone tries to attack me. And I'm not interested in any money—just my friend."

The old man smirked.

"So you say. But what if those who would attack you cannot be seen, how will you defend yourself then?"

Pandy had no idea.

"I just will," she said at last.

"Very well, since you will not listen to my advice and turn away, hear this: when the door is opened, you must summon all your courage to find your way into the first room, which will then be lit as bright as day. Pass through the room as quickly as you can and pay no attention to anything you may hear. Anything. And above all, touch nothing. I shall repeat, although it never does any good: do not listen and do not touch. Do you understand?"

"Yes," Pandy replied. If it was just voices, how bad could that be, she mused.

"Then come," said the man, unbending his legs and rising. Pandy noticed that, while the old man had been talking, all the snakes had simply disappeared. Moving swiftly to the golden door, the man gave the gentlest push and it swung silently inward, revealing nothing but blackness beyond.

Pandy looked to Iole, Homer, and Douban, her smile weak but her fists clenched firmly. Then she walked into the darkness. Remembering that she had forgotten to ask anything about the garden itself, its size, shape, or where exactly to find Alcie, Pandy turned back, but the golden door was swinging shut and, suddenly, she was in pitch—pitch—black.

It was then Pandy recalled the words spoken by the head of Douban's father: "the deadly corridor." And she flashed back to the first words of advice the old man had just given her: "You must summon all your courage to find your way into the first room."

Pandy had just assumed that she would be in some sort of rocky passageway, much like the one she and the others had passed through as they descended the stairway into the earth from above. Why would she need any courage? Couldn't she just walk?

Then, as her eyes were trying to adjust, trying to find even a pinpoint of light to lead her, she heard the sound. So very soft. All around her, a rustling, but not harsh—whisper soft. It was the sound of things gently rubbing together, oh so slowly.

Tentatively, she put out her hand, trying to find a wall with her fingers. Nothing. She edged forward, slowly. Finally, her middle finger brushed against something soft and dry. Pandy pulled her hand back, then stretched it out again cautiously, feeling again the papery softness.

Then she felt it move.

In the blink of an eye, just before she jerked her hand away, she felt the tiny but strong muscles contract. She knew exactly what it was. And she flashed on all the small heads turning toward Douban, fangs bared.

All the snakes that had disappeared from the alcove were now surrounding her; her skin rose up in prickles along the back of her neck and down her arms and legs. She remained frozen for—she couldn't say how long. She hadn't known this particular type of fear before: to be completely unable to see the enemy, to see what was coming at you. Then she remembered that her feet hadn't come into contact with anything so, perhaps, shuffling along the floor wouldn't be dangerous. Her legs felt like they were made of bronze. She forced herself to go onward until her shoulder grazed a wall and she felt a mass of long shapes on her upper arm.

"*Okay. Okay*," she mouthed to herself. "This is not the way. I could be in here forever, bumping into walls. Think!"

Without knowing why exactly, only that she was, naturally, curious, she gradually raised her right arm into the air over her head. Her elbow was still bent when she brushed against a ceiling writhing with long, slender bodies—so close to her head.

She gritted her teeth and hesitantly put out her hand one more time.

"If I can just move along a wall," she mumbled.

She closed her eyes; there was no point in keeping them open, she knew she could only rely on her fingers and her sense of touch. She lightly traced over a mass of snakes slithering on a wall. Moving forward, she delicately swept her forefinger along one particular snake or another, always avoiding the head. This worked until she headed into a corner and her nose rammed between two snakes clinging to the wall. Instantly, she flung her head back but not before her cheek felt a tiny fang, bared and ready to strike.

Around and around she went. She lost any sense of time. Into dead ends, oddly angled corners, and wide, sweeping curves. At one point, the ceiling sloped downward and a hanging tail lightly struck the top of her head. She was beyond tired. She got on her knees, still keeping her arms stretched out, mashing her knees into the hard ground as she willed herself onward.

"Alcie's alive and, by Zeus and all the gods, I'm going to find her," she said aloud, not caring if the snakes were at all disturbed.

Then she felt it.

The air became ever-so-slightly cooler and less stale.

Pandy had an urge to speed up, but resisted with all her might. She kept her pace even, but felt over her head and realized she could stand again. Then, all at once, she felt a bare spot on the wall to her right and her fingers touched only stone. Then more stone as the gaps between snakes grew wider, then she placed her palm on the wall and felt only smoothness. Impulsively, she raised her left arm and felt the ceiling, devoid of snakes.

Suddenly the wall and ceiling ended and she was standing alone in the blackness. She opened her eyes. There was nothing to cling to, no focus point. She began to lose any sense of direction, becoming uncertain of which way was up and which way was down. Just as she began to stumble forward, a light was lit in a room, the opening to which was directly in front of her. Immediately, she stepped into the archway and, steadying herself against a wall, turned to look behind her.

There was nothing. She had seen this kind of blackness only once before, when she'd been sucked into the void of the heavens. She'd seen the great masses that formed the constellations up close, but beyond them, a darkness that went beyond an ordinary moonless night. This corridor or chamber . . . or whatever she'd just passed through had been exactly the same.

Pandy turned back into the long room to find that it was now awash in light. There wasn't a soul in sight, but many oil lamps hanging from the ceiling were now blazing, turning the room red. Pandy realized that the walls and ceiling were covered entirely in copper. Beyond this room another archway led into darkness, but Pandy knew that Alcie was close by. She headed quickly, in a straight line, for the archway, only glancing at the huge jars, close to the walls on either side, full to bursting with red copper coins. She wasn't ten steps into the room when the first voice whispered in her ear.

"Take one—who will know?"

Then another voice in her other ear.

"Aren't they pretty? And you could use them, no?"

Suddenly the voices were all around her. Some were light and airy, others sweet, but all were playful.

"Just a handful." "We won't tell." "Come, over here!" "This way!"

Then, a voice crept in that was anything but sweet.

"Stop her. Stop her before she goes any farther!"

Both Pandy's courage and footsteps faltered for a moment.

"There! You see? She's listening. Tell her! Tell her what we will do to her if she takes another step." "Do not let her pass!" "Take a coin, just one."

Pandy remembered the words of the old man and walked straight across the long room. The tempting words and the threats died out quickly as she reached the entryway to the second room, which was magically lit before her.

"Okay," she murmured to herself, glancing back into the copper room, now completely dark. "Not bad. Not great, but not bad."

She peered into the new room. It was blinding white, covered from top to bottom in silver. Large jars piled high with shiny silver coins lined the walls, and there were many more black stones on the floor around them. She squared her shoulders and walked ahead. Only five steps into the room, however, and the voices were back.

"Where does she think she's going?" "What does she want here?" "Such beautiful coins—take some."

The voices grew in ferocity and temptation.

"Catch her!" "Kill her!" "The coins are enchanted, such powers they would give you!" "The death of a thousand cuts!" "Your eyes will be torn away!" "All of this silver is yours, take it!"

With a start Pandy realized that she had stopped in the middle of the room and was staring at the gleaming piles of coins.

"That's it!" "Take one, ten—take them all!"

She couldn't remember the last time she had seen so much silver. Even the silver merchant in the market-place had not such a quantity.

"Figs," she said absentmindedly. And that word brought her right back to Alcie. Alcie, only one room and a few measly trees away! She turned her steps toward the entrance to the third room and, reaching it, didn't even bother to look behind her; she knew the silver room was now dark, and if it wasn't, she didn't care. The third and final room lay before her, made entirely of gleaming gold and now ablaze with the light of dozens of oil lamps. So many jars of beautiful golden coins lined the walls, three or four deep in places, that she lost count. She had never in her life seen so much money. She'd seen splendor, to be certain, but never simple, pure golden *money*. There was so much it was even piled in heaps on the floor. And so many black rocks. There were more rounded rocks in this room than in the first two combined.

She took a quick glance around; the only physical difference to this room that she could see was the absence of a far wall. Instead, the room opened onto an expanse of blackness. Then Pandy narrowed her eyes and stared hard. There was a twinkle to the left, then a sparkle to the right, and then a flash, and then another and another, all accompanied by a delicate clinking sound. Finally, her eyes made out the large trees with low-hanging fruit that tinkled and glinted in the lamplight. And far beyond the trees, a single candle or lamp or flame of some sort sputtered in the blackness.

"The garden!" she gasped.

"Hey! I see a light!" came a voice from somewhere deep in the grove of trees.

"Alcie!" yelled Pandy.

"Pandy?" yelled Alcie in return.

Without another word, Pandy broke into a run, but she was only two steps into the room when the voices began screaming in her ears; shouting and shrieking, cursing her and threatening her so violently that her hands flew up to cover her ears and she stopped, petrified.

"Assassin!" "Thief!" "I shall tear your arms from their sockets!" "I shall feed you your tongue!" "One more step and my knife shall plunge into your heart!"

Pandy was immobilized, shaking and unable to focus. Then soothing voices took over and calmed her.

"Pay no attention to those brutes!" "No one can harm you now." "Do you see what lies here? All this is yours." "We have been waiting for one such as you!" "So courageous!" "This is your gift!"

Then, from out of nowhere, but close enough that Pandy whipped around, came a voice that sounded exactly like that of . . .

. . . her mother.

"How wonderful to see you at last."

It felt as if a knife were, indeed, going straight into her heart.

"Take a coin, dear one. It is more precious than you know. Only one will buy you the world. Come."

Pandy turned to the nearest cluster of jars. She wanted to see her mother more than anything else in the world. And there were so many pretty coins. She missed her family. She stared at the gleaming piles.

"Come."

As she took one tiny step, she heard Alcie's voice, far

in the distance; so far that Pandy couldn't make out the words. Something about—help.

"Come. With these, you'll be able to do anything. Come."

She'd be able to help. Help Alcie. Help them all. They would be able to travel safely and in style. She would be able to buy information regarding the remaining Evils. With so much money, she might even be able to buy back the Evils themselves. What would it hurt if she just took one or two? She could buy anything—everything. And they were all so shiny.

"Come."

"One more step and I'll sever your head!"

"Hush! Ignore him. Come."

She reached out toward the closest jar, mesmerized, and felt her fingers curling around a small golden disc.

Instantly, within a heartbeat, the world was being sucked into a vortex somewhere on the floor at her feet. The next moment, the long room was silent and empty, as if no one had been there in ages. No sound and no movement.

Except . . .

Against the base of the jar of golden coins, there was one more black stone rolling to a slow, lazy stop.

CHAPTER NINETEEN
The Garden of the Jinn

"Your friend is dead," said the old man. "Now go away."

Iole, even with her brilliant brain, was certain she hadn't heard correctly, so she had no reason to be alarmed, only surprised.

"I'm sorry?" she said, almost sweetly.

"Leave this place," the old man said. "The girl is dead."

Douban's entire body went rigid. Iole sprung away from Homer, on whom she'd been leaning for the past hour because the walls were pocketed with snake holes.

"What!" she screamed, not getting too close, but trying to appear that she was bearing down forcefully. "What do you mean? *Who* do you mean? *Which* girl?"

"The one with whom you arrived," he said, a smile playing across his lips. "No one listens. No one ever listens. Now go."

"Okay," Homer said, turning out of the alcove.

"Homer! Stop right there!" Iole commanded.

"Okay."

"Please explain, sir," Douban said, fighting to keep his voice even.

"Only your father listened. Only your father could move through untempted," said the old man to Douban. "His was a will of iron."

"Pandy is *dead*?" Iole yelled. "How? How did she die?"

"You bore me," said the man, uncrossing his legs as if to stand and go.

"I don't care if I put you to sleep!" Iole said, totally surprised by her own vehemence and authority. "You're not going anywhere! Let me in there!"

She marched over to the golden door and stood squarely in front of it, waiting.

"I'm going in," she announced.

"No," Douban said, "let me go. I can do—"

"Anything you can do," Iole cawed at him, "I can do—with greater skill, efficiency, and nerve! All the tales we've told you over the last few days? Well, it wasn't half of what we've been through. And that 'we' includes me. So I am very capable, thank you very much, to discover what happened to one friend and save another!"

She turned to the old man.

"Now open it!"

With another slight smile, he rose, walked to the golden door, and pushed it open. As the door swung back, Iole marched through without another word and immediately found herself in inky blackness. In the alcove, Douban turned to the old man and Homer.

"I only meant that if I am truly my father's son, I might have had a better chance at avoiding whatever traps lie beyond."

"Naturally," said the old man.

"Okay," agreed Homer.

Alone and unable to see, Iole followed the first idea that came to her. She crouched low to the ground and wrapped her arms around her knees. Like Pandy, she looked for any glimmer of light, the faintest twinkle, and when she saw nothing, her ears pricked up. She even stopped breathing through her nose, choosing to inhale and exhale slowly and silently. There was nothing.

At first.

And then she heard the rustling. Like two layers of silk barely glancing off each other. Iole held her breath and strained her ears. With a start, she realized it was coming from every direction. And then, like Pandy, she realized that the snakes had disappeared from the alcove and, while they probably *could* have gone many places, there was only one place they *did* go and they were now completely surrounding her.

She dug her fingernails into her knees and tried not to cry out.

The one thing Iole had never mentioned to anyone was her intense, paralyzing fear of snakes. Before her family had moved from Crete to Athens, she had made the mistake, when she was only a little girl, of telling some other children that she didn't particularly like the slithering creatures. The next day, two young boys held her to the ground while another girl teased and tormented Iole by holding a snake only millimeters from her face as Iole screamed. Finally, the girl tossed the snake onto Iole's shoulders as she and the boys ran away. Iole fainted on the spot, only to be found later by her father.

When she arrived in Athens, before Pandy and Alcie became like sisters to her, she vowed never to reveal this terror to anyone. Then, because there were so many other things to talk about, it became somewhat of a non-issue. She could laugh about Alcie's aunt Medusa, with snakes for hair, because Medusa had been killed long ago. And she rarely left well-traveled roads and pathways. If they had come across any snakes in the months since they had begun the quest, Iole had simply clenched her fists and had walked around them, remaining silent. Trying to laugh and be brave. Even in the alcove, when she had essentially climbed onto Homer, she hadn't screamed; she'd just acted rather "girly," never letting on that her insides had become liquid.

But this.

This was her worst nightmare coming true.

She began to cry, imagining the bites, the stinging, the attacks that were sure to happen. And she waited, trying to cover the bare parts of her legs and arms. Then, when nothing happened, Iole gingerly felt the ground in front of her. Nothing. No snakes. She felt off to each side. Again, nothing. Then, as she reached to feel the ground behind her, her hand brushed against her girdle and the decorative ties around her waist.

One of which was coarse and thick.

Puzzled and distracted from the serpents all around her, she felt the tie encircling her tiny body. It couldn't be . . .

. . . but it was!

The magic rope!

She had never taken it off and Pandy hadn't asked for it. Pandy had recounted the story of how she and Homer had tied the four of them (Dido included) together during the monstrous sandstorm that had hit them in the desert. She also told of how the rope had begun behaving oddly and had ultimately snapped in two but for some inexplicable reason Pandy hadn't taken Iole's length of it back. Perhaps she thought she already had and had just forgotten. Iole had been focusing on other things and had just put it back on after bathing or sleeping.

And here it was.

Instantly, Iole's brain went to work.

"Rope," she said softly, "untie and . . . make a small coil in my hand."

The next moment, the rope was unwinding itself from around Iole's waist in a movement that, sickeningly, made her think of snakes slinking all over her. But that moment passed quickly as the rope coiled around her neck.

"No!" Iole whispered. Then the rope expanded to ten times its size and pushed Iole against a snake-covered wall. Then, immediately, it shrunk and nestled into her palm.

"One end," she said, "tie around my wrist."

As soon as the words were out of her mouth, the rope tied itself around her ankle, then back around her waist and only then around her wrist. Iole suddenly realized that her section of the enchanted rope did two incorrect things before it did what it was asked to do. She needed to trick it into doing what she wanted the first time.

"Now," she said, "pay attention. Lead me into a wall covered with snakes. But I'm going to be crawling so go swiftly. Please."

She felt the free end of the rope move out from her palm and moments later there was a gentle tug at her wrist. Gradually, her head down, her eyes closed and her breath coming in short bursts, the rope slowly led Iole not into a wall but out of the snake-infested corridor. There was only one moment when a snake broke loose from its grasp on the uneven ceiling, its tail swinging down and falling across the back of Iole's neck. She flung her body forward on the ground, her knees tucked under. The rope stopped moving until she found the courage to rise up and crawl onward.

Finally, she was in the open space between the corridor and the first room. Seeing the lamplight, she herself tied the rope around her waist again before it could lead her into a snake-covered wall and entered the room of copper coins. She passed easily through it, completely unswayed by the voices, the taunts, and the tempting words. She was not curious at all about the black stones littered about the room. She was only looking for Pandy's body.

Iole entered the room full of silver. Surveying the length of the room and not seeing Pandy, she began to cross when, out of nowhere, a voice that sounded like her father's whispered in her ear.

"We have missed you so, my dear."

She stopped and turned toward one wall, stunned. It was only then that she comprehended the vast amount of gleaming metal within arms' reach.

She slapped herself, hard, across the cheek.

"Stop it!" she said loudly and moved on.

At last, she came to the room full of gold. She hadn't

taken one step into the room before the lamps were blazing. And that's when she heard Alcie's voice.

"Pandy? Where did you go?"

"Alcie! Alcie!"

"Iole? Is that *you*?"

"I'm right here!" Iole called.

"Where's Pandy? She was here and then she was gone and everything went black."

"I'm trying to find her!"

"Well, come get me and we'll find her together. Lemons, she can't be far. I don't think there are many ways to get out of this place."

"I'll be right there!"

But with Iole's first step, the spirits surrounded her with such ferocity and intensity that Iole lost the sound of Alcie's voice. She tried to keep her goal in focus and was past the midway point, her eyes glued to a glittering apple tree in the dim garden ahead, when a soothing voice crept into her ear.

"I'll show you where your friend is."

Iole whipped her head and was instantly overwhelmed by the gold.

"Where?" she said, her lip quivering.

"She's been taken prisoner. But we can help. You'll need some of this to set her free. She's so close. Almost at your feet. Take one, take it all—it's all for you. For your friend."

Mesmerized, without another thought, Iole drew closer to the first jar she saw and stretched out her hand.

In the alcove, the old man smiled and shook his head.

"Young girls," he said with a sigh. "They simply cannot resist bright, shiny objects. It is almost a disease."

"These girls can," said Douban without even knowing why the old man spoke.

"Well," the old man smirked, "perhaps they have been misled, but only a little. In any case, the second one is dead. Now go."

"Wow," Homer said.

"What!" yelled Douban. "What is going on in there? What traps have you laid for them?"

"Only the trap of their own immaturity," said the man.

"Very well," said Douban. "I should have gone in the first place. I am nothing if not my father's son. I will get to the very bottom of this. Now, if you please, open the door."

For a third time, the old man rose and gave the golden door a light tap. After Douban disappeared, Homer stared at the snake holes in the alcove walls, and the old man stared at Homer until he grew tired of watching Homer poke his fingers in and out and closed his eyes.

Moments later, as Homer sat with his back against the door, the old man opened his eyes and sighed.

"He was not his father's son."

"Huh?"

"Dead, dead, and . . . dead," said the old man, spitting onto the dirt floor. Then he looked at Homer, a gleam in his eye. "And then, there is you. The last. The one with the problem—blowing whichever way the wind takes you. I suppose you will want to go in now yourself, hmmm?"

As he scratched at his nearly healed wound from the blood scorpion, Homer couldn't decide if he wanted to go because the man had just told him he would want to and he was still infected with the lesser evil of "gullibility," or if he wanted to go because he wanted to search for his friends. He only knew he wanted to go.

"Yes," Homer said, standing. "I do."

"And you will not listen to my warnings?"

"No. I mean yes. I mean, what do you mean? Whatever you say. I will not—do you want me to? What?"

The old man chuckled and slipped past Homer to rap on the door, which swung wide for a fourth time.

"Have fun," he said.

Homer had to duck through the doorway and, like the others, instantly found himself in pitch-black. Without listening or trying to get his bearings, he straightened up and banged his head on the ceiling of the enclosed space, knocking loose several snakes, which began to slither across Homer's shoulders. He brushed them off as if they were raindrops and stumbled forward, crashing into first one wall, then another. It didn't take him long to realize that the space was crawling with serpents, but he didn't bother to think about where they had come from, only that they were in his way. He felt, roughly, along the walls, batting away tiny, fanged heads, clearing large spaces with a sweep of his palm. He pulled them off his legs as they wound their way up his calves. Like Pandy, he got backed into oddly shaped corners and down dead ends, but he plowed his way through so fast and so furious that it was almost no time at all before he was standing at the end of the walls, clean air on his skin, and lamplight in a room just ahead of him.

As he set foot in the room full of copper coins, the voices began to whisper.

"How strong!" "How handsome!" "Come this way. Over here." "Take some of these!"

Homer began to stumble in a different direction with each new voice. And then an alarm went off in the very back of his mind. The effects of gullibility were still strong—too strong, and Homer wouldn't be able to resist unless he did something. So he did the first thing that came naturally, the first thing anyone would do if they heard a noise they didn't like or knew they shouldn't hear.

Homer put his fingers in his ears.

🍇

In the alcove, the old man smiled, nodded his head, then laughed once . . . and disappeared.

🍇

Homer made it safely through the rooms full of copper and silver. Then he came to the room of gold and one particular glint of lamplight off a single coin was so bright that he took one hand away from his ear and shielded his eyes.

"Hello?" came a voice from beyond the room. Homer heard a soft tinkling, like glass beads hitting together.

"Hello?" he answered.

"HOMIE!" Alcie cried.

"Alcie!"

"Oh, Homie . . . *what* is going on? Pandy and then Iole and somebody else, I think, were where you are right now and then they were gone!"

"Hang on," yelled Homer, "I'm coming to get you!"

He stepped into the room and the voices swirled around him like leaves in a vortex.

"This one is mine!" "Attack him!" "Assassin!" "Hand-some youth, come this way." "No, over here." "Gold—all for you!" "Listen to me . . ."

Even with his fingers in his ears, Homer could hear everything that was being said. He turned in so many different directions, he began to get dizzy. He wanted to go one way first, and then another . . . he believed everyone and everything that was being said. He was an assassin, and a handsome one, a thief and murderer; he should go this way, no! *That* way. The voices began to blend into a continuous roar, so loud and so persistent that Homer did what he always did when things became too confusing. He just stopped thinking altogether. Then something—some *thing* wound tightly around his brain—snapped, and in the middle of the chaos Homer suddenly knew that none of these other voices mattered, especially when the one voice he truly wanted to hear was so close.

"Alcie!" he called.

"What?" she cried back.

"Keep talking!"

"What do you want me to say?"

"Anything," Homer yelled.

"Figs! Neat! Okaaaayyyy . . ."

Alcie proceeded to recount her adventures in the underworld with Persephone and Hades as Homer tried to focus in on her voice only. Twice, the spirit voices led him to a jar full of golden coins and twice he stretched his fingers out to take a bright piece of metal. Twice he had almost forgotten the warning of the old man not to touch any of it. And twice Alcie brought him back. Because it wasn't the money that he was after ultimately. It was her. The voices became more cunning, taking on the sounds of his mother, father, and teachers. Taunting him, tempting him. Playing upon his gullibility. He shouted for Alcie to keep talking, not to stop. Sing, if she had to. He fought the voices: the incredible delights that were promised him, the shiny money and the fear of a dozen horrible deaths, as hard as if he were back in the training ring at gladiator school. He sweated buckets as he forced his mind not to be swayed. He slashed at the air with his fists, as if his opponent were flesh and blood, not unseen tormentors trying to break his mind.

As he crossed the midpoint of the room, the dark garden spread out before him; he felt a strength return to his mind as the last of gullibility seeped in perspiration through his pores.

The spirits saw that they were losing their chance and redoubled their efforts. But with no gullibility in his body, Homer lowered his hands; there was no one to fight. He lowered his head; he had no need to look around. Gold was nice, he supposed, but somewhere in the garden, Alcie was talking, and he was on his way.

He walked straight to the end of the long room and out into the dark grove of trees. Immediately, the lamps in the room of gold were extinguished, making it almost impossible to see.

"Oh, pomegranates," Alcie said, half to herself. "And the lights go out again and *again* I am stuck in the tree and no one is around."

"I'm here," Homer called from below.

"Homie!" she squealed.

"Hang on," he said. "My eyes, like, need to adjust."

"Yeah," Alcie called. "There's a tiny light way over that way. You can just make out big shapes. Should I keep talking?"

"Absolutely."

By the single flame of the far-off lamp, Homer felt his way around each tree. As Alcie was coming to the part of her story where she had tasted the roasted garlic and snail custard, Homer was standing underneath the tree in which she was stuck. He started to climb.

"Ooof," she said, looking down as he jostled the tree. "There you are!"

"Keep talking," he said.

"Oh, okay. Well, then I ate some more and then I met Lachesis, who gave me my life-thread. Oh, yeah, tangerines, I got my very own life in my pouch! Then I contacted Pandy the first time."

Homer climbed way out onto the branch on which Alcie was sitting.

"Hi," he interrupted.

"Oh!" she said with a start, not realizing he was so close. "Oh, hi."

"Hi," he said, grinning.

"Hi," she said, smiling back. "Do you want me to keep talking?"

"For the rest of your life," he said, and leaned in to kiss her quickly and very gently.

"Guess what?" he said as they broke apart.

"What?"

"I'm not gullible!"

"Okaaay," she replied, not having the faintest idea what he was talking about. "And I'm not an eggplant, so we both win!"

"Oh, Alce," Homer said, tears in his eyes. He just sighed deeply and shook his head.

"I know," she said, reaching with her far arm to stroke his cheek. "I know. But, apples, do I have stuff to tell you!"

"I have to get you out of this tree first," Homer said, wiping his eyes.

"That's not going to be so easy," Alcie said. "Hades and Persephone both said I might end up stuck somewhere. I kinda thought they were joking at first, but look."

She pointed to her right shoulder. Sure enough, a small branch, about the diameter of a string bean, was growing into her shoulder from the back and sprouting out from the front in several smaller branches from which hung two clusters of hard red cherries.

"Actually, the tree is in me."

"Does it hurt?" Homer asked.

"No, that's the weird part."

Homer pulled a short knife from his pouch and began to cut the tree branch about a centimeter away from Alcie's back. Homer sawed fast, keeping the blade away from Alcie's skin. At last, Alcie was free. As she went to throw her arms around Homer, she nearly fell out of the tree.

"I think I'll wait until we're down," she said.

Descending as fast as they could from branch to branch, Alcie not wanting to let go of Homer even for a moment, at last their feet hit the ground. Alcie threw her arms around Homer, then immediately drew back.

"Ouch!" she cried, staring down at the tiny branches poking through her shoulder.

"Gods!" he said. "I'm sorry."

"Don't be sorry," she said, gazing at him. "Don't ever be sorry. Just be careful."

Homer pulled her left side close to him and draped one arm lightly around her neck. They stood like that until a breeze shook the fruit around them and brought them back to reality.

"First things first," Alcie said. "We have to find Pandy and Iole and whoever else that was."

"His name is Douban and, man, is *his* story wild!" Homer replied. "We need to be able to see. Let's go check out that light."

He led the way through the grove to the far wall of the garden, where a single flame burned low in a dull, brass lamp. Alcie went to reach for it, when Homer suddenly stopped her hand.

"Wait," he said. "I just remembered. Douban's father said something about this lamp. He said that a genie might be living in it. And it's a bad genie. Like, not good."

Alcie now regarded Homer as if he had gone mad.

"Excuuuuse me?" she said. "In this? Something lives in this?"

"Or he might have escaped."

"Well, I have no idea what a genie is, but I don't care if the Minotaur itself is inside, I say we use it," Alcie said. "We got nothin' else."

Removing the lamp from its niche, Alcie carried it back through the grove of trees. Now, even with such a tiny source of light, the fruit on the trees sparkled brilliantly.

"What in the name of Hercules are these things?"

Homer asked, catching bright flashes of red, green, and purple. He was trying to keep up as Alcie, nimble as a dryad, hurriedly picked her way around the thick tree trunks.

"Don't know," she called back to him, moving fast. "Don't care right now."

At that moment, Alcie nearly tripped over an over-sized root growing several centimeters out of the earth. Homer neatly caught her just before she fell flat.

"I've missed doing that." He smiled.

"I'm not *that* clumsy," she said.

"Whatever you say," he said, and he threw his arms around her again.

"Come on," she said, breaking away with a laugh.

Reaching the large opening to the room of golden coins, Alcie stopped abruptly.

"You came through here, right Homie?"

"Yep," he answered.

"Well, this was the last place I heard both Pandy's and Iole's voices, so they have to be here."

"Yeah, but there are other voices in here, too," Homer began, trying to warn her of malevolent spirits.

"Good," she interrupted him. "They can help us look."

"Or not," he said softly. "Alce, don't touch anything. I mean it. There's lots of gold . . . like, coins. We have to be careful not to touch any of it. I think it may have something to do with Iole's and Pandy's disappearance."

"I am not interested in gold," she said, surprising herself. "I have to find my friends."

She stepped into the room and held the lamp high.

"Wow!" she said, surveying the enormous piles of coins. "You weren't kidding."

"Do you hear anything?"

"No," she answered.

"Good. Let's see if we can get some light. There are lamps hanging from the ceiling," Homer said.

He took the brass lamp from Alcie and, reaching as high as he could, tried to get the oil to catch. But the room remained dark and cold. Taking back the lamp, Alcie doggedly, and very carefully, picked her way around the jars of golden coins, mindful not to touch a single piece. She moved deeper into the room, calling for Pandy, lifting the lamp high and low as Homer trailed after her.

"Oh," Homer said, remembering something. "I forgot to tell you. Watch where you step."

"What? Why?" Alcie asked, turning back. In that instant, a voice whispered into Alcie's ear.

"Assassin!"

"Ahhhh!" Alcie cried, whirling around, stumbling and pitching forward as her foot caught on a smooth black rock. She managed to hang on to the lamp as its stopper banged about on its thin chain, but a tiny drop of oil splashed out and hit the rock she'd just tripped over.

197 ▣

"What was that?" she cried.

"I'm sorry," Homer said. "I forgot to tell you. There are rocks on the floor."

"No!" she cried. "There was a voice."

Her own voice trailed off as, without any warning, the black rock lying next to her began to vibrate, shaking back and forth. Suddenly, it began to grow and change; even in the dim light of the lamp, Alcie and Homer quickly made out colors and fabric. Then skin and fingers, then an arm, then a leg. The rock changed within seconds and soon a young man, dressed in fine, costly robes stood before them. He was quite dazed, but before Alcie or Homer could speak, a wide grin broke out on his face and he grabbed Homer by the folds of his cloak and wept joyously.

"Thank you, my friend," he sobbed. "Thank you for my liberty. You have no idea how long I was trapped in that horrible form. A thousand blessings upon you."

"Uh," Homer said, slightly shaken and pointing to Alcie. "She did it."

The young man lifted Alcie off the floor with such speed that Alcie didn't know what to say. It was only when he went to embrace her that Alcie found her words.

"Okay," she said, struggling to keep the man at arm's length. "Okay . . . that's good, that's enough. We're good."

"Yeah, she's good," said Homer, taking a step toward them.

"How can I thank you?" the man said, his eyes still wet.

"You can tell us what's going on. A moment ago you were a rock."

"I have been imprisoned for so long. I hardly know where to begin. I am a prince from a neighboring kingdom. For years I have heard the story of the Garden of the Jinn. I traveled a great distance but I came to the garden only to look at the trees. I swear, that was my only reason. I was able to pass safely through the rooms of copper and silver."

He pointed behind him as he spoke and in the distance, Alcie saw the entryway to another darkened room.

"But I became bewitched by the gold. I ignored the warning and I listened to the voices around me. This gold belongs to the genies of the garden, but I thought it could do no harm to take only one piece. There is so much, they would never miss it. I barely got my fingers around a single coin and instantly I was transformed."

"That means," Alcie said, realizing, "that all of these stones are people, just like you?"

"Yes," the man said.

"But what did I do?" she asked. "How did I bring you back?"

"Just before I transformed," he said, "I felt something hot. It was a burning sensation on the back of my leg."

He turned, lifting the bottom of his garment for everyone to see. There, in the dim light, was a small stain. Touching it, he rubbed it between his fingers.

"Oil," he said.

"When I tripped, it must have spilled from the lamp and landed on you." Alcie said.

"The oil inside must be charmed," said the man, his eyes growing wide.

"Well, if it worked on you, it's gotta work on the others, right? Homie, I'll wager fifty drachmas that Pandy and Iole are rocks. Let's do this!"

She knelt on the ground so as to be more precise and not waste any oil. One by one, Alcie released a teensy drop of oil onto each of the black rocks. Up sprang princes, beggars, common workers, and royal advisers. There were young men and old, those who were born in Baghdad and those who had come great leagues to see the magical garden, only to be caught by the spell of the money to be had. None of them were inherently greedy; all of them shunned the sight of the precious metals once they were restored. Some were furious at their captivity and pounded the walls of the large room at the time that they had lost, even though they had not aged a day. Some were so relieved at their liberty that they fainted. Some, as rocks, had been so resentful that they were the voices that had enticed others to join their fate. Others had not known exactly what had happened and so blamed the next person to visit, crying out "assassin" and "thief."

But all were grateful to Alcie and Homer for their freedom. In fact Homer had to prevent most of them from rushing upon Alcie, hugging her, kissing her feet or her hands and generally disrupting her task.

"Homer!" she cried at one point. "Keep them back! I hardly have enough light as it is!"

Alcie was more than a little surprised when one young man, after being transformed, rushed at Homer and threw his arms about him.

"This is Douban," Homer said, looking at Alcie's surprised expression. "It's a long story."

"I am Douban the Physician," the handsome youth said, bowing ceremoniously to Alcie. "It is my pleasure, Alcie. You are just as beautiful as Homer said."

Alcie, again, was completely stumped. She stood for only a second, shaking her head in utter incomprehension.

"Hi," she said, her tone more bewildered than frustrated. Then she knelt and went back to pouring oil on the stones in no particular order. Dozens and dozens of men were restored before her eyes. Then at the very moment, when seeing a young man appear had become so commonplace that she had actually turned back to ask Homer if Pandy had recaptured Rage yet or if she had any clue as to where Rage might be hiding, Alcie heard a soft voice just above her.

"Oh, Alcie!"

Iole stood staring down at Alcie. Alcie looked up and that was all it took. The competition for Pandy's affection, the snarky little comments, the trivial insecurities, all of it vanished. In that one moment, Alcie realized how much Iole meant to her and she was on her feet in a flash. Iole went to throw her arms around Alcie when Alcie stopped her short.

"Careful," she said, pointing to her right shoulder, not taking her eyes off her friend.

"Incredible," Iole gasped, staring the tiny branches and the red cherries. "Are you all right?"

"As far as I know," Alcie replied. "We'll deal with it later. Right now . . ."

She halted as Iole put her hand on Alcie's arm. Then the two girls embraced as best they could, leaving Alcie's shoulder alone. Alcie felt a relief like none other; she clung to Iole's neck and held on as if she were drowning and Iole was a rope that had been tossed to save her. Without warning, Alcie and Iole were sobbing and choking and sputtering, each trying to say something, trying to talk over the other, but nothing came out.

Iole looked about.

"Pandy?"

Instead of answering, Alcie looked at Iole with an expression of astounding determination. The next moment, Alcie moved Iole away from her.

"Homie!" she yelled. "Start bringing the stones to me! We're losing too much time if I have to crawl around. New guy! Don't make me say it again—hold everyone *back*!"

One by one, Homie set the black stones in front of Alcie and the seemingly endless supply of enchanted oil. At least a hundred men of all shapes and sizes had been restored, but there were hundreds of stones still left. One at a time the men were liberated and every one of them, after hearing the story told by Iole and Homer, about the young girl who came back from the dead and who was now setting them free, chose to stay and watch the miracle. At last Homer stood before her empty-handed. There was no stone left.

Alcie began to panic.

"Could she be in the room of silver?" asked Douban.

"No! NO!" Alcie screamed, startling everyone there. "I heard her voice in *this* room! *This* room was lit up. She has to be here!"

The men began chattering and moving about.

"Stop!" Alcie shrieked. "Nobody move!"

Everyone froze.

"Don't move a muscle," she said, her voice carrying the ultimatum with quiet authority. Slowly, the lamp in her hand, Alcie began to walk the perimeter of the large room, in between all the jars heaped with the still untouched gold. Everyone held their breath, following her and the minute flame only with their eyes.

At last, wedged in between two jars, partially sunk in a pile of golden coins, Alcie saw a black stone.

"One of you melon heads kicked her over here," she softly cursed at the men standing closest. Alcie reached for the stone, careful not to touch the piles of gold.

Placing the stone in the center of the room, she let fall a little drop of oil. In an instant, the fabric of a cloak appeared followed by two legs, then a silver girdle, then two arms, and then a head of long brown hair.

CHAPTER TWENTY

Restored

Pandy's first conscious thought was that there were so many people now standing around her in the dark, whereas it seemed as if only a moment ago, she was alone in a brightly lit room, reaching for something sparkling. She shook her head to clear it; she remembered the snakes and the gold and her mission to find Alcie. As it all came back, she noticed a figure resembling Homer standing a short distance away. Then, turning her head slowly for fear of becoming dizzy, she saw Iole, and then, standing so close Pandy could see her red hair glinting in the lamplight, she saw Alcie.

They looked at each other for a long, long time. Iole stood back and let it happen with joy in her heart. Homer was rapt. Douban, who wanted to rush forward and hold Pandy tightly even for an instant, held his ground. The men around them, without knowing why, complete strangers to the two girls in the center of the room and one another, were humbled by the moment. They were only vaguely aware of something immense and endless, yet quiet and simple passing between the maidens as they stood, face-to-face.

Then, without any signal or sign, Pandy and Alcie reached out at the same time and fell upon each other without words or tears. Alcie twisted her shoulder slightly so that the twigs in her flesh wouldn't get in the way; she wanted to explain nothing in this moment.

Pandy, in that split second, realized that her friends were the family that she had given herself, that no blood sisters could ever be as close as she, Alcie, and Iole. And that nothing would ever change that.

Not even death.

They broke apart and stared at each other again.

"What happened?" Pandy asked.

"You were a rock. I poured a little oil on you. No biggie."

"You brought me back?"

"It's what we do," Alcie said softly.

"There's so much to tell you," Pandy said.

"You know it!"

"We have no time now," Pandy said. "Rage may be hiding at Mahfouza's house. Maybe not, but it's a good place to start."

"Okay, so you haven't found it yet. So, then, I didn't really miss much, right?" Alcie asked.

Homer chuffed and Iole laughed until she looked at young Douban, his face grim. It only took a little time to transform the remaining stones in the rooms of silver and copper, and soon the men began to disperse, feeling their way into the darkness and out of the treasury. Each one thanked Alcie as he left; some were so grateful and relieved they even thanked Pandy and Iole.

The girls, Homer, and Douban were readying to leave when Alcie, adjusting her carrying pouch and checking its contents, got the strap caught on the branches in her shoulder.

"Ow."

"*What is that, Alce?*" asked Pandy, noticing for the first time the small red fruit emerging from Alcie's body.

"When I left the underworld, part of me got stuck in this—or this got stuck in me."

"Alcie," said Iole, amazement in her voice, "I think those cherries are . . . are . . . rubies!"

"Figs, no way," Alcie said, looking at her shoulder.

"Indubitably. I'd wager anything," Iole said. "Rubies have a particular sparkle no matter which way they're cut, and these have it."

"Look," Alcie said, turning to Pandy, "I know we have to get moving. But we probably won't be back and as long as we're here, wherever this is, let's just see what's so special about this garden."

Pandy paused, her brow furrowed. She had no idea what lay ahead, if going to Mahfouza's was even the right path. But her curiosity was so strong it was making her fingers tingle, and Mahfouza said that the trees were the most amazing feature of the garden.

"Five ticks on a sundial, okay?"

"Follow the lamp!" Alcie said as she headed toward the trees.

Young Douban spent an extra moment retying the sash around his waist, so when he finally caught up to the rest, he was surprised at the silence as everyone stood, gaping, underneath the nearest tree. He followed Pandy's gaze and there, hanging so low that anyone could touch it, was a perfect pear.

An emerald pear.

The most beautiful jewel any of them had ever seen.

Alcie reached out her hand, but Pandy stopped her.

"I'm not going to pick it," Alcie said. "I just want to touch it."

But her fingers hadn't even grazed the surface when the pear dropped to the ground and landed at her feet.

"You saw!" she said, looking at Pandy's wide-eyed expression. "Not my bad! I didn't even get close!"

"I know," Pandy said. "I'm just waiting to see what will happen."

But nothing happened. No one turned into a rock, no monsters crept from secret places, no thunder.

"Finder's keepers," Alcie mumbled gleefully as she picked up the jewel.

She moved to the next tree full of topaz oranges. This time she only lifted the lamp to give everyone a better view and again several fruits dropped to the ground.

"It's as if they've been waiting for us; as if they're meant for us to have," Iole said, focusing on two oranges, watching them vibrate and drop as she moved close by.

"I'm not saying no!" Alcie said, scooping them up.

"I guess it's okay, then," Pandy said, but she still craned her head all around, up and down, searching for any sign of trouble.

Each tree was more stunning than the last. There were amethyst plums, opal peaches, ruby apples and cherries, citrine lemons, garnet pomegranates, and sapphire figs so blue as to almost be black. The fruit literally fell off the tree if they so much as looked at it. Pandy and Iole were only taking one or two of each, but Alcie was taking as much as she could carry. Her carrying pouch began to bulge with gems, so she thrust a few into Iole's hands.

"Keep them for me."

"You want *all* of these?" Iole asked, passing a few oranges and lemons to Douban.

"They'll make nice hostess gifts when we get invited to bacchanals and sacrifices back home," Alcie said. "If we get home."

"Girls and their bright, shiny objects," Homer chuckled, echoing the words of the old gatekeeper.

"Something you would do well to remember, my good man!" Alcie shot back, handing him pears, apples, and plums.

"Come on, guys," Pandy said, heading back into the golden room. "We all have enough for a fruit salad. Alcie, let me have the lamp; I know this route."

She led them through the three rooms, all now eerily quiet. When she arrived at the deadly corridor, she stopped.

"I didn't do so well in here," Pandy admitted.

"I only made it through because I had a little help," Iole said. "Oh, by the way, I think you may be missing this."

She loosened the magic rope from around her waist and handed it to Pandy.

"What's in there?" Alcie asked, looking into the darkness of the corridor as Pandy tucked the rope into her bag.

"Snakes," Pandy and Iole answered simultaneously.

"I'm goin' *back* to my tree," Alcie said, starting to turn.

"You're going nowhere," Homer said. "Pandy, let me have the lamp. Now, everyone hold hands and close your eyes. Douban, you're on the end, okay?"

"Yes."

"When I say move, move fast. Follow the person in front of you and just, like, stay calm."

Homer led them into the blackness, prepared to swat, swipe, sweep, and crush if he had to. But there were no snakes anywhere. The corridor was empty and actually a very short distance from the exit to the entrance. In no time, Homer was pushing against the golden door and suddenly everyone was standing in the alcove, which was also completely empty; no snakes, no gatekeeper. Just a message in gold on the walls, written in beautiful, flowing Arabic.

It is ours once again.
Maidens of Greece, may the fruits
of our labor repair the ruined
and vanquish your foes.
Depart in peace with our thanks

"Watermelons," Alcie said. "What does *that* mean?"

"Maidens of Greece," Homer said, tying the lamp to his waist with a cord. "Someone knew you were coming, or here. Or whatever."

"Repair the ruined?" Douban questioned softly.

"Well," Iole said, "we were right about the jeweled fruit being a gift, for one thing."

"'*It is ours.*' What's ours . . . theirs?" Alcie asked.

"The garden," Pandy said. "Every human is out of it. They've taken it back."

The next instant, the earth began to shake violently and there was a deafening crash behind the golden door as if something was being blown apart. Everyone tried to run for the staircase, but all were thrown to the ground and could do nothing but cover their heads. At last the noise subsided and a small puff of dirty air shot through a space at the bottom of the golden door. Homer pushed on it, but only succeeded in opening it a few centimeters. He could see nothing but black rock resting against the other side. The entrance to the garden was caved in. It simply didn't exist.

"Is that what the message meant? Do we have to repair *that*?" Alcie asked.

"No. They destroyed it," Pandy said.

"Utterly," Iole agreed.

"Who?" asked Alcie.

"The genies who built it in the first place," Douban answered.

"Why?" Alcie asked.

"My guess is that they have had enough of mortals poking around," Pandy said. "I'll bet the genies moved the garden someplace else, and this time they won't tell *anyone* where it is. That's also why we've been asked to depart."

"Okay, grapeseeds," Alcie said. "What or who is a *genie*? Everyone knows but me."

"In Persia, genies, or jinns, and their female counterparts, peris, comprise the main group of immortal beings," Douban began.

"Douban," Pandy interrupted, "tell us all on the way out of here. We have to get back to Baghdad."

Douban began to relate everything that his father had taught him about genies and peris as Pandy led them all back up the earthen stairway and into the cold air of the predawn desert.

CHAPTER TWENTY-ONE
The House of Mahfouza

"Just give it to me once more," Alcie said.

"From the beginning again?" asked Douban.

"No, not from the beginning!" She huffed. "I've got all that. Persia has mortals and immortals. Just like Greece, duh. Largest class of immortals are the genies and peris—got it. But still I don't understand the eggs. Wait, Pandy, wait!"

Alcie stopped walking and leaned back against a low stone wall.

"I just gotta catch my breath. Maybe I lost some, like, stamina or something when I was in the underworld. Just gimme a tick."

It had only been a short time since they left the ruined courtyard and the crumbling fountain. The sun was still well below the horizon line, only the faintest glow beginning in the east.

"You okay?" asked Homer gently, looking down on Alcie as if he were seeing her for the very first time.

"Yes, Homie," she said, and Iole could have sworn that Alcie actually batted her eyelashes. "Okay, Douban—go."

"Think of it this way: your gods in Greece have someone or something more powerful than they are, correct? Someone or something that they call 'master'?"

"Well," Alcie said after a moment, "the only thing more powerful than the gods is the one god, Zeus. He is more powerful than all the Olympians put together. So I guess Zeus would be to the Greek gods the same as a roc would be to the genies. Except they don't call him 'master.' Some call him 'father' or 'Sky-Lord' or 'brother.' I think there was a rumor that Hera called him 'dummy' once. We didn't hear much about Hera for a while after that. Iole, am I even close?"

Iole, who had moved ahead slightly to talk to Pandy, turned back over her shoulder.

"You're comprehending quite nicely, Alce. It's a tricky concept, but you've got it."

She turned back to Pandy.

"More importantly, do you have any idea about Rage?"

"I don't," Pandy sighed. "Nothing solid, that is. I would have thought we might have gotten it out of Douban the Physician after his head was cut off. That was so stupid, so unfair, and just plain wrong—it would have enraged me! But he was kinda calm about the whole thing. So, no, I got zilch. Mahfouza's mother and father are dead—at least Mahfouza thinks so—and apparently they were very well loved. I think it's a good place to start. And Mahfouza has a big family. Her brothers and sisters might know something. Besides, we have to get Dido. Alcie? You good?"

"I'm good," Alcie called ahead.

Following the map Mahfouza had given her, Pandy led the way through the darkened, empty streets of the poorer side of Baghdad to one of the wealthier quarters of the city. Here, ornate lamps hung from bronze chains in front of every house, still lit in the predawn hours. Behind the immense walls, some with decorations of gold and silver, the domes and turrets of the homes rose high enough to be silhouetted in the faint morning light. Flowering plants and thick, leafy vines tumbled over the walls, indicating no shortage of water in this tiny section of the dry desert. Even the few servants that they encountered, those who rose early to prepare meals, seemed lavishly dressed and bejeweled. It was still too dark to see much of anything clearly, but squinting her eyes, Pandy could just make out the indicators that Mahfouza had written on the map.

"Winding street, okay we're on it," she mumbled

to herself. "Wall with vines with orange flowers. Uh-huh." Then she tried to look over one large wall. "Guys, does this house look sorta greenish? The one over this wall?"

Homer lifted Alcie on his shoulders.

"Ooof! Watch the—watch the cherries!" she said as he swung her up. "Yeah, it's greeny, kinda."

Pandy crossed to the other side of the road.

"Okay. Then Mahfouza's house should be this one, right . . . over . . . here. Yipes."

They stood in front of a large iron gate bordered by a high white wall covered in grime. The abundant vines overflowing from the garden and entwined in the gate were blackened and dead. The tops of the trees were bare, the hinges on the gate were rusty, and the house was completely dark.

"Great Athena," Pandy whispered. "This couldn't be right."

Iole took the map, stared at it, then looked at Pandy. "It is."

"Maybe, but it looks one hundred percent wrong," Pandy said as she pushed against the heavy gate, which swung open slowly.

As Douban passed her, he brushed her arm lightly. After an involuntary shudder, Pandy once again thought of her responsibility and that, ultimately, the quest was hers alone.

"Douban, if you don't want—I mean, you don't have to go in."

Douban paused to look her right in the eyes.

"As you say, Pandora," he smiled, "it looks wrong, and dangerous."

He stepped into the garden.

Pandy didn't know whether to feel elated or guilty. He was obviously doing this just for her, but his death, if it came to that, would be a source of yet more guilt that she would shoulder for the rest of her life.

The garden surrounding the house was enormous. There were many date palms, pomegranates, and other trees Pandy couldn't identify. There were two fountains at either end, but the water wasn't flowing so much as spurting. There were also several piles of a whitish material that Pandy thought might be stones or leaves.

But what everyone noticed immediately, from the smell, was that everything in the garden was dead or dying.

"Figs. This garden looks like one of the rooms in Hades' palace," Alcie said. "Only that was kinda beautiful. And it didn't stink. I think."

"Ares' shield," Pandy whispered. "Something's happened here, all right."

Then she turned toward the house for her first good look; now Pandy saw it was truly massive. It rose out of the ground into an elaborate concoction of turrets, arched doorways, and balconies; yet everything was in wretched condition, as if the house had spent years simply decaying. Some of the tall windows still had tattered silk curtains billowing gently, while others were covered by thick dead vines. At one end, the main wall had fallen outward into the garden and lay in a heap of rubble. Ornate, decorative ironwork around the windows and doorways was mangled and twisted, sharp ends jutted out into space like some sort of makeshift barricade.

As Pandy began to follow the remnants of a formal walkway, everyone heard a low moan coming from the right side of the garden, far off in a corner amongst a clump of low trees. Hurrying toward the sound, Pandy nearly ran headlong into a large object hanging low in a pomegranate tree.

The object moaned again.

"Who's got a light?"

Homer had completely forgotten about the brass lamp hanging from his waist and innocently remained silent. Pandy felt around on the ground and picked up a dead branch.

"Allow me," Douban said, producing two vials from the fold of his robe. He sprinkled the powders inside into his palm where they ignited into a red flame.

"Quickly, please!" he said.

At once, Pandy lit the end of the branch and held it close to the hanging object.

Everyone gasped.

A young man was suspended from a high limb, his body caught in a net like a catch of fish. He turned toward the light and all could see the thousands of bright red and white bumps covering his face, neck, and arms. He opened his mouth to speak and his tongue rolled slowly out, covered with the same horrible bumps.

Pandy was about to demand Homer and Douban cut the youth down when a wail erupted from the house that made everyone's blood turn to ice water. The youth moaned again and Pandy turned back to see that he was motioning with one free finger, flicking it in the direction of the main doorway.

"You want us to go in?" Pandy asked him.

The young man nodded weakly.

"Okay," she said. "But we'll be back. We'll get you down."

In that moment, saying something like that, Pandy felt heroic and important. It only occurred to her as she was racing toward the house that she had no idea if she would even be alive to get back to the youth. It just seemed like something a hero would say—and perhaps it gave the distressed man a little hope. It was the best she could do.

They got within two meters of the front entryway when the wailing began again, louder and sharper, and stopped them in their tracks. It was a wail of despair, certainly, but now there was something underneath; something vicious and brutal and angry—it was terrifying. Iole grabbed hold of both Pandy and Alcie.

"That's the most horrible thing I have ever heard," she said.

Pandy looked at the others, Homer had thrown his arms around Alcie, and Douban was shaking slightly. Creeping up the last few steps to the open, arched entry, Pandy craned her neck inside to look deeper into the house. Holding her little torch high, she saw a large room, its far wall blown out into the garden. At the other end of the house, Pandy saw what had been a magnificent and richly appointed salon. Now cushions and couches had been shredded, chairs overturned and tables broken. Pandy motioned to the others to follow her across the marble floor toward the back of the house. The wailing rose again and, again, they froze midstep. Alcie clutched Pandy's arm.

"It sounds like it's coming from inside the walls!" she whispered.

"I know!" Pandy mouthed back.

She was about to move forward, but the moment the wailing died off, they heard a soft sobbing coming from the salon. Pandy, with a surprised glance to the others, immediately changed direction. Picking her way around a few couches oddly bunched together, she came upon a young girl, seated on a couch in a corner with a thin tapestry thrown across one shoulder, leaving the other arm exposed. The girl didn't move when she opened her eyes, wet with tears, and saw Pandy staring down at her.

"Uh, are you okay?" Pandy asked.

The girl only sobbed softly in reply.

"I'm Pandora and I'm looking for Mahfouza. Is this her house?" Pandy went on, feeling stupid for some reason, as if the questions she was asking were the wrong ones. The girl nodded almost imperceptibly.

"What's wrong? What's happened?" Pandy asked.

Instead of answering with words, the young girl drew aside the tapestry with her free hand. Alcie gasped and turned her head into Homer's cloak. Iole took such a huge breath of air that she almost started to choke until Douban steadied her. Pandy just gaped in horror.

The girl's head, neck, left arm, and shoulder were perfectly normal. But the rest of her body was coarse gray stone. Suddenly, the girl winced and in the light of the torch, Pandy and the rest saw the left side of her neck drain of color and harden. Pandy was afraid she would turn completely to stone before her eyes, but then the transformation stopped.

Before Pandy could open her mouth, the wail erupted again, so loud this time that the pain in her ears made her think she might go deaf. Suddenly, Iole's eyes went wide.

Without warning, one of the walls, bare of tapestries or decoration, had developed large wet spots in several places. As the wailing continued, the spots grew larger until the water pooled and overflowed—in the exact shape of large tears—and ran down the surface. Each wail brought more huge teardrops.

"Is the wall weeping?" Pandy asked Iole.

"I think so," she replied.

"Only one way to find out," Pandy said, extending her fingers to catch some of the liquid.

"Don't touch it!" came a cry off to her right.

Everyone turned to see a mammoth pale spider with flowing black hair scuttling backward into the center of the house.

"Come! This way!"

"That sounds like Mahfouza," Pandy said.

"Well, *that* most certainly was not Mahfouza!" Iole said, eyeing the spider as Pandy took off.

Completely forgetting the poor girl turning to stone behind them, Pandy and the rest flew after the creature, rounding a corner just in time to see it disappear behind a privacy curtain far down a long corridor. Racing to it and pushing the heavy fabric aside, Pandy, Alcie, Iole, Homer, and Douban found themselves in a large room, one that had obviously been used for storage when the house had been functioning normally. Now, with the glow of one lamp burning somewhere, unseen, in the room, Pandy could tell that everything here, too, had been overturned, spilled, or ruined.

"Pandora?" came a voice out of the clutter.

Suddenly, there was a bark from the direction of the lamplight.

"Dido! Quiet!" said the voice in a soft but insistent tone.

"Mahfouza?"

"Here, but be careful—all of you. Do not cry out when you look upon me. It is almost daybreak. We must be silent."

"Uh, okay," Pandy said, then dropped her voice to barely a whisper. "I mean, okay."

Picking her way around a jumbled pile of low brass tables, vases, screens, and overstuffed floor cushions, Pandy followed the glow until she spied movement on the other side of a multicolored glass panel. She froze, looking through the pane in shock. Perhaps the glass and the colors were distorting the image of the objects on the other side. She couldn't possibly be seeing correctly; she prayed to Athena that she wasn't. She jumped when, out of nowhere, she felt a soft tongue licking her hand. She looked down into Dido's face and knelt to wrap her arms around his neck.

"Hi, boy. You gotta be quiet for me, okay? Good boy. Let's go. Take me to Mahfouza."

Pandy slowly walked around the edge of the pane

and, staring at the sight in front of her, felt every muscle in her body seize up. Iole's hand flew to her mouth. Alcie opened her mouth to scream and, thinking quickly, Douban turned her to face him, his finger on his lips. Homer just gaped for a moment, then closed his eyes.

Mahfouza was . . . wrong.

Her long, lean dancer's body had been taken apart and reassembled with everything in the wrong place. Her legs were where her arms should have been, and her arms were functioning as her legs. Her head was in the middle of her stomach, her chin pointing to where her neck used to be. Her nose was in place of her right eye and her mouth was on the side of her face. She was forced to sit, lean, or bend backward for her eyes to be able to be able to focus on Pandy.

"Gods," Pandy murmured.

"It must be a shock, I know. I am grateful I cannot see myself."

"Does it hurt, Mahfouza?" Iole asked.

"I am not in any pain. Uncomfortable, yes, but my muscles are in good shape. It is only the joints that are strained. But, please, we don't have much time. He will wake soon and he cannot find you here. You must take Dido and go."

"Who will wake soon?" asked Pandy.

"Giondar. The genie who inhabited the lamp in the the Garden of the Jinn."

"You mean this lamp?" Homer said, lifting the lamp hanging on a cord at his waist.

"Oh no!" said Mahfouza. "You must go! I have no idea what he will do if he sees it!"

Suddenly, everyone heard a hissing sound, as if air were slowly escaping from something. Turning to a low pile of rugs against a wall, Pandy saw a child with dark, wrinkled skin and huge eyes looking at them all.

"How did you get in?" said the child. But on the instant it spoke, Pandy realized it wasn't a child. "Mahfouza, ask them how they got in."

"Zoe, lower your voice," Mahfouza cautioned.

"Mahfouza," Pandy whispered, stepping closer. "What in Hades is going on? We found a guy in a tree. There's a woman in the front of the house turning to stone. And now you? I mean . . . ?"

Mahfouza sighed and sank against a floor cushion.

"Tell them," said the creature on the rugs. "It is already too late. The sun may be up by now and he will never let them leave. Better still, let me tell them."

"Pandy," Mahfouza said after a moment. "This is my older sister, Zobeide. Zoe, this is Pandy, Alcie . . ."

Mahfouza paused and a smile passed over her lips, contorting her beautiful face even further.

"Alcie. It is so good to see you again. Your friends were quite desolate without you," Mahfouza said sweetly.

Alcie burst into tears. She'd had no "alone" time with

Pandy and Iole since she'd come back from the underworld. The last few hours had been filled with so much tension, excitement, and stress. And now, this wrecked creature, whom Alcie had only known as a lovely woman, was being kind even in her own misery. Alcie just fell apart. Homer wrapped her tightly in his arms.

"Zoe," Mahfouza continued, "Homer is the one with his arms around Alcie. This is Iole and that is Douban."

"The Physician?" asked Zoe.

"Yes," answered Douban. "But I am the son of the Douban you are thinking of."

"Ah, then it came to pass and your father did lose his head. I am sorry. We have not any news. Before Giondar did this to me, I would stick my head up and over the outer wall to get snippets of the news from the city. That was some time ago. But tell me, how did you get past the outer gate?"

Pandy, Alcie, and Iole looked at one another.

"We walked in," Pandy said with a shrug.

"That is impossible. Giondar laughed when he told me that he'd enchanted the house and grounds with secret spells. That he'd imprisoned us all. That no one could get out and no one could get in past the gate or over the walls. No one, that is, but the final member of the family or someone with powerful magic. Then he chanted over me and did this."

There was silence in the small space.

"Bring the lamp closer," Zoe said.

Pandy picked the small lamp up off the floor and walked slowly to where Zobeide lay. But it took several moments of staring at the woman to actually see what had happened to her. Her skin had been wrinkled, but not merely so: it was now so thin, her bones were distinct. Then Pandy realized there was almost no flesh under the darkened, dead skin. More than that still, there was no fluid in her body whatsoever. She was completely dehydrated. She was being "dried."

"Zoe was one of the last to be attacked," Mahfouza said after a moment, her voice the only thing that broke Pandy's stare. "And then I came home yesterday. Now all of my parents' children have been deformed in some way."

"But why?" Pandy asked. "And what about your mother and father?"

Mahfouza looked to her sister.

"Zoe . . ."

Everyone looked again at the shriveled mass staring from the pile of rugs.

". . . tell them."

CHAPTER TWENTY-TWO
The Tale of Zobeide

"Many years ago," Zoe began, "my mother and father received an enslaved peri named Deryabar in a cut-glass wine bottle as a wedding gift. Dery, as we called her, was extremely beautiful, very caring, and became something of a second mother to everyone. We children loved her greatly, especially our littlest sister, Zinebi. But we were not the only ones: a powerful genie named Giondar also loved her and she him. In doing so, they both had committed one of the greatest sins of their kind. For a genie to love a mortal is almost unheard of; but for a genie to love a peri is unthinkable. Their offspring could be so powerful that no one knows what destruction could follow. But Giondar and Dery had fallen in love many, many years before. As punishment, Giondar's master, his roc, imprisoned him in a small lamp in the Garden of the Jinn. Dery was confined to her bottle. Dery was released often to serve our family; we were good to her, she lived happily (so she said) and never tried to free herself. But Giondar had been all but forgotten by his roc. And then, he learned how to escape his lamp. He had been visiting Dery, unknown to us, for years, but always at night when the family was asleep. To be honest, even if we had known, we wouldn't have cared; we loved Dery that much.

"Then, one morning many weeks ago, Zinebi woke in a strange mood. She was the baby of the family; we pampered her and she had become a little spoiled, but this morning, her temper was greater than usual. She was spiteful and petulant. One of our serving women asked what Zinebi wanted to eat and our sister threw several carving knives at her, driving the woman from the room. I heard the commotion and, along with our sister Amina, arrived just in time to see Zinebi smash Dery's wine bottle on the floor. Instantly, Deryabar appeared in a panicked state. She was confused and, although not frightened for herself, alarmed at Zinebi's condition.

"As children we would always ask our parents' permission to open the bottle; the rule was that whoever let Dery out would be the one whose wish or task she would complete. Since Zinebi had released Dery, even by smashing her bottle, Dery had to listen to Zinebi. Dery asked our sister what she wanted and without hesitation, Zinebi said that she wanted a meal made of eggs. Dery began an incantation to create my sister's request, but Zinebi stopped her cold. From behind her back, Zinebi produced a small bowl containing several eggs—one of which contained Dery's roc. Dery recognized her master's egg at once. She wailed and flew about the room, howling that she could not grant such an evil request. But Zinebi insisted. Amina and I pleaded with our sister, but Zinebi would not be moved. Then she held the bowl over her head and threatened to smash all the eggs on the floor. Dery cried out for her to stop! Dery knew that her master would never permit such an action and would kill Zinebi before its egg ever hit the ground. Zinebi again demanded her dish of eggs and Dery agreed, knowing what her fate would be. One by one, Dery incanted over the eggs, turning each one into a bright yellow scramble in the bowl. The roc egg was last and Dery looked at Zinebi, tears streaming down her face. We, Amina and I, pleaded with Zinebi again. She was like ice. Dery began her incantation, but had not spoken two words before a screech was heard from inside the egg and Dery was turned into a solid block of marble, which then exploded into dust before our eyes. She had been utterly destroyed by the commands of the person who supposedly loved her most, and Zinebi picked up the steaming bowl of eggs and calmly walked from the room."

"Olive pits," Alcie said. "What a brat!"

"She was infected, Zoe," Pandy said. "I'll wager my mother's silver girdle that Zinebi was acting that way because of the lesser evils of spite . . . and, what was the word you used? P—something?"

"Petulance?" Zoe replied.

"Yeah, petulance, and it sounds like there's something else in there as well. Iole, what do you think?"

"If I were to guess, I would state that your sister was plagued by a severe case of entitlement. She felt she deserved special treatment just for being . . . her."

"Yes, yes. You have said it!" Zoe said.

"Zoe, your voice," Mahfouza cautioned.

"And I'll also bet that the morning all of this happened is the morning I took the box to school," Pandy said.

"Yes," Zoe said, then her voice took on a somber tone. "Mahfouza has been telling me all about you. So, we have you to thank for all of this."

"You'll never know how sorry I am," Pandy said, and she was right. They never would. It was that big.

"Zoe, continue," Mahfouza said.

After a moment during which Zoe just stared at Pandy, she went on.

"Our mother and father rushed in. They saw the pile of marble dust on the floor. Amina and I told them what had happened, and they began weeping and tearing at their hair. Our brother Noureddin rushed in and discovered Zinebi's wickedness just as Zinebi reappeared with her empty bowl and sweetly announced that her eggs were so good, she'd like more. Noureddin picked up a knife and charged after Zinebi until our mother stopped him. There was much screaming and yelling; no one knew what to do. Just as the shouting reached its peak, the house shook violently three times. Then we all heard a tremendous crash and a wail such as none other coming from the largest room, the one directly across from this room. Standing in the middle of that room, surrounded by rubble that used to be the ceiling, was Giondar. His face was a mask of anger—no, more than that."

"Rage?" Pandy asked.

"Precisely. In a booming voice, he asked what had become of his beloved Dery. My father told him the entire tale and Giondar incinerated him on the spot. My mother began to scream and she, too, was reduced to ashes in an instant. And then the horror began for my brothers and sisters. We were immobilized while Giondar went about the house looking for the servants. They all tried to flee through the garden, but Giondar caught them."

"Those are the piles of ashes we saw?" asked Iole.

"They are."

"But he didn't destroy the entire family. I don't get it," said Pandy.

"Figs, the mom and dad are bad enough," Alcie said.

"Oh, but he is destroying us. But he is doing it one by one, very slowly and in a way we cannot understand. His incantations over all of us have been the same and yet we are being murdered in different ways."

Pandora had so many questions running through her head, she couldn't focus on just one.

"After he had dispatched the servants, Giondar caught our brother Noureddin trying to scale the garden wall to get help. Those of us there were forced to watch as he held Noureddin in the palm of his great hand and said only a few simple words. And then, Noureddin . . . changed."

Zoe paused.

"What, Zoe, what did he say?" asked Pandy.

Zoe spoke low, as if repeating the phrase might do more harm.

"And so to these children, who killed my beloved, my curse is a prison which you cannot flee. The cure for your ruin, that which you resemble, hangs low in a garden which you'll never see."

"Weird," said Pandy.

"Oogly-boogly," Alcie whispered.

"Then Noureddin was suddenly held fast in a net, his body crunched into a ball, and reddish white bumps began to appear all over his body."

"We saw him," Pandy said. "As we came in."

"Giondar disappeared and for days we neither heard nor saw anything. The rest of the family returned to the house, unaware of the danger, only to be held hostage. We could not help Noureddin, but we thought it was over and that Noureddin was his final act of vengeance. Then one week later, at sundown we heard wailing, which seemed to come from within the very walls. The next day, Giondar appeared and again we all were forced to watch as he cast his spell over Amina and she slowly began to turn to stone. Days later, Hassan was taken out to the garden. Seeds began to pour out of his mouth and they will not stop. He cannot eat or drink. He can barely breathe. And so it went on. Giondar weeps through the night and roams the house during the day, checking on all of us to make certain we are suffering. Zinebi was his last victim, until Mahfouza arrived. Now no one can help us."

"Except someone with very powerful magic," Pandy said. "That was part of what Giondar said. Well, if we're here . . ."

She turned to the others.

". . . what do we have?"

"All I have is what I've always carried," said Alcie. "Except a travel bag of dove hearts."

Pandy and Iole whipped their heads in unison, but before they could get a word out, Zoe began to shake her head.

"It has to be something all of you carry, because you all passed through the gate."

Iole gasped. She turned to Pandy, an enormous smile on her face.

"The fruit."

CHAPTER TWENTY-THREE
"That Which You Resemble"

"What fruit?" Mahfouza asked.

"Of course!" Pandy said, grabbing her carrying pouch. "And now the message on the wall makes sense!"

"What fruit?" Mahfouza asked again.

"From the Garden of the Jinn," Pandy replied, taking an opal peach from her pouch.

"You took the *fruit*!" Mahfouza almost shrieked.

"Shhhh!" Pandy quieted her. "We didn't take it. It fell at our feet. And good thing, too. We found a message on the wall when we left that said something about the fruits of labor repairing the ruined and vanquishing our foes."

" 'The cure for your ruin, that which you resemble,

hangs low in a garden,'" Iole chanted softly. "This fruit is the cure!"

"How?" asked Zoe.

"It's all in one phrase," said Iole.

"'That which you resemble,'" Pandy said, looking to Iole for confirmation.

"That's it," Iole agreed.

"What do I resemble?" Mahfouza cried out. "I resemble no piece of fruit!"

"Shhhh!" Pandy cautioned.

Mahfouza was right. She looked nothing like a piece of fruit. She was in pieces. She was *parts* of herself.

And then something clicked in Pandy's brain. Without any warning, Pandy found herself tensing as if she were on the edge of a cliff, and her father's words on her last night in Athens came rushing back: *". . . . your powers will start coming into their own . . . the power to think things through, to see the big picture, not just the small scene . . . the power of your mind might manifest itself in interesting ways."*

A whole new way of thinking suddenly presented itself. It was as if a light went on in the darkness. Immediately, she started to think of Mahfouza's body not in the sense of literally looking like a piece of fruit . . . but what did her particular affliction represent? What were the traits that could be applied to a piece of fruit? Parts, pieces, segments.

"Lay them all out," she said. "One of each."

"You must hurry!" Zoe said.

"Come on, everyone, faster!" Pandy said, almost sputtering. "Open your pouches!"

Quickly, nine pieces of fruit were placed on a small rug. An apple, an orange, a pomegranate, lemon, pear, peach, cherry, fig, and plum. Pandy studied each piece intently. The only piece of fruit that could be divided easily into parts—into segments—was an orange. Trusting her instincts, she picked up the orange. Nothing. She waved it over Mahfouza's body. No change. But when she approached Mahfouza's face, the beautiful hard topaz became soft and pliable. Suddenly she was holding a real orange in her hands. Quickly, Pandy peeled away the rind, broke off a juicy segment, and carefully fed it to Mahfouza. Then she stood back.

The transformation was instantaneous.

Mahfouza's legs and arms quickly glided into their proper places as her facial features rearranged themselves and her head slid on top of her torso. All of this was done before Mahfouza had time to take a breath.

"No way," Homer whispered.

Mahfouza faltered back, leaning heavily on an overturned couch and nearly knocking over the colored panel of glass. Righting herself, she was stunned for a moment; she stood with her arms held straight out in front as if to ward something away. When she fully realized that she had regained her true shape once again, she grabbed Pandy's face in her hands and kissed her on both cheeks. In all the excitement, Dido leaped up to put his forepaws on Pandy.

"Oh, Dido," Mahfouza cried softly. "He's been so good, Pandy. So quiet. I found him just tied up outside the gate yesterday. Oh, clever girl . . . thank you, thank you."

"Guh-roovy," Alcie said, keeping her voice low.

"How did you know?" Iole asked.

"Giondar's curse. She didn't really look like an orange, but she was in pieces. Only thing she resembled like that was an orange. Had to be."

Iole looked at Pandy as if she had never seen her before.

"You're brilliant," Iole said.

Pandy smiled awkwardly as Mahfouza stifled a laugh. Zoe coughed lightly to be acknowledged.

"Zoe!" Mahfouza said.

"Okay," Pandy said. "Can't get ahead of myself. What's shriveled? What's dried?"

"Nothing," said Alcie, kneeling to look more closely at the rainbow of fruit.

"Nothing, normally," Pandy said, her brain whirring, her hand passing over the remaining eight pieces of fruit. "But Zoe's still alive."

"Barely," Zoe said.

"What can be dried and still be good, like, eaten?"

"Genius," said Iole softly, standing to the side, watching Pandy in awe.

"What do we have . . . pear? No. Peach, no. Apple? Not really. Cherry, maybe, but they're not great. Fig? Could be."

Pandy reached her hand out to pick up the sapphire fig and a spark shot out from the center of the fruit, catching her in the middle of her palm, sending her sprawling backward. Then the fig shattered.

"Pandora!" Mahfouza almost shrieked as Douban and Alcie, who were closest, bent to help her.

"Wrong," Pandy said, picking herself up. "Not a fig."

"You okay?" asked Alcie.

"Little fire can't hurt me," Pandy said, shaking her head to clear it. "Good thing we have several of each fruit."

"And I think we know who to thank for that," Alcie said.

"Okay, what's next? Pomegranate, nope. Lemon . . . don't think so. Plum. *Plum.* Dried plums are great! I love 'em. My dad does too—says they keep him regular, whatever that means."

Her hand hovered above the plum. Slowly she lowered it until the amethyst became a soft, real piece of fruit. Then, before their eyes, the plum became a dried, wrinkled mass not even half its original size. Instantly,

Pandy picked it up and gently fed it to Zoe, who had become so weakened by telling her tale Pandy was scared she might not be able to chew. But as the tiniest bit of dried fruit slid down her throat, the flesh grew back on her bones, ligaments and tendons repaired themselves, and her organs, now full of fluid, began working again. It looked to everyone as if she was being inflated with air. In almost no time, the shriveled mass was gone and in its place sat a gorgeous woman, only slightly older than Mahfouza, with long black hair falling to her waist. She fell back on the pile of rugs, feeling her arms, legs, and face. Then Zoe sat up.

"Water."

Douban was at her side immediately, offering his water bag, and she gulped greedily until the bag was empty.

"I'm sorry," she said sincerely.

"There is more where that came from," he answered.

"We're in a desert," she said.

"Ah, yes . . . right."

"Who's next?" Pandy said, picking up the six pieces of fruit from the floor.

"Here," said Alcie, putting a new fig into Pandy's hand.

"Come," said Mahfouza, helping Zoe to stand. "This way."

After Pandy commanded Dido to stay and hide until

she came back, Mahfouza led everyone out of the storage room. Then Mahfouza crept back down the long corridor to the large salon. She turned, motioning for everyone to follow fast as she pointed outside at the quickly lightening sky. Silently she approached her sister who was turning to stone.

"Amina," Mahfouza said softly to the dozing girl. "Amina, wake up!"

Slowly Amina opened her eyes, nearly crying out when she saw both Mahfouza and Zoe.

"Shhhh!" Zoe said. "This girl is going to help you."

Pandy set the seven pieces of fruit on a nearby couch. She couldn't speak her thoughts aloud; she had to think it all through. Stone. Hard. Something that was half stone, half real? No. Something that was gray, like this stone? Nothing. Not that. Think! What was it definitely *not*? Not a pomegranate. Lemons—nothing stonelike. Pear, nope. Peach! A peach has a hard stone in the middle of it! She was about to reach for the opal peach, when suddenly Iole's hand came out of nowhere and stopped her. Pandy looked at Iole, who, for the very first time that Pandy could recall, didn't look at her like she was making the biggest mistake, but instead, like she was an equal and just needed a few more seconds to make the right decision.

The cherries.

A peach has a pit, but cherries have stones.

Pandy smiled and Iole winked at her. Then, just as Pandy went to reach for the several cherries on the couch, Giondar wailed again and a huge tremor shook the house. Furniture began to topple, a window exploded inward, and several beams fell from the ceiling. Pandy and Iole threw themselves on the couch to keep the fruit from crashing onto the floor, covering everything except the cherries. They bounced onto the hard marble and rolled loudly across the room, where they came to rest against the back of an overturned chair. But just as Homer moved to retrieve them, another huge beam fell from the ceiling, crushing the ruby cherries underneath.

Pandy looked to Iole, who rifled through her pouch. She looked at Pandy and shook her head; she had no cherries left. Douban and Homer checked their fruit stores and came up empty. Alcie had no more either. Pandy looked to Mahfouza and Zoe, not knowing what to do, then looked at Alcie again.

All Alcie knew in that moment was that Pandy's expression went from panic to relief, but she didn't know why.

Pandy marched over to Alcie and plucked a cherry right off of Alcie's shoulder.

It didn't hurt Alcie in the slightest, but still her mouth flew open. In complete indignation, she mouthed the word "OWWWW!" as big as she could.

Taking the cherry to Amina, Pandy indicated that she should open her mouth. As before, the ruby became a real piece of fruit and, after looking to Zoe, who nodded emphatically, Amina ate the cherry and spit out the stone. This time, as the stone receded and her body quickly became flesh, it seemed to cause extreme pain, and Zoe and Mahfouza both had to cover Amina's mouth and hold her tightly to keep her from crying out. Finally, she was whole again, but she'd been incapacitated for so long that she could barely stand, and walking or running was out of the question. Pandy motioned to Homer to pick up Amina and carry her.

Hearing Giondar's wails growing louder, they raced outside to the young man hanging in the corner of the garden. Pandy didn't even need to think about this one. The cherries were gone and the apple didn't have bumps. The youth resembled a pomegranate. The beautiful garnet became real at Pandy's touch and yielded numerous juicy seeds, which Noureddin ate hastily. Seconds later, Homer was cutting him down and helping him to stand; his muscles, too, had lost their strength but with Douban's assistance, Noureddin could keep pace.

"Told you we'd be back," Pandy said with a smile.

Noureddin was too stunned to say anything.

As Homer picked Amina up again, everyone, following Zoe's direction, rushed around to the back of the house. Alcie tugged on Pandy's toga and gestured to the piles of ashes, the gnarled trees with pointed limbs and black leaves, and the rank, fetid stench.

"The whole garden has been changed by Rage," Pandy thought. At that moment, the wailing of the genie stopped abruptly.

With a look of panic toward the house, Zoe brought them to another young man, only slightly younger, it seemed, than Pandy herself. He was tied to a charred tree stump, his skin was yellow, and seeds were pouring out of his mouth nonstop. Somehow he had learned to breath solely through his nose and was calm, almost motionless, as Zoe and Pandy approached him, a citrine lemon in Pandy's hand.

"Hassan," said Zoe. "Can you clear your mouth?"

Hassan shook his head gently.

"He has to eat it," Pandy said.

"But he can't," Iole said, stepping up. "Which must mean—"

"That it has to work differently this time," Pandy interrupted. "The cure has to have a . . . a . . ."

"Alternate method of delivery," Iole said.

"What she said," Pandy echoed, looking at Zoe.

The citrine lemon in Pandy's hand became soft and fleshy as she moved it toward Hassan's body. The numerous lemon seeds flowing from his mouth turned into a torrent and Hassan began to choke.

"Gods!" Alcie said, reaching forward to brush them off his chin and away from his face.

"Knife!" Pandy demanded.

Homer began to set Amina on the ground in order to get to his pouch, but Douban produced his knife in an instant. Pandy cut deep into the lemon and, without thinking, began to squeeze the juice over Hassan's head.

Nothing.

"It has to get inside," Iole said. "Choose another orifice—opening."

"Eyes! No," Pandy cried, looking at the poor boy vomiting up seeds by the hundreds. "Ears! Hassan, tilt your head!"

Hassan did and began to gag in desperation. Immediately, he righted his head.

"Mahfouza, help him!" Pandy said.

Mahfouza swiftly and gently tilted Hassan's head. The boy began to thrash, but not before Pandy squeezed a few drops of lemon juice into his right ear. At once, the flood of seeds lessened to a trickle and then stopped completely. The sickly yellow color left his skin and Hassan was unbound from the stump. He threw his arms about his sisters and then rushed from Pandy to Iole to Alcie, jumping with joy.

A crash, followed by two small screams, followed by a gigantic roar from right inside the house made them all jump.

"That sounded like Saouy!" Mahfouza said.

"Look!" Douban said, pointing to the roofline.

The straight line of the roof was interrupted by something huge moving behind it.

"Giondar," whispered Amina.

"Here we go," said Pandy, heading toward the house. She turned back to stop only for a moment.

"No one has to come with me."

"As if!" Alcie said. "Death doesn't frighten me. I've been there. We get snail custard and liver pudding! Let's go!"

Both Noureddin and Douban hurried to keep up with Pandy and Alcie. Homer, with Amina in his arms, provided a substantial buffer for Mahfouza, Zoe, and Hassan, but nobody stayed behind.

Pandy slowed slightly as she entered the house. Noureddin, feeling bizarrely territorial, moved ahead as if to usher her forward. Pandy motioned him and everyone back against a dividing wall, then peered slowly into the room.

Giondar was in the middle of the devastated salon. Bits of the ceiling were teetering on his shoulders while other bits still clung tenaciously overhead. The air was filled with dust. Giondar was so enormous that his head and shoulders were sticking out of the open roof, yet his body below his thighs was only a thick trail of smoke, much like a tail, in the bright green color of his pantaloons. His skin was such a dark blue as to be almost black or purple. He had rings in both ears that were easily the diameter of chariot wheels. His mammoth brows were pinched closely in the center and curved up at the ends into neat circles. His eyes were black, but ringed in red, and his hair was piled high in a knot on top of his head. He was bare chested, but his neck, upper arms, and wrists were adorned with thick bronze bands.

"He has grown even larger since the last time I saw him," whispered Zoe from the shadows deep in the corridor.

Being so colossal, his movements were slowed, and it took him several moments to notice Pandy's little head peeking from the entryway.

"Hah!" he said, blowing the word out with spiteful laughter as he put his hands on his hips. His teeth were huge, sparkling white, and flawless.

And he had a giant spike through his tongue.

"Undoing all of my work, I see," said Giondar, spotting Mahfouza and her restored siblings who had come to stand behind Pandy. "Who are you that you would be so arrogant, reckless, and stupid?"

Emboldened without the faintest notion why, Pandy stepped into the center of the entryway.

"I am Pandora Atheneus Andromaeche Helena of the House of Prometheus of Athens and—"

Just then Mahfouza shrieked, startling everyone.

"Saouy!"

Amina, who was able to walk by this time, and Zoe each went to Mahfouza's side as she pointed to the far wall of the salon.

"Hush now," said Amina.

"She did not see him yesterday, Amina!" replied Zoe.

Pandy and the others peered past the misty tail of the genie to see what had so alarmed Mahfouza. Even Giondar slowly turned his massive body.

Against the wall were two tall, impossibly thin beings. So thin that Pandy thought at first they must be some sort of strange new animal; they simply couldn't be human. Then she saw, as they cowered in the corner, shafts of light from the open roof playing upon their skin, that they were indeed human—they were indeed a person. More to the point, they were two perfect halves of one person and as such, they moved in perfect sync as if they were still connected. One leg, one arm, one eye, one ear, half of a mouth, half of a nose. Skin covered the portions of their bodies where they had been split, but they were a mirror opposite in every respect. A matched pair.

Pandy was dumbfounded, but the motion of Giondar as he turned back to her, a malicious upturn to his mouth, brought her mind back into focus.

"That is who I am, Giondar," she said, standing straight.

"It is of little consequence," Giondar began, then he

broke off and stared at Alcie, who was still in the shadows but visible as she stood just behind Pandy . . .

. . . rolling an emerald pear in her hand.

Pandy followed his gaze.

"What are you *doing*?" she whispered frantically.

"What?" Alcie whispered back, ticking her head toward the two half-beings. "I'm just ahead of you all. Big deal. Four fruits left. They're a pair, right. Pair . . . *pear*?"

"Get back!" Pandy said, using her forearm to push her into the shadows as Homer stepped up to drag Alcie back. Giondar spotted the lamp hanging from Homer's waist.

"My *lamp!*" Giondar screamed, shaking the house. "Thieves! You have plundered my garden!"

"Not *your* garden, Giondar," Pandy said, feeling certain that she could dodge or outmaneuver any blow the genie might deliver. It was how to get him into the box that concerned her. "And now, it's destroyed."

"My brethren have not forsaken me!" he cried, shaking the house again.

"Oh, but they have!" Pandy said.

"I shall deal with the scum of the household first and then with you, infidel!"

His eyes narrowed a bit as he focused his gaze on Mahfouza. Quickly, Pandy stepped in front of her, blocking her from Giondar.

"Mind telling me why you're doing this?" she asked

with such a casual tone that even Iole was forced to look sideways at her. But Pandy was trying a new tactic: yes, he was gigantic, but Giondar's physical movements were almost painfully slow for such a powerful being. She had a hunch—she hoped, rather—that his brain was, perhaps, a bit "casually paced" as well. She was going to try to keep him mentally off balance. And, as if to confirm her suspicion, as soon as she'd asked the question, Giondar closed his eyes and folded his massive arms neatly across his chest. Pandy took that moment and quickly turned to Iole and Douban.

"Go!" she mouthed and pointed to the upper floors of the house. "Find the others!"

Douban nodded and quietly stepped back into the shadows and hurried down the long corridor, already fumbling for the remaining pieces of jeweled fruit. But Iole looked at Pandy fearfully, questioning if Pandy knew what she was doing. Pandy winked.

"Go!"

With a single backward glance Iole caught up to Douban, waiting at the foot of a large staircase, and headed up to the second level.

As Pandy turned again toward Giondar, her gaze passed over those around her; Alcie, Homer, and five members of a tortured household all depended on her next movements.

"I have no need to tell you, traveler," Giondar boomed.

"That's true," Pandy said. "But you have your freedom. You could be anywhere, doing anything. And yet you stay here, hurting people who have done nothing to you."

"Nothing to me!" Giondar bellowed, his face turning black as his speech picked up speed. "You are as ignorant as a camel! You know less than a beggar's dog! This family took from me that which was most treasured—my love. You are too young to know a loss such as mine. Until you feel pain such as I do, you will never understand my *rage*!"

There was the word. Giondar had actually spoken it, knocking several beams loose from the roof with the timbre of his voice, sending up splinters and clouds of dust as they crashed to the tiles beneath.

But the word "loss" had sent Pandy's thoughts back to one single event that had taken place only weeks before: the moment when she'd felt Alcie die in her arms. Giondar assumed she didn't know "loss," didn't know rage. The loss of her best friend had crushed Pandy so completely, she knew there would never be any recovery. Even though Alcie had actually returned from Hades, very much alive, Pandy still remembered the feeling of a knife plunging into her heart when she saw Alcie's head fall to the side and the light go out of her eyes. And *then* to discover that Hera had murdered Alcie out of sheer spite and was joyful about it, loving every moment of the aftermath; Pandy felt a rage so great that she had, on pure impulse, set the goddess on fire. She had been on the verge of doing the very same thing to Homer when he questioned her despair over Alcie's death. And now Giondar assumed she knew nothing?

"You don't know me!" Pandy cried, startling everyone. "You have no idea what I have gone through! You don't know what or who—"

Giondar flung out his right arm and hurled Pandy into a wall.

The pain was so intense that for a moment Pandy saw the entire room begin to swirl before her eyes as if it were water circling a drain. Then her vision began to dim and blur. She was only vaguely aware of Mahfouza high overhead somewhere. She began to slide down the wall and felt a pain in her left shoulder so sharp that she couldn't decide whether to let it take her out completely or shock her back into consciousness. The next moment, her vision cleared and she heard Amina and Zoe screaming as Giondar held Mahfouza high in the air, laughing as he tightened his grip on the slender girl.

Without thinking, Pandy focused her mind directly on the middle of Giondar's torso, waiting only an instant for the silence she knew would come. She felt a cool tingling down her right arm and stretched her hand out toward the cackling genie. At once, a white hot fireball shot out from the tips of her fingers and exploded into Giondar's chest. He was blown back, dropping Mahfouza onto the cushions of an overturned couch. Pandy didn't wait for him to recover; she blasted him again straightaway, this time throwing him into a far wall, which blew outward, sending him flying into the garden. Pandy tried to get up, but a tapestry hanging by a thread above her head came crashing down over her, sending her into the dark. As she pulled the fabric off her head, the pain in her left shoulder made her cry out and slump against the wall. She looked at her left arm and saw that it was dangling at a funny angle. She tried moving it, but not only was the pain unbearable, the muscles wouldn't respond.

By this time, Giondar was upright and moving back inside. He flung his arm out again and sent his own fireball straight at Pandy. She saw it coming and, instead of letting it hit her, she sent out her own fire wall to meet it. The two forces of fire met only a centimeter above her skin and formed a cloak of white flame. Pandy realized the effect this might be having on Giondar and with great effort, forced herself to her feet.

Walking toward the amazed genie, she tried to spread her arms wide for a greater spectacle, without having the slightest notion of what to do next, but when her left arm refused to move, she abandoned that idea and just tried to stay as tall as possible. But she was unable to clearly see objects in her path and suddenly her left arm knocked into a marble table. The shooting pain made her lose focus and the flames went completely out.

In a flash, unexpected given his previous slowness, Giondar had her in his hands, both of them squeezing her tightly to prevent any movement. Pandy screamed as his enormous thumb pressed against her shoulder.

"You must be a spirit of some importance and power in your land," he said, looking at her curiously. "But I see no roc egg about you, so I will assume that is the extent of your abilities, ignorant one."

"I'm not ignorant!" Pandy cried. "You aren't the only one who has ever suffered, you stupid blue . . . thing."

She felt the pressure of his grasp on her lungs.

"People suffer loss all the time," she gasped. "But they don't usually kill people to make themselves feel better."

Just as she realized she had run out of air and couldn't take another breath, she also realized that it was incredibly foolish to try to reason with a being under the influence of one of the great Evils. She felt the pounding of blood in her temples and knew that at any moment, she was going to pass out. Then she felt Giondar relax his grip only a tiny bit.

"I shall grant you a wish, brains-of-a-dog," Giondar said, staring at her, turning her about like a toy. "And when you tell me what you wish, I will trouble this family no further."

"Huh?"

"Hear me, traveler. I am going to grant you one wish."

"A wish?" Pandy said.

"Yes," said Giondar. "Even though you are as a flea in my armpit, you obviously possess some extraordinary powers. Out of respect for your abilities, I shall grant you a wonderful favor."

"What's that?"

"The luxury of telling me how you wish to die."

🍇

Douban moved ahead of Iole up the staircase, on the watch for any surprises. The second level was in much better shape than the first; statues were still upright and whole, walls were still in one piece, privacy curtains had not been shredded.

"He must not bother himself with this section of the house," whispered Douban, walking slowly down the corridor.

"Perhaps there's no one up here," Iole said softly, looking at a wall hanging, stunning even in the dim light. Inadvertently, she bumped into Douban standing at the entrance to a sleeping chamber.

"No," he said, staring into the room. "We are in the right place."

Iole followed his gaze. In the middle of the room, a woman—or a man, Iole couldn't tell—was sitting, or standing, perfectly still. The bottom half of the person was bloated to at least five times normal size and had been covered in various places with pieces of clothing and fabric. But the skin was dark, almost purplish. The upper half, by contrast, was shrunken and distorted so that the head and neck were almost of the same shape and thickness and curved slightly to one side. The skin went from purple at the torso to yellow as it covered the neck and face. In fact, only the tufts of black hair at the back gave any indication of where a face might be. In Iole's mind, there was absolutely no question.

"She's a fig."

"Yes," said Douban, the large sapphire fruit already in his hand. As they approached the person, two eyelids flew open, causing Iole to put a hand over her heart. The person gave a tiny squeal in what was, unmistakably, a woman's voice.

"Do not be alarmed," Douban said, his voice supremely calm and even. The woman looked at Douban, and Iole saw the lines of fear around her eyes relax. Even Iole was settled at the sound of the young man's words, thinking to herself what a wonderful manner this physician had.

"We are here to help you," he said, placing his hand where the woman's shoulder should have been, but feeling only hard yellowed skin. "Please, be so kind as to eat this."

Without a word and completely trusting a man she didn't know, the woman took a bite of the blackish purple fruit, even though only moments before, she'd seen the hard stone change into a pulpy fig.

At once, her bloated legs and feet began to shrink and lighten to a normal color. Her head was redefined from her neck and the skin on her upper half lost all its yellowness. Her hair grew long and full and her beautiful face came fully into view. It was more than beautiful, Iole noticed. This woman, who used to be a fig, was almost as beautiful as Aphrodite.

"We are fully aware of the situation," Iole said, watching Douban's eyes go wide. "We are trying to help the rest of your brothers and sisters."

"We know about Giondar and his vengeance on your family," said Douban, his voice taking on an altogether different tone. "What we do not know is your name."

Out of the blue, Iole felt something utterly beyond her comprehension. Douban was being more than nice to this lovely young woman; he was *flirting* with her. Death and destruction all around them, Pandy downstairs quite possibly getting killed, and this youth—who had all but *driven* Iole from the desert sand dunes not two nights before—was now flirting with some girl he'd just saved from slow death as a fruit. Without warning, Iole became furious, protective, and exceedingly territorial on behalf of her best friend.

"We can obtain that information later."

"I am called 'Fair Persian,'" said the young woman, now rising from a chair that had been hidden by her previous form.

"Delightful," said Iole. "Charming in oh-so-many ways. All right, Fair, are there any—"

"Fair Persian," said the woman in a tinkly voice. "It is all one name. Apparently, my appearance has elicited this response from many a young man who has—"

"Yes, I am enthralled, mesmerized, and cannot wait to hear the end of your story," said Iole, turning and practically shoving Douban from the room. "But we must attend to the rest of your family. If you have other things to do, like finding some decent clothing, we certainly understand. Don't let us detain you."

"Fair Persian," said Douban, "can you help us to find . . . I believe there are two unaccounted for—a brother and a sister."

"I did hear a commotion several weeks ago from a chamber down the corridor," Fair Persian said as she flew past Iole toward the entryway. "Let us go and see."

"Oh, by all means," Iole mocked to herself through clenched teeth as she raced after Douban who was racing after Fair Persian. "Let us go and *seeeeeeee*. . . ."

"That's my choice?" Pandy mumbled, even as she felt the tiniest bit of air inflating her lungs. "I get to choose how I wish to die?"

"It may be as painless as you'd like," Giondar said, casually flinging Homer, who'd begun to circle around behind the genie, out into the garden. "But choose!"

"Then I choose to die many years from now on my own sleeping cot!" Pandy huffed, watching Homer get to his feet.

"You insist on being clever?" said Giondar, clenching his hands again. "How clever will you be when I dismember you slowly, roasting each limb over hot coals as you watch?"

Suddenly Pandy saw a glint of morning sunlight bouncing off something *on* Homer as he crept back into the large salon.

The lamp.

Without warning, and utterly surprising in the midst of her current situation, Pandy involuntarily tried to imagine the enormous genie squeezed into that tight little space.

And then it hit her.

"Very well," she wheezed as his thumb pressed again into her shoulder. "I'll tell you how I wish to die. But first . . ."

CHAPTER TWENTY-FOUR

Hurrying down the corridor on the second floor, Iole stopped at a blown-out opening in the wall that looked straight down into the salon precisely at the moment when Homer had been tossed into the garden. She saw Pandy held fast in Giondar's grasp. She was about to scream when she felt Douban's hand on her arm, pulling her away.

"Pandy!" she mouthed furiously to him.

Douban watched the scene below, a look of despair on his face.

"She's trusted us," he said finally, turning to Iole. "We must have faith!"

"Gods," Iole thought, following him into a chamber at the end of the house. "He's starting to sound like me! Either that or he just doesn't care about Pandy anymore."

She was about to spit her thoughts out to Douban when she stopped cold, speechless once again. Fair

Persian was talking softly to a young man cruelly chained to a wall, large black spots covering his thin body. She was wiping his brow and cradling his head, telling him that Douban and Iole were going to help him. Gently Iole approached the youth, trying to keep silent so as not to betray her growing revulsion.

The black spots were actually indentations. Something or someone had been scooping out his flesh little by little and black was the color of the congealing wounds. Some were fresher than others and, as they watched, a small chunk of flesh flew out of the boy's upper arm and a small pool of blood began to form. With a cry, the boy almost passed out.

"Hurry!" urged Fair Persian.

"Which is it?" Douban asked Iole.

"Quiet!" she said, then dropped her voice. "Let's solve it logically. I have one pear and a peach."

"I have an apple, another fig, and a pear," Douban replied.

"It's not the fig. And I think Alcie was right about the pear being for—for whoever's downstairs. That leaves the apple and the peach."

"Please, try both!" pleaded Fair Persian.

"We can't," Iole said as if she were talking to somebody who really should have been more informed. "We only have one of each here, and if we use the wrong one, it would be disastrous."

"What does he resemble?" Douban asked.

"Nothing that we have," Iole replied. "So that line of thinking is out. But what is being done to him? Why is his flesh being taken? He's being pocked, cratered, indented, excavated, dimpled, dented, scooped, dug into . . ."

"Pitted," Douban offered.

"Stop!" Iole commanded. "That's it!"

"What?" said Fair Persian.

Ignoring her, Iole rummaged for the opal peach.

"What do you do to a peach when you eat it?" she asked Douban.

"You remove the pit. You pit it."

Gingerly Iole moved toward the young man, feeling the cold hardness of the opal melt away.

"Kerim," said Fair Persian. "Kerim, you must eat this."

But Kerim was in such pain he could barely lift his head.

"Help him, Douban," Iole said.

Slowly and gently, Douban lifted the young man's head and opened his mouth. Iole broke off a small piece of the beautiful, ripe fruit and placed it delicately on his tongue. Kerim's head lolled forward again and the bit of peach dropped out of his mouth. Hitting the floor, it crystallized into a small opal and rolled into a corner. Iole broke off another bit of peach and again placed it in Kerim's mouth. This time Kerim managed to swallow it without chewing and the transformation, as every time before, was instantaneous. Kerim opened his eyes, his face a mask of increasing relief. Every indentation in his flesh began to fill in, the hard, congealed blood dropping to the floor like dark leaves. However, he was still chained to the wall and there was no lock or key to be seen. Then Iole noticed that the manacles weren't as tight as they could have been and if Kerim could just . . .

"Oil," Iole said. "I need oil."

Fair Persian fetched a small lamp from a nearby table.

"Pour it on his wrists," Iole said, stepping up to the weakened youth. "I'll wager you haven't eaten in weeks. There's space for you to wiggle out. Think you can do it?"

Kerim smiled at her.

"My family used to tease me because I was rather . . . thick," he said, working his slick wrists and hands through the manacles until at last he was free. "Not anymore."

"I should think not," answered Fair Persian. "Come, we must find Zinebi."

It was at that moment they all heard the words "Watch. *Then prepare to die!*" followed by Giondar's malevolent laugh, rising up from the lower floor and reverberating through the house. Iole's blood ran cold. Without another word, she made a run for the staircase.

🍇

Giondar relaxed his grip.

"But first?" Giondar asked.

Pandy's thoughts were going so fast she was surprised her brain wasn't leaking out of her ears. She had one idea. Only one, but if it worked . . . Giondar was a little slow, but he wasn't stupid. If it didn't work, if he caught on and saw what she was trying to do, then he would kill everyone in the house on the spot, she was sure of it. What would her father do in the same situation? (Well, he would never *be* in the same situation, duh! Because he wasn't dumb enough to take a box of evil to school like she did!) But if he was, he would act swiftly and decisively, even if he was uncertain of the outcome. Simply by having the right attitude, he would make everyone around him think he knew *exactly* what he was doing. What did he used to say to her when she was much smaller? Something about . . . failing. Then Pandy remembered:

"If you're gonna fail, honey, and you will," Prometheus had said, "then fail BIG and most people will never know the difference. Then get up and fail again. Only next time, fail better."

Pandy looked Giondar square in the eyes.

"But first," she said, her voice even, "I would like you to answer one question and swear by your roc master that you'll tell the truth."

Giondar raised one eyebrow ever so slightly, surprised and a bit alarmed that she invoked his roc.

"Ask your question and be quick."

"Do you swear that you really lived in that little lamp? Homer! Hold up the lamp!"

Homer untied the lamp from around his waist and held it high for all to see.

"Do you really think that we're all stupid enough to believe you could fit in there? Your little fingernail, okay, I could see that. Maybe. But not all of you. So, do you swear it?"

"By my roc master, even though he has forsaken and abandoned me, I swear that lamp was my prison. Now, how do you want to—"

"Nope," Pandy sighed. "I don't believe you. And if you kill me now, I will die thinking that you are a liar."

Mahfouza and Amina gasped. A genie's word, once given, was beyond reproach.

"You dishonor my word," Giondar said, softly, almost hurt. "You dishonor me."

"Yeah, and killing an entire family of innocent people for the . . . the crime of one little girl who probably didn't know what she was doing in the first place isn't dishonorable, right? Oh well, I guess you'll just have to be dishonored. 'Cause I think you're a liar. And I always will."

She paused. This was the moment.

"Unless I see it. With my own eyes."

Pandy blinked at Giondar several times.

"These peepers. So go ahead, liar. Kill me. Let's see, how do I want to—"

"Very well," Giondar spat. "Since you have questioned my word after my oath, I shall *prove* it to you, unclean dog with the fleas of a thousand camels! Watch, *then prepare to die!*"

With a laugh so loud it shook loose another beam from the ceiling, Giondar tossed Pandy to the ground. She landed on her injured shoulder and came close to passing out, biting her lip in pain. She got to her feet just in time to see Giondar dissolve into an enormous cloud of black smoke that extended itself far out into the garden. Then the cloud began to condense into a fine, swirling stream.

"Homer!" Pandy yelled. "Gimme the lamp!"

Homer sent it sailing through the air. Pandy caught it, setting it on the cracked tiles in front of her. The black stream had formed a spiral over the garden, and as everyone watched, it shot back toward the house like a bolt of lightning.

"Here we go!" Pandy cried.

Giondar flew back into the house, crashing first into

a table, which disintegrated. Then a couch, which splintered. Then the black stream sizzled through a tattered privacy curtain, sending it up in flames, before it ricocheted off the corridor wall and flew back into the parlor, narrowly missing Noureddin and Amina. The black stream of smoke that was Giondar then exploded off one wall and onto another.

"It's just smoke. It shouldn't be doing all this damage," Pandy thought, mesmerized. She was so focused on the careening ribbon that she didn't react fast enough when it caromed off the floor and headed straight for her.

In an instant, as it hit her with full force, she knew why the smoke was destroying everything in its path. It was Rage. Pure, unadulterated Rage. Then her mind went as black as the smoke driving through the middle of her body. Her stomach twisted into a knot and she felt as if she were going to vomit. The next moment, her rage at things she hadn't thought about in years was so great, she wanted to kill, maim, shred, dismember everything and everyone around her. The other girls and maidens who'd laughed at her for any reason at all. Her mother for not understanding *anything* about her. Her teachers, all of them, for every cruel, useless, cutting remark meant to mortify her when she'd failed in some way. Every boy that had ever been unkind. Her face for being her face. Her girl's body for being ridiculous. Then she flashed on Hera. She'd thought she'd been angry at Hera before. But now, if the goddess were in front of her, Pandy would tear her *limb from immortal limb.*

And then it was over.

The pain in her stomach disappeared as the last of the black smoke left her body, but her breath was labored and she realized she'd been crying. Hard. She watched from the floor—how had she ended up on the floor?—as Giondar hovered above the lamp, then slowly and evenly filtered into the tiny, tapered opening until nothing remained.

On her knees, Pandy was motionless except for the great rise and fall of her chest as she tried to catch her breath.

"Stop it up!" Alcie shouted.

Pandy looked up at Alcie as if she didn't understand what she'd said. Then her mind cleared and she leapt forward; ignoring the stabbing pain in her shoulder, she grabbed the stopper on its chain and pushed it deep into the opening, sealing the lamp with Giondar inside.

Mahfouza, Amina, and Zoe screamed with delight, then screamed louder at seeing Kerim and Fair Persian rush in, fully restored. Noureddin and Hassan hugged each other as Alcie and Homer hurried to Pandy.

"Can you stand?" Homer asked.

"Yep," Pandy said, getting to her feet.

"Gods," Alcie whispered. "Look at your clothes—and your hair. Pandy, you just dropped to the floor. When that smoke was going through you, you fell on your knees and you were shaking so hard. Are you okay?"

Pandy nodded her head, then she looked down and saw that her toga was burnt brown, its edges singed. Her armband was hot on her flesh and she could have peeled the metal away as if it were soft cheese. Her hair was dry and brittle, her nails were black, and the skin was peeling on her knees, shins, and elbows. Her sandals were basically lumps of burnt leather and ash.

"How can I still be alive?" she asked.

"Because, doofus, you're semi-immortal, remember?"

"Oh yeah."

"Can I be Iole for just one moment and say buh—," Alcie began.

"No, you can't, because I'm right here," Iole called as she and Douban flew into the salon from the corridor.

"Did you see it?" Alcie asked.

"Only the smoke," Iole replied. "We ran from the staircase and it came within millimeters of hitting us. Douban was thrown onto his head."

"Are you all right?" Pandy asked.

"I am fine," he replied, and Iole was quick—and delighted—to notice the slightly dreamy tone in his voice as he looked at Pandy.

"I got knocked back against the wall," Iole went on.

"I lost my breath for a bit and I lost a little hair, that's all. So, even though I wasn't here to see how you induced Giondar to turn into smoke, for whatever you did, may I just say buh-rilliant!"

"Thank you," Pandy said.

"As I was just *about* to say," Alcie huffed. "It's even more amazing than you think, Iole. Wait till I tell you what she did, how she outsmarted him! Pandy, are you certain Giondar was Rage? The *big* Evil, the giant falafel patty, the huge wheel of cheese?"

"Oh yeah," said Pandy remembering her thoughts and feelings as the smoke was coursing through her. "He was it."

"Then it's box time!" Alcie cried.

With her one good arm, Pandy went to open her leather carrying pouch and found the flap so hardened by the effect of Rage that it was almost wooden. She felt for the box and grabbed a handful of objects as hard as pebbles. She pulled out burnt, stony chunks of dried fruit.

"We couldn't eat it anyway," she mumbled.

She removed the box, also slightly blackened, and handed it to Alcie.

"Pandy?" Douban asked, watching from a distance. "What is the matter with your arm?"

"I think it's . . . loose," she replied.

"Let me look at it," he said, moving forward.

"Not right now, Douban," Pandy said, then she smiled

at him, holding up the box for him to see. "*This* is why we're here. This is the most important thing. You can look at me later."

"Need the net?" asked Iole.

"Don't think so," Pandy said. "I touched the lamp. It's a little hot, but it doesn't affect me. Ready?"

Mahfouza and her brothers and sisters crept up beside the girls as Alcie held the box while Iole slid the hairpin out and flipped the clasp. Pandy picked up the lamp from where she'd left it on the floor. It was hot. It was very hot and becoming hotter. Perhaps she should have used the net; she was beginning to get a little . . . angry.

"Okay, let's do this," she said testily. "One, two . . . three!"

Alcie opened the lid, Pandy threw the lamp into the box, and Alcie snapped the lid shut again. And there it was: the sizzle, the sound of Evil evaporating into a fine mist. But this time, just as the fizzle and sizzle began to subside, there was a long, low, faraway laugh as Giondar bubbled into nothingness.

Pandy thought back to the moment when they had first captured Jealousy: the whooping and cheering. This time Mahfouza's family was exuberant, Homer was whirling Alcie and Iole around in the air. But she was just exhausted. She sank to the floor, leaning her back against the a wall. If she could only sit, even for a moment. And maybe find something to eat. She couldn't remember the last time she—or any of them—had eaten! Could it have been—no! Was it the first meal in the caravan camp yesterday morning? Had it been two full rotations of a sundial? Suddenly, they all heard a strange sound from the corner of the room.

Hands, clapping awkwardly.

They all turned their heads to see the two deformed, mirror-opposite figures, hitting their hands together as hard as they could, at once cheering Pandy's cleverness and begging for attention.

CHAPTER TWENTY-FIVE
The Last Two

Pandy struggled to get to her feet, but Alcie gently knelt beside her and sat her back down again.

"I've seen you do it," Alcie said. "Sit, for Athena's sake. Let me. I promise I won't goof it up."

Without warning, tears formed in Pandy's eyes.

"I know you won't."

"Why are you crying?"

"Gee, Ares' armpits, I don't know! One of my best friends is alive again, my arm is totally useless, I've seen more bad things happen to good people than I could ever think of, and I just felt Rage and wanted to kill everyone. Think that could be it?"

"Dumb question?" Alcie asked.

"Duh."

"Okay, I'm gonna go help this guy. Let Douban try and fix your arm."

"Cool," Pandy said, slumping back against the wall as Douban bent over her.

"I'm just going to feel," he said, his fingers gently pressing her shoulder as she tried not to scream. "Oh, my. The bone has been dislocated. I can join it again, but it will be painful."

"Go ahead," Pandy said. "Can't use it any other way."

Douban placed the strap of her leather carrying pouch between her teeth.

"Bite," he said.

She bit, then he shoved her arm bone back into the shoulder socket.

When she regained consciousness, Pandora looked at the strap of her pouch where she'd almost bitten it in two. Then she looked at her bare feet and the lumps of blackened sandal leather she'd kicked off to one side. She looked at her damaged arm now in a sling made out of Douban's sash. Finally she looked at Douban.

"You blacked out," he said softly. "Not long. Five heartbeats at the most. You thrashed a little, but now everything is fine. Your shoulder will heal and Alcie is taking care of Saouy."

Pandy closed her eyes for a moment, then realized the fusing of two opposite halves of a person back into a whole was something she didn't want to miss. Slowly, with Douban's help, she stood, then hid behind a pile of ceiling debris and ruined furniture, watching the scene in the corner of the room.

"Iole," Alcie asked, "you think I'm right, right? It's the pear?"

"I think you have deduced it flawlessly," Iole replied. "Yes."

"Tanger . . . ," Alcie began, then she did something Pandy had never seen before. Alcie purposefully stopped herself from swearing. She didn't make a big, showy deal of it; she didn't slap her hand over her mouth or *humph* or roll her eyes. She simply stopped saying the word "tangerine" and closed her mouth.

"Okay," Alcie continued. "Mahfouza, get on his right side, please. And, what's your name?"

"Fair Persian. I am called that because my appearance and form have elicited that response—"

"Aprico—! Ummmm. Yes, okay, don't really need the backstory at this moment," Alcie said as Iole suppressed a giggle. "Just need you to get on Saouy's left side. Now the two of you bring the two of him as close together as possible."

"Good girl!" Pandy thought.

"Saouy," Zoe said, "these maidens will help you. Do as they say."

The two halves of Saouy's head nodded.

Alcie approached with the emerald pear. Immediately, it became soft in her hands. She broke the fruit in two and placed the halves in the two separate hands.

"At the same time," Iole cautioned.

"Right," Alcie said. "Now eat."

The two halves of Saouy placed the fruit in their half-mouths at precisely the same moment. Instantly, his flesh melded together as if he were being sewn up the middle of his body with incredible speed. His clothes even mended themselves. Almost at once, a handsome young boy was standing before them without so much as a scar.

The family rejoicing was exuberant, but short-lived.

"Zinebi?" Zoe asked.

"We only restored Kerim and your sister," Iole said, with a glance Fair Persian. "We came down to be of assistance."

"Then we must find her," said Mahfouza. "Zoe says Zinebi was one of the very last to be transformed. She should not be too hurt."

Pandy and Homer went with one group to search the remainder of the second level. Iole, Alcie, and Douban went with another to hunt through the rest of the garden and the lower level, coming at last to . . .

. . . the food-preparation room.

On the second level, Pandy heard the screams of Zoe and Amina and flew downstairs. She arrived at the entryway just in time to see Kerim holding Noureddin's head over an urn as he became sick with dry heaves. Looking past them, she saw Zoe holding a weeping Amina as Douban and Iole crouched over a small body on the floor. Pandy saw Iole hand a juicy red apple with one bite taken out back up to Alcie.

"It's done," Pandy heard Iole say.

"They're all moving back into place," Douban said.

Pushing past other family members, Pandy finally saw Zinebi; the little girl was lying on the floor, bound by her hands with cords to a small table, essentially on the very spot where she had shattered Dery's glass bottle. As Pandy looked at her, she saw nothing whatsoever the matter with the child. Then, very subtly, underneath her silken robes, Pandy saw an object slide into a shallow trough that ran up and down the girl's midsection. Then she saw the trough disappear.

Zinebi was wide-eyed but silent as tears ran down her face.

"Somebody start talking," Pandy said. "Please."

"She was an apple," Douban said, rising.

"I know. I know, it was the last fruit left," Pandy said. "But what was that moving into her body? How was she an apple?"

"What does one do to an apple, Pandora?" Douban asked, lowering his voice for those family members who had arrived late on the scene with Pandy. "Her major organs were all on the outside of her body, as if she were being—"

Pandy's mouth fell open, she held up her hand for him to stop.

"*Cored?*" she finally said in horror. "You've got to be kidding me."

"I am afraid not," Douban said. "But after we convinced her to eat the apple, everything has returned to its proper place. What you saw was her heart finding its way home. And Zinebi claims she was in no pain at all."

"Gods," Pandy murmured, looking at Hassan trying to loosen Zinebi's ties. "Wait. What do you mean you *convinced* her to eat? She didn't *want* to?"

"No," replied Douban. "And she doesn't want to be moved. She wants those things on the ceiling to fall on her."

"What are you talking about . . . ," Pandy asked.

Then she looked up at the ceiling and saw three bright blue objects, shaped almost like daggers, dangling over the little girl by the slenderest of threads. They reminded Pandy of the odd pointy-down things that she would see in caves when her father took the family on hikes back in Greece.

"Okay!" Pandy called out. "I want everyone out of the room . . . NOW!"

Mahfouza and the rest of her family were so startled, they simply stared at her.

"Homer, Douban, get them out. Alcie and Iole, you stay."

"Duh," mumbled Alcie.

"Come, Fair Persian, come, Amina," Mahfouza was saying on her way out.

"But," Amina protested.

"Pandora knows what she is doing," Mahfouza hushed.

With her good arm, Pandy withdrew her net and handed it to Alcie. Then she took out the box and gave it to Iole.

"Look," Iole said, pointing up.

One of the blue daggers had begun to vibrate over Zinebi's body.

"No, please," the little girl cried. "I deserve it!"

Pandy couldn't even comprehend why the child would even be thinking something like that, let alone saying it. She dragged a chair underneath the blue things and, wrapping the net around her hand, stepped up. She grabbed the first one and became aware, even through the net, that it was soft but freezing to the touch. And she was instantly assaulted by a sharp, rancid smell—as if she'd just opened a jar full of goat cheese and lemon rinds that had been left to bake in the sun. As she pulled it off the ceiling, another one began to shake itself loose.

"Box!" she cried as Iole slid out the hairpin and readied the lid.

"Now!" Pandy yelled and tossed the blue substance,

which felt slimy and gooey, inside the box as Iole snapped the lid shut. Looking back up to the ceiling, Pandy caught the second dagger just as it was falling, and Iole reopened and closed the box with perfect timing. But when Pandy had turned for the third dagger, it had already broken loose and was plummeting downward toward Zinebi. In a flash, Pandy was off the chair and Alcie had kicked it underneath the falling blue goo. It hit the edge of the chair and for one terrifying moment, no one knew whether it would fall on Zinebi or roll into the center of the chair. Risking infection by . . . whatever it was . . . Alcie reached in and tipped the chair, forcing the goo into the center, where Pandy scooped it up and flung it into the box, where it sizzled away with the others.

"Nice save, Alce. We're getting pretty good at recognizing the lesser evils," she panted.

"You are," said Alcie. "I just thought it was interesting Persian decorating."

"I'll bet Poseidon's trident," Pandy said, "that those were Spite, Entitlement, and Petulance."

"I'll bet you're right," agreed Iole.

"Why did you do that!" Zinebi began yelling. "I wanted them back!"

"Okay," Alcie said from between her teeth. "Crazy time. Not all the way back to normal."

"Hush," said Pandy, looking at the little girl intently. "Guys, gimme a moment."

"You're certain?" asked Iole.

"Yep."

Pandy waited a few moments after Alcie and Iole had left the room. Then she found a sharp knife and knelt down beside Zinebi.

"Good! Please kill me! It's what I deserve," Zinebi cried.

Pandy just stared at her.

"I'm not going to kill you," she said at last, beginning to cut through the cords. "I'm just super curious why you want to die. Or why you thought you should be—Gods, what's the word—uh, reinfected with those things on the ceiling. And why you didn't want to eat the apple to restore you, and they had to *convince* you. Y'know, just curious."

Zinebi began to cry again.

"Because I killed our peri. Well, I got her killed, which is the same thing. And now my mother and father are dead. My family has been hurt. Our house is nearly gone. And it's all my fault. Something bad should happen to me."

Pandy regarded Zinebi with something close to awe. When she was this girl's age, she would have done anything she could have to blame someone else for her mistakes and very often did. Not that she ever got away with it, it was simply the first place her survival instincts told to her to go. But this girl wanted to pay, as if her death could somehow make things right.

Freeing Zinebi at last, Pandy helped her to sit.

"Look," Pandy said after a long moment. "I get it. I do. If anyone gets it, it's me. But here's what you gotta understand: your death won't bring anybody back. Not your parents or your peri. In fact, you letting yourself become spiteful and stuff all over again is the worst thing you could do. 'Cause you wouldn't, like, be in control and you might cause other bad things to happen. You have been punished enough, okay? Something bad *did* happen to you. And you saw what happened to your brothers and sisters. There's only one thing you can do now to make it right."

"What?" asked Zinebi, wiping away tears.

"You can never forget what you did and you have to work really hard every day to make sure that nothing like it ever happens again. In fact, you have to work double hard to be a better person—grown-up—than your parents or your family ever thought you could be. It sounds silly, but it's like their death will have had some purpose if you do that. Y'know, make them proud of you. Even though they can't see you. Can you do that?"

Zinebi stared at Pandy for a long moment and Pandy saw that the girl was thinking very hard.

"Yes," said Zinebi.

"Cool," Pandy replied. "I thought so. Okay, let's find the others."

CHAPTER TWENTY-SIX

"Did You Really Think I'd Just Blow Away?"

Pandy fetched Dido from his hiding place in the storage room, then she and Zinebi joined Alcie, Iole, and Mahfouza in the large salon. The rest of the family was scavenging in the garden, trying desperately to find something, anything, to eat. No one wanted to leave the property; they were all overcome with a desire to be close to one another, but the trees were bare and any vegetable, root, or herb they found was blackened, shriveled, or rotting. Finally, Kerim caught a rabbit and, dispatching the creature quickly and painlessly, brought it into the food-preparation room. Pandy lit a fire in the grate (to the amazement of no one—not after what they'd seen and experienced) and a short time later, the entire group was sitting around several tables in the large salon, picking at tidbits of the little roast and marveling at Pandy, Alcie, Iole, and Homer's adventures.

"I will go to the marketplace tomorrow for supplies," Mahfouza said. "I simply am too tired to do it now."

"Will you stay, Pandora?" asked Fair Persian. "The house is in shambles, but we can make you comfortable. You must rest a little while."

"So sorry," Iole answered, just as Pandy opened her mouth to speak. "Tempest fugit, you know. Oh, you must forgive me. That's Latin. Just a little something I picked up. It means 'time flies.' We really should be off now. Tight schedule."

"Yup," said Alcie, her mouth full of rabbit as she looked from Fair Persian to Douban.

Pandy stared at Iole as if she'd just grown another head.

"I think we can at least stay one night," she said, looking back to Mahfouza's family. "Thank you. Although, Hermes' helmet, I don't even remember how many days we have left."

"And we don't know where we're going," said Homer.

"Probably far away," Iole said softly, tossing a bone onto a platter. "Need to be ambulating."

"Well," Pandy said, removing the blue bowl from her pouch, which was slowly regaining its suppleness. "Let's find out."

The bowl had several dark blue veins now running

through the colored marble—an effect of Rage, Pandy mused. But other than that, it looked fine.

"Uh-oh," she said, holding up the vial of her tears. "It's empty."

"Do they have to be your tears, Pandora?" asked Fair Persian. "I have become an expert at crying when needed."

"Sheesh," mumbled Alcie.

"I, too, can cry at will," said Zinebi. "It always got me everything I wanted."

"What did we talk about?" said Pandy, looking at the young girl.

"Oh. Right. No more of that kind of thing," agreed Zinebi.

"Thank you, everyone," Pandy said. "But they have to be mine. I just don't know if I can think of anything right now that will make me—"

Out of nowhere, Alcie slugged Pandy on her wounded arm—not enough to knock it out of place again, but enough that Pandy doubled over. When she raised her head to look at Alcie, there were fresh tears spilling out of both eyes.

"Alcie!" yelled Douban.

"Gimme the vial," Alcie commanded.

Quickly Iole grabbed and handed it to Alcie, who drew it upward over Pandy's face, catching many big, wet drops.

"Sorry," Alcie said. "We could have told sad stories and blah, blah, blah. This was quicker."

"Right now, I love you and I hate you. Equally," Pandy said, through gritted teeth, as Douban checked her arm.

"I'll live," Alcie said, catching one of Pandy's tears on her forefinger. "Iole, a little water if you please."

Iole emptied her water skin of its last few drops into the map, barely enough to cover the bottom of the bowl, as Alcie shook the tear off her finger. The concentric rings of the bowl began to spin, slowly at first, as if they had been rusted or fused by Rage. Then they spun faster and faster until at last three symbols lined up with the familiar illuminating light.

"Fifty-four days left, including today," Pandy said. "We're looking for Greed and we're going to Rome."

"I LOVE ROME!" shouted a voice, suddenly piercing the quiet of the salon.

Everyone turned to see Hera hovering above the tiles, close to the blown-out wall.

"The weather is perfect this time of year, lots of feasting going on and on and on, and when in Rome, as the saying goes! And of course, we have family there . . . Neptune, Mercury, Venus, and my personal favorite, Juno. They say she looks a lot like me, although those who actually know say I'm much prettier. Oh, won't we all have such fun! Well, when I say all of us, I don't really mean you, Pandora, or your filthy, bratty little friends, because I am going to kill you all today—this minute—if it is the last thing I do!"

The next few moments happened so fast and blended so seamlessly that, afterward, Pandy would never be able to fully recount the exact order of events. As Hera was talking about how much fun it had been to finally explode the head of Douban's father ("I'm sure some pieces flew all the way back to Greece!"), Pandy suddenly felt something snake into the palm of her hand. She looked down as Hera was gesturing wildly and saw the magic rope, frayed to points on either end, bumpy in the middle where it had woven its two lengths together, and slightly reddish—like a little worm. The rope had come to her unbidden—but it had obviously been affected by Rage. And now it was . . . waiting. Pandy knew that giving the rope an order could mean an opposite action, so she directed only one thought into her hand.

"Do whatever you want, friend."

The next instant, the rope flew out of her palm and, in midair, enlarged itself to the thickness of a horse rein. It wrapped itself around Hera as she was rearing back to let fly some horrible torture on all of the stunned faces staring back at her. The rope started at her broad shoulders and worked its way down her body, binding her arms to her sides and her legs together. Then, seemingly endless in length, the rope doubled on itself and wound its way back up her body, binding Hera to just below her chin. Her screams nearly brought down the rest of the roof.

"What do we do!" yelled Pandy, knowing that the rope wouldn't hold the goddess forever.

"Her ears!" shouted Douban. "Get the eggs!"

As Pandy rushed forward, Hera rose into the air. Homer sprang up from the table and grabbed Hera's foot just as it was almost out of reach. She was unable even to kick at him as Homer pulled Hera back down until Pandy could reach out and snatch the eggs off of her ears. Hera tried to bite Pandy's hands whenever they got close, until Alcie raced in and grabbed the back of Hera's head by her still-short red hair, jerking her into submission.

Pandy swiftly loosed the roc eggs from Hera's earlobes. Instantly, Hera lost her ability to stay airborne and crashed to the ground.

"Zinebi?" Pandy said. "Please hold on to these until we figure out what to do with them."

She turned to give the roc eggs to the little girl and found instead two baby birds fluttering about in her grasp. The tiny chicks, still wet and slimy, flew up to Pandy's shoulders, one on each side, and clucked for all to hear.

"A thousand blessings upon you," said one, staring at Hera rolling about on the floor like a boar stuck in mud. "I could not have tolerated that creature one instant more."

"The most foul mind of an immortal I have ever encountered. That includes the genie I was punishing. And that's saying something, I tell you."

"I shall never recover from being so close to that brain. So base, so petty," said the first.

"And yet so little goes on in there," said the second roc. "She doesn't like you at all, mortal maiden. So naturally, that puts you in very good standing with us. Before we go to join our fellow hatchlings, what may we do for you?"

"I know!" said the first. "Let's restore the enchantments on all her personal items!"

"Brilliant . . . and done! And done for her companions as well," answered the second roc. "But we can do more. Speak up, maiden. What would you like?"

While Pandy was taking all of this in and trying, at the same time, to think of something she needed above everything else she needed, Homer stepped forward.

"She needs new sandals."

"Tasty!" agreed Alcie.

"Oh, Gods," Iole said, with a fleeting look of apprehension.

Pandy would have never thought of such an idea by herself; in fact even now she hesitated. They were far from Mount Olympus and Zeus might not even know or care about his wife's current situation. But anything that Pandy did to the Queen of Heaven, if not officially sanctioned by Zeus himself, could have serious consequences. But if she let Hera go . . .

Iole, somehow, read her thoughts.

"I can't think of any other idea, Pandy. And you know we can't release her."

Pandy glanced sideways at the tiny chicks.

"We all could use new sandals," she said. "Would you please transform the goddess into some appropriate walking gear?"

"Thick soles," said Alcie.

"Good arch support," Iole put in.

"Speed," Homer finished.

"With all of those things. We would like sandals that will help us leave Persia in . . . two days," Pandy said.

"Three!" Iole interjected. "Let's not kill ourselves."

"Of course not," Pandy replied. "Let's save that for Zeus when he finds out what we've done. Three days of walking. Please."

"Four pairs of Goddess Go-Swiftly with comfort cushioning coming up," said one chick.

"Five, please," said Iole. "Douban is coming, too!"

Pandy turned to Douban.

"I must return to my family soon, but it would be my pleasure to accompany you at least as far as the Syrian border," he said.

"Darn tootin'," Iole whispered as Alcie grinned.

"As you wish," said the other chick.

The rocs let up a cacophony of calls, screeches, and whistles, and Hera, much to her surprise, began to dissolve into a mist before everyone's eyes.

"Pandora! How DARE you! I command you to stop this at once!" Hera wailed.

"Or what?" Pandy asked, never imagining she could have been so bold with anyone, let alone the Queen of Heaven. Hera's eyes narrowed into tiny slits as she tilted her now-transparent head to stare down at Pandy.

"My husband will never forgive you for this."

"Probably not, Hera," Pandy retorted, speaking to the wife of Zeus as if she were a common criminal. "Then again, he just might."

Within moments, Hera was gone completely and the magic rope fell loosely to the floor, where, not waiting to be called, it shrunk itself and slithered back into Pandy's leather pouch. Alcie, Iole, Homer, and Douban found themselves wearing supremely comfortable sandals made of beautiful peacock blue leather. Pandy looked down at her own feet and saw that the leather of her new sandals was bright copper in color.

"Gods!" she said, looking up at everyone. "That's the color of her hair; I'm standing on her head!"

Without warning, Alcie and Iole began to laugh.

"We'd better enjoy this while we can," Pandy said,

giggling. "I have a feeling this is gonna land us in some serious trouble."

"Not until you reach the border," said one chick. "She will remain a nonthreatening, powerless foot protector until then. And now we shall join our fellow hatchlings far away. Be well, Pandora!"

The chicks flew off so fast, no one really saw them go. All anyone saw was a flicker of two silhouettes against the sun.

The rest of the day and into the evening, Pandy rested as Alcie and the others helped Mahfouza's family put things in order about the house. Homer helped the brothers re-set window frames, right overturned statues, and clear away debris as Douban checked out the entire family to see if there were any ill effects from Giondar's punishments. Mahfouza didn't wait until the following day to venture to the marketplace; late in the afternoon, she, Zoe, and Fair Persian returned with vegetables, a little meat, sweets, juices, and a fresh supply of water. And not a single piece of fruit.

Pandy was lying on a couch in a room on the upper floor, going over her mother's cloak and silver girdle centimeter by centimeter, checking for any damage done by the effect of Rage. The girdle was, miraculously, fine and the cloak had only lost a bit of embroidery, nothing more. Pandy lay back and closed her eyes, trying to sleep amidst a few tattered but cozy pillows, but she found it difficult with the aromas of cooking food wafting up to the second floor. Suddenly, she felt another presence in the room.

"Hi," said Alcie, sitting down beside her.

"Hi."

"This is from Zoe," Alcie said, holding a bowl full of a yellowy paste.

"Looks gross," Pandy said, scooping a bit out with two fingers. "But I'm starved."

"Not for eating, plebe-o," Alcie said. "It's for your fried hair. It's fat and olive oil. She said to put it on your head and your skin. She wants you to moisturize."

"Thank Apollo," Pandy said, smoothing the paste on her hair. "I might have gagged."

"Okay," Alcie said. "Iole and I were talking and we are both, like, very confused. The pouches and the rope and the bust of Athena didn't work here. They were glitchy. And even Hera had to get a couple of birds to be able to use some of her powers, right?"

"Right."

"Then how were you able to use your power over fire? And why did the map work?"

Pandy sighed and shook her head.

"Believe me, I have been sitting here trying to figure that out. And the truth is, Alce, I have absolutely no idea. At the moment I used them, I didn't think about how my powers might be wonky, I just went ahead. But

I have no idea how they worked—or the map. I mean, none of us even considered that it might not work, right? I just . . . don't know."

Alcie looked at the floor for a long moment.

"Do you forgive me for slugging you?"

"Not yet, but I will. It was very smart."

"Oran—uh. Yes. Thank you," Alcie said, biting her lip.

"Okay, that's the third or fourth time I've seen you do that."

"Do what?"

"Stop yourself from swearing," Pandy answered, wiping her greasy hands on her toga. "What gives?"

Alcie was silent for a bit. Then she reached into her leather pouch and pulled out the cobalt blue enamel and gold box.

"I have decided that swearing is not maidenly," she said. "It used to be funny, I know. But I've seen the ugly side of fruit in the last few ticks of the sundial, and . . . and I am simply not going to do it anymore, using fruit or anything else. At least I'm gonna try."

"But it's part of your curse!" Pandy said. "It's part of the effect of you standing so close to the box when it was opened! You don't have a *choice*."

"Yeah, well, that's where you're wrong."

Alcie gently opened the blue and gold box so that Pandy could see inside.

"It's a string," Pandy said, unimpressed. "A nice string, Alce, but I'm just sayin'."

"No," Alcie said. Then she broke into a wide grin and a look crossed her face that Pandy hadn't seen since they were little girls. It was a look of sheer astonishment.

"It's my life-thread. The Fates gave it to me. I was never supposed to be in the underworld, not for a while anyway, but they'd already cut it, so they gave it to me. Pandy, I'm the only one who has their own thread. Lachesis said that."

"*Lachesis*? You met her?"

"Yep. And she said that my life was in my own hands now, to do with whatever I wish. And I think I'm going to try to start being a little more responsible. Starting with the swearing."

Pandy was dumbfounded. Suddenly she heard Fair Persian, Douban, and Iole in the corridor outside.

"Perhaps you could come back, Douban," Fair Persian was saying. "Baghdad has need of an excellent physician, now that your father is no longer."

"He can't," Pandy heard Iole snap. "He is coming with *us*, as I have already communicated to you."

"Yes . . . but," Fair Persian began.

"No *buts*," Iole said as their voices trailed off down the corridor toward the stairs.

"Gods!" Pandy said. "What's going *on* with her?"

"Puh-leeze!" Alcie said. "You can't see it? She thinks Fair Persian is trying to steal Douban away from you."

"Steal! He's not mine! I haven't even . . . looked . . . at him."

Alcie just looked at her with a big, goofy smile on her face.

"Oh no? I've seen you! Listen, my friend, you can't fool me. I wasn't born yesterday, you know. Well, in a way, I was, but never mind that. I've seen the way he looks at you. He obviously adores you."

"You think?" Pandy said, smiling.

"I have been known to, yes."

Pandy gazed at her friend.

"I am so proud of you," she said, finally.

"Mutual," Alcie said as the call to evening meal came up from below.

CHAPTER TWENTY-SEVEN
Outward Bound

The next morning, washed and well fed, Pandy, Alcie, Iole, Homer, and Douban, accompanied by Mahfouza's entire family, made a quick stop at the marketplace to replenish their supplies and to introduce Alcie to the silversmith who had lost his cat. They presented him with a ruby apple as payment for Hera's destruction of his shop, which very nearly caused him to faint again.

The group walked to the very edge of the city and faced west, the river before them and the wide Arabian desert beyond that.

"I will send the others home," Mahfouza said. "And I will wait with you for a barge to take you across."

"No need," Pandy said, slipping a garnet pomegranate and a sapphire fig into the hands of the beautiful girl. "We're fine. These are to help you rebuild your house and thank you. Oh, Mahfouza, thank you for everything."

"Pandora, my dearest, thank *you* for restoring my

family. But do you not want at least one piece of fruit as a remembrance of your time in Persia?"

"We're not leaving with nothing," Pandy said, then she nudged Alcie to open her pouch. Mahfouza saw many pieces of the glittering jeweled fruit inside.

"Everyone else is carrying food," Alcie said, speaking low and looking around as if there might be thieves. "I have the important stuff."

After many hugs all around and promises to return one day if at all possible, Pandy turned toward the river, about to sit and wait for a boat.

"It would be groovy if we could just walk across."

At once, her legs began to move on their own and she was ten meters across the river—on top of the water—before she knew what was happening. When she realized she wasn't sinking, she turned around in surprise and saw Alcie, Iole, Homer, and Douban right behind her. With a laugh, she threw up her arms, waving madly to Mahfouza's family. Stunned for only a moment, all nine brothers and sisters began waving and cheering, shouting for good luck and safe travels.

Three days later, having slept and eaten upright, as the sandals continued their march and Alcie told of her adventures in Hades' kingdom, they reached the border between Persia and Syria. Shortly after the sun had reached the midpoint of the heavens, the sandals slowed, then came to a complete stop.

Without thinking, Pandy was about to simply walk into Syria, when she heard Alcie cough slightly behind her. Turing around, she saw Alcie cock her head to one side. Then Pandy looked at Douban. Then it hit her. He was leaving. Actually leaving. And it was doubtful she would ever see him again.

As Iole, Alcie, and Homer began to, obviously, look down into their pouches, checking for things they already knew were there, mumbling to one another and staring into Syria, Douban took Pandy by the hand.

"It is very likely that I will never have another chance to say this," he began. "You are the most remarkable person I have ever known. Your courage and determination are inspiring. Even my father thought so. Your respect for duty and what is right is, with the exception of your face, the most beautiful thing about you."

Three days of uninterrupted walking and her legs felt fine. Now they were beginning to wobble.

"And, if you will permit me, I should very much like to come and visit you in Athens one day."

"That," Pandy managed to get out, her voice squeaking before it settled. "That would be fine . . . lovely. If I'm alive."

Douban laughed and leaned in.

Pandy's mind went nowhere and everywhere all at once. "What is this?" she thought with a shiver of excitement as she instinctively tilted up her chin. "This—oh,

Gods! Is this it? This is IT! My first KISS!" But it wasn't the rush of girly excitement she'd been expecting at this moment. It was more natural, as if this was absolutely the way it was supposed to be. Her first kiss would be with someone she didn't just have a schoolgirl crush on, but with someone who knew her well, respected her, and whom she really cared for.

Then she heard Alcie scream.

Immediately, the spell was broken. Pandy and Douban quickly turned to look at Alcie and Homer, both having stepped over the Syrian border, both now barefoot. In front of Alcie, lying in the sand, was Hera's right leg complete with one golden sandal. Lying at Homer's feet was Hera's left arm, her rings and bracelets glinting in the sunlight.

No one spoke for a long, long time.

Then Pandy had an idea.

"Iole and Douban, please remove your sandals," she said, taking off her red-leather footwear. Then, with her hands, she dug a shallow pit and buried all three pairs.

"Pandy!" cried Iole.

"Well, what do you suggest?" Pandy cried desperately. "We can't have her following us!"

"No, you can't," said a familiar voice. "At least not for a while."

With a start, Pandy whipped her head to see Hermes standing a short distance down the borderline. Feeling tremendous relief, she ran straight to him, but he put his huge hand out to stop her.

"Not so fast," he said, a frown creasing his perfect face. "You would really leave her here? In the sand? Not a wise move. Zeus sent me simply to check on you. And if you had done well, maybe give you a little help getting to—where are you going next?"

"Rome," Pandy answered.

"Rome, eh? Good times! I barely had time to make it to the Bureau of Visiting Deities in Baghdad. I'm zooming over the horizon, I look down, and here you are holding hands with that nice young man and the Queen of Heaven is in pieces all over the desert. What kind of a report am I going to give to the Sky-Lord? Not to mention your father when he hears about the holding hands part. What am I going to say, huh? Answer me that."

"I didn't know what else to do," Pandy said, now fearful that word of her actions had somehow gotten back to Zeus and, quest or no quest, Pandy was as good as dead.

"No," Hermes said. "Zeus doesn't know yet. But he will. Because she'll have to be restored, Pandora, and you know that."

Without waiting for her to answer, Hermes caused the buried sandals to rise out of their pit and fly to him. Then he shrunk Hera's arm and leg and, along with the sandals, put them into a peacock blue silk pouch he simply materialized out of thin air, then tucked it neatly away into the folds of his silver toga. He turned back to Pandy.

"Personally," he said with a little smile, "I love it. I wish she could stay buried for the next few thousand years. But I can't speak for Zeus. He might be, shall we say, put out. Or he might tell me to drop her in the Tigris. I don't know. And I don't want to know for a while. I have a bit of time before Zeus wonders where I am, so I'm going to take a little walkabout. Perhaps see that this young man gets home to his family in one piece. That should take up a few days, but I'd get to Rome fast, if I were you."

"How?" Pandy asked.

"Iole, step across the border, if you please," Hermes said. "Are you all across now? Yes? Good. Say good-bye to the nice youth. Special smile from you, Pandora. Don't think I can't tell what's going on. That's right, wave to him. Bye-bye! How do you get to Rome, Pandora? Like this."

He blinked.

And they were gone.

Epilogue

High above Rome, on a cloud bank, Jupiter sat and studied his friend, his brother and, in almost every way . . .

. . . his near exact double.

"They're *all* coming?" Jupiter asked.

"Most of them," the other figure said. "I haven't taken a head count lately. But surely it's not a problem."

"Not at all," Jupiter said. "Well, not for us at any rate. Happy to have you. I am simply concerned about the populace. What will they do when they see various sets of two almost identical beings—should they happen to see us."

"We do adorn ourselves a bit differently," said the other, brushing back strands of silver hair being tossed about by the high winds.

"True, true," Jupiter acknowledged. "But then there's the matter of lodgings."

"Yes, I have been meaning to talk to you about that.

We actually have a *home*, you know. Mount Olympus. It's lovely."

"Of course," Jupiter said. "I've been, remember? Deity Family Day, several centuries ago?"

"But my point is, it's fortified, remote, no humans trespassing. Why don't you build yourself a nice palace somewhere close to Rome and secret it away. Invisible walls, that sort of thing. With spacious quarters for guests. I'll help. Let's do it together, right now!"

"Not so fast, dear brother," Jupiter said. "Romans don't necessarily think of us, their gods, as having a distinct home. We are merely the sponsors, the benefactors, the protectors of various aspects of their human existence. And in that respect, we must abide by the perceptions of the people who do us homage. Your Greeks are different and for that, you and the others are lucky. But Juno and Venus and Mars and Mercury and the rest, well, we exist on the wind as it were."

"If I tell Hera she has to sleep on the wind, I won't hear the end of it for eons."

"Oh," said Jupiter, looking away for a moment, "Hera's coming too?"

"Yes. And, Jupiter, please try not to act so disgusted."

"Does it show?"

"Only because it's what I see in my own looking glass every sunrise."

"Here's a thought," Jupiter said, gazing down from

the dizzying height into the heart of Rome. "Why don't we all camp in the city? It'll be easier to help the girl. We can all be together. We can meet up faster if need be. I know a wonderful bakery for morning rolls. Dare I say it will be fun!"

"None of this is fun, brother. You know what is at stake if Pandora fails."

"I do," Jupiter said, his face becoming somber. "But Hera can't possibly still be thinking of harnessing all the remaining evils for her own purposes at this point, could she? We're all sort of in the clear, aren't we?"

"Two, maybe three large Evils are still free," said his counterpart. "But the final one is the biggest of them all. And if *that* is left loose in the world and remains fixed, it will only be a matter of time before the others are fabricated out of mankind's extremely fallible mortal nature. Hera won't hesitate to pounce on that opportunity."

"I don't know why I am surprised," Jupiter said. "Juno has been following right along with everything that Hera has been doing. The only words out of her mouth for the past few months have been 'Good for Hera!' and 'That's what I would have done!' or 'Smart move, sister!' We married badly; I've taken to drink more than usual."

Finally, Zeus smiled.

"Pandora's got at least four evils in the box. Five at this point, for all I know. And I would certainly hope so, considering the strings I had to pull with the Persian Bureau of Visiting Deities to get an emergency override for her power over fire and that map they're using. Do you know, Jupiter, that I had to agree that a contingent of rocs be allowed to come to Greece on a fact-finding mission—to see how we immortals 'do' things back at home. At any rate, that's four more evils than any of us expected. Personally, I thought she'd be dead within a week when she started. She's rather remarkable, this girl. But none of it has been a gambol in the forest. And Greed, if she gets to Rome, will prove exceptionally difficult. Which is why some of us from the Greek contingent are going to be here. But the help must be specific and subtle. Tiny. Nothing general, no broad strokes, if you will."

"I understand."

"I think it might be entertaining, rather amusing, to live among mortals for a bit. I like your 'camping in the city' idea."

"I'll arrange everything," Jupiter said.

"Good. So it's set, then," Zeus said, rising to go. "As soon as I hear from Hermes that Pandora's still alive, those of us who're coming will be on our way. Greek and Roman gods together."

He laughed in spite of himself.

"However this works out, it should prove very, very interesting."

GLOSSARY

Names, pronunciations, and further descriptions of gods, Demigods, other integral immortals, places, objects, concepts, and fictional personages appearing within these pages. Definitions derived from three primary sources: Edith Hamilton's *Mythology: Timeless Tales of Gods and Heroes*; Webster's Online Dictionary, which derives many of its definitions from Wikipedia, the free encyclopedia (further sources are also indicated on this Web site); and the author's own brain.

arboretum (are-bore-EE-tum): a room or building (often made of glass) used to cultivate, house, and display trees, shrubs, plants, and/or flowers. An arboretum is primarily used for scientific or educational purposes but may also be for simple enjoyment.

genie (GEE-knee): a spirit (sometimes invisible but not always) mentioned primarily in ancient Persian lore and the Koran; may take the form of a human or an animal.

jinn (GIN): alternate name for a genie; may be a good or evil spirit.

peri (PEAR-ee): a female genie; in the nonspiritual sense, a peri may refer to a beautiful or graceful girl.

scimitar (SIM-ih-tar): a curved Oriental sword with the sharp edge on the outside of the curve.

shade (SHADE): a ghost or spirit; the soul after it leaves the body.

ACKNOWLEDGMENTS

Thanks to Scott Hennesy, Richard Overton, Cynthia Preston, Simon Lewis, Debby O'Connor, and Dominic Friesen. Of course, I am deeply grateful to Caroline Abbey, Deb Shapiro, and Anna Dalziel at Bloomsbury.

To "the gang of four": Gracie Kirschbaum, Zoe Hanket, Olivia Villegas, and Iris Burson . . . the Pan-fans who keep me honest.

As always, special thanks and love to Sara.